Lydia's Song

The story of a child lost and a woman found

Katherine Blessan

Sept 2016

First published in Great Britain in 2014

Instant Apostle
The Barn
1 Watford House Lane
Watford
Herts
WD17 1BJ

British Library Cataloguing-in-Publication Data

A catalogue record for this book is available from the British Library

This book and all other Instant Apostle books are available from Instant Apostle:

Website: www.instantapostle.com

E-mail: info@instantapostle.com

ISBN 978-1-9097-2819-6

Printed in Great Britain

'Each heart knows its own bitterness, and no one else can fully share its joy.'
Proverbs 14:10 (NLT)

Acknowledgements

For a novel that was eight years in the making, there are many people to thank for help given during that time, both significant and seemingly insignificant.

Thanks to Manoj Raithatha for accepting my manuscript for publication. Thanks to my editor Nigel Freeman for his insightful suggestions to improve my manuscript and to Nicki Copeland for her expert copy editing, which reminded me that there's always more to learn about sentence-crafting!

Thanks to my husband, Blessan, who loved and encouraged me throughout and gave me space to develop my writing. Thanks also to my brother, Symeon, who encouraged me and supported the publication process.

Thanks to Liz Evershed and Alison Hull for reading sections of my earlier drafts and making helpful suggestions for improvements.

Thanks to Alli Mellon from the Hard Places Community for taking the time to meet me and share her stirring personal account of work done with child prostitutes in Cambodia. Thanks to the other NGO staff whose names I forget who met me to talk about their work with trafficked children.

Thanks to Gary A. Haugen for your true-life story about trafficking and freedom. Your book inspired me in my own writing.

Contents

Part 1

Lydia's life

Chapter 1
England, October 2036

Lydia turned over in bed and sighed, plumping up her pillow for the umpteenth time. She listened to the clock ticking, each pulse beating a rhythm of time passing inescapably, and suppressed a moan.

It's too late. It's not too late. It's too late. It's not too late. It's never too late. It's far too late.

She clenched her jaws and picked up the alarm clock. 04:43. Well, at least that was one thing that wasn't too late. With little hope of any more sleep, Lydia put on her dressing gown and slippers and shuffled over to the window. The street was bathed in a yellow glow, and outside her house the street lamp rattled in the light wind of the early morning. She opened the window wide and breathed the cool October air in deeply, hearing faint laughter coming from the house just opposite where the newly-weds Joy and Phil had recently moved in.

Wonderful. Just wonderful.

Lydia didn't see herself as someone who begrudged other people their happiness, but just now she felt like pulling down the carefully erected fence of their garden of delight and trampling on it: a cruel revenge against an unwitting rejection.

The tightly coiled knot which had lain in the depths for so many years was being mauled at, and the pieces were slowly unravelling. Lydia tightened the belt on her dressing gown and went to have an early morning shower.

Some time later, Lydia sat curled up in a chair with her ePad on her lap. *I would like very much to meet with you.* Lydia reread these words in the Facebook message over and over again as if she could not quite believe them. It was that simple, and yet impossible to wrap her thoughts around. Unlike her thoughts, the message wrapped itself around the screen and bounced repeatedly in between rereads. That Song should want to meet her after all that had happened and in spite of the intense feelings of betrayal she must have felt was the antithesis of sense to her. Or maybe it was just that she would have to climb the steep wall of guilt that she had internalised, and the strain of doing so was too much for her. Conversely, Lydia remembered the warmth of the young girl's arms around her neck and the way she had grown to trust Lydia implicitly, and she felt a combination of curiosity and desire to see what she was like now. It would be preferable, though, if she could observe herself watching from a distance and not actually have to bear the pain of the experience.

The message was brief and gave away little. She couldn't figure out how much trouble it had taken Song to track her down. One part of her thought and secretly hoped that she had gone to a lot of trouble. Yet, these days, when the lines between public and private information were so fragile that it was relatively easy to find out practically anything you wanted to about anyone, why had she waited 30 years? Something significant had to have happened in the intervening years that had led to her decision to make contact with the woman who had become like a second mother to her.

Lydia had read the message for the first time yesterday, her immediate shock turning to a kind of numbness, and she was undecided about how she should respond. In between rereading the lines of Song's message again and again, she clicked aimlessly between her Facebook account and a distracting game of patience.

The phone rang sharply, piercing the silence and providing a welcome relief from her thoughts.

'Lydia speaking.'

'Oh, hi there, Lydia. I was wondering if you'd mind me popping around for a chat. I've got something on my mind and I was hoping for a good ear to offload on.'

It was her young friend Sally, whom she knew from her teaching days. It floated into her mind to say, 'Well, that's a relief because I've also got something I want to offload on you!' but she heard herself saying breezily, without a word about her own state of mind, 'Of course, dear, that's absolutely fine. When would you like to come over? I've got no plans, so any time will do.'

'You're such a star, Lydia. Well I guess now is as good a time as any, if that's ok with you.'

'Well, why not? I'll put the kettle on and see you in five!'

'How are you, darling?' crooned Sally, planting an affectionate kiss on Lydia's cheek before she flung a pretty embroidered bag from her shoulders onto the floor and kicked off her shoes.

'Better for seeing you,' Lydia chirped, feeling like a young woman again, and revelling in the niceties that plastered a superficial normality over the crumbling walls of her life. At that moment, she resolved that she wouldn't tell Sally anything about Song's message but would focus herself entirely on Sally and whatever was bothering her. Somehow, reaching out empathetically would ward off the barrage of self-doubting thoughts that little bit longer and shroud her in her default setting of calm, reliable, supportive Lydia.

Sally was 31 years old, just a year older than Lydia had been when she had gone out to work in Cambodia all those years ago. They had met while Sally was doing her NQT year at the school where Lydia worked. Sally had come straight from university, and stayed in that same position for the next few years until Lydia retired. Sharing a very similar outlook on life, and a common sense of humour, the two had become close friends in spite of the 30-year age gap.

'So what's been happening?' Lydia said, drawing towards Sally on the sofa.

Sally curled her legs under her, and holding both hands snugly around her steaming cup of tea, she began to divulge.

'It's a long story,' she sighed.

'I'm in no hurry. Got myself trenched in with ammunition and food to last a few days,' said Lydia straight-faced.

Sally giggled and warmed herself up to it. 'Hmm, well you remember I told you about the new deputy head, Angela Whittington, who started at Newbury at the beginning of term?'

'Yes, I vaguely remember something...'

'Well, she's really, like, manipulative and plays all the staff off against each other.'

'Really? In what way?'

'One example... Ok, Patrick O'Kane and Amina Wasseem?' Lydia nodded her head in acknowledgement. 'They both teach maths, right? She's extremely good at her job, and without being rude, he's not quite so effective in his teaching methods.'

Lydia had some recollection of occasions where pupils had been known to run riot during Patrick's classes, while he could be heard through the walls shouting, 'Johnson, get your arse on your seat, right now. Gabby, quit flashing your tits over that table like a slapper and maybe you'll get somewhere in life,' and there would be a roar of laughter and an indignant Gabby shouting, 'Sir, that's abuse, that is!'

'So O'Kaney isn't known for the best boundary-setting techniques in the whole of teacherdom, but I'll give it to him – he can convey his subject in an entertaining way, so he's certainly not the worst of teachers. But Amina is a relatively new teacher and uses a highly disciplined approach with her classes. I like her a lot. She's a good laugh outside of the classroom and keeps her head out of the staff gossip columns, which I respect her for.'

Lydia turned her head to the side slightly in that empathetic way she had and Sally glanced at her appreciatively, seeming to know exactly what it signified.

'So Angela frequently asks Amina to cover for classes that O'Kaney is supposed to be teaching by telling her that O'Kaney is going to be late, and then he turns up a mere five minutes late, in his usual casual style, and discovers that his class has already been started by Amina. Of course, his style and technique can never compete with hers, so he ends up being humiliated. In the meantime, Angela is in her sly way sucking up to O'Kaney by telling other people what a wonderful storyteller he is in the classroom. Naturally, O'Kaney hears about this, and he's getting really frustrated by the mixed messages he's receiving. On the one hand, his authority is being undermined by Angela, while on the other she is praising him to high heaven! What do you make of all this?' Without waiting for Lydia to answer, Sally continued breathlessly with her tirade. 'The thing is, this isn't the only instance: Mrs Oh-so-high-and-mighty-Whittington is causing problems among teachers and staff throughout the school.'

Lydia fingered the rim of her coffee cup and said, 'It sounds tricky, and I certainly wouldn't be happy in such an environment. But I can't quite figure out how all this affects you personally – you haven't mentioned yourself so far in this tale.'

'Well, both O'Kaney and Amina are my friends, so it feels a little bit like I'm stuck in the middle, hearing different sides of the story from different people and trying to stay professional in the situation, when all I feel like doing is confronting Angela directly and having a yelling match with her! That would, of course, not be appropriate, but that witch is making me so angry!'

Lydia suppressed a chuckle, put her coffee cup down on the side table and held Sally's hand in her own. As if through a glass window, she could see herself dispensing fairy-godmother-like advice to Sally, while Sally listened keenly. In flawless mimicry of the Cambodians among whom she'd lived for several years, she maintained face the whole time, not a glimmer of a crack appearing in her walls.

'I love you, Lydia. You always manage to say exactly what I need to hear and make me feel so much better about the whole situation. I wish you hadn't retired and we could still have fun together in the staffroom like we did before.'

'I know, but then we wouldn't be having so much fun discussing this now. I'd be too heavily involved myself and bitching with you about that old witch by the photocopier.'

'Like you'd ever bitch about anyone!'

'I used to be a serial bitch, don't you know, moving from one school to another spreading slander and lies.' The two women laughed freely together, knowing what nonsense this was. Throughout the process Lydia was only just managing to maintain her composure, while under the foundations an earthquake was stirring.

Lydia waved goodbye to her young friend, grateful that she'd managed to hold herself together while the past was catching up on her and gnawing away at her innards. Lydia opened out the foldaway kitchen unit, designed to save space in a modern home, picked out a small pan and began stirring a jar of pre-prepared pasta and sauce into it. She spilt some over the edge onto the kitchen surface and tutted at her carelessness.

The dinner was one of the tastiest of the ready-prepared meals that she habitually bought, but this evening it tasted like white packaging foam. Out of mere habit she watched TV that evening. Her eyes were unable to focus, and she could see and hear nothing other than a blur of colours flickering across the screen and a comforting hubbub of sound, as voices from the past clamoured for attention, making her feel seasick. 'Don't send me back to him!' 'Even if you were ten years older than me, you'd still be as beautiful.' 'That's just what I don't want … a comfortable life.' 'You're not her mother.' 'It's nothing to do with you.'

After hours of turbulent thought, she made a resolution, and went to sleep with a certain stillness of mind, knowing that a decision had finally been made.

England, November 2036

Bonfire night fireworks crackled and whizzed in the distance as Lydia put the final preparations to her outfit, smoothing her flyaway hair and adjusting her tights. Her mouth was dry and she kept sipping on her glass of mineral water. Nothing could minimise the pounding in her chest cavity.

At exactly seven minutes past six, the doorbell chimed through the house and Lydia glided down the stairs to the door, knowing that this was her reality and that she couldn't hold off that truth any longer. As she reached the door, her shadow loomed large in the light from the teak standing lamp, an heirloom from her great-great-grandmother. Lydia unlocked the Chubb and, while her shaking hands fumbled with the chain, the doorbell rang again, impatiently. Lydia opened the door and stood with a frozen smile on her face as she looked without saying a word at the woman standing in front of her. Here she was, after 30 years, as beautiful and as innocent as ever. Only a slight sadness in her eyes and grey shadows of sleepless nights gave a slight hint of something else. Her dark, glossy hair was cut short so that the edges feathered around her jawline. She smiled softly at Lydia in an attempt to break the ice.

Lydia collected her faculties and spoke after what felt like minutes but was probably only a few seconds. 'Please come in, Song?' she said with a questioning tone, as though she was not sure whether this stylish woman was the same girl she had known.

'Yes, it *is* me, Aunty,' Song replied, reaching forward to give Lydia a hug. Lydia held her body stiffly and patted Song on the shoulders like one would pat a dog.

I need to loosen up. I shouldn't punish Song for my own feelings of guilt. 'How are you, my dear? It's been so many years. I have so many questions to ask you.' Lydia pushed past the pain to reach out.

Song didn't say anything. She just held her hand on Lydia's shoulder and drew her into the house as though she were the host and not the guest.

Chapter 2
Cambodia, April 2006

A red haze filled the horizon. Lydia opened the door of her relatively cool apartment and braced herself against the oven-like heat of the early April evening. She picked her way past the haggle of motodop drivers calling out to offer their service, smiled and told them she wasn't going far. 'You crazy foreigner!' joked one of them to her, a weather-beaten, wide-smiling man called Sakoeun with whom she had often ridden.

'I know, I know. I should be locked up for it!' she laughed back at him. Everyone in Phnom Penh thought you were crazy if you wanted to walk from place to place, especially if you were Western and could afford a ride. The concept of wanting to walk for the sake of walking and for some exercise was alien to most Khmer people: walking was usually associated with poverty, and thus to walk was accordingly a status-smasher. With it as hot as it was in April, you could understand this to some extent, but she really only had a five-minute walk and it was hardly the middle of the day.

It was two years since she had first moved to Cambodia to work with Volunteer Opportunities in Asia (VOA) as an English teacher, and in that time, once she'd familiarised herself with the layout of the roads and the crazy but functional traffic system in Phnom Penh, she had bought herself a moped. However, she didn't like the hassle or see the point of taking it on short trips. Whenever the motodop drivers saw her come out of the house without her bike, they would immediately jump on her as a potential customer. She almost felt guilty not riding with them as she knew how poor they were, but as her friend Simon had pointed out to her, 'You can't fix everyone.' Thankfully, the men on her street were friendly and reasonable.

Simon, an American expat, had told her that the drivers on his street were becoming quite spiteful about him and his day-to-day movements, and niggling among themselves about the amount of money he would pay them for the smallest of journeys. He had only been in Cambodia six months and hadn't bought himself a moto yet, but having to deal with the negative attitude of his regular moto drivers was pushing him in the direction of buying one. Lydia herself was lucky to have a pleasant group of motodop drivers in her own locality, so while they would joke with her, she never felt that this came from any maliciousness or vindictiveness in them, which left her feeling comfortable to banter back. Nevertheless, as a Westerner used to going about her daily life with little comment or observation from others, she had had to get used to them knowing her every move. Her life was not her own in the same way that it was back home in England; it was a far more public affair.

'Lydia, thanks for coming over at such short notice. You're phenomenal, you know that.' Brian kissed her on both cheeks in his usual desultory fashion and waved her over to the chair on the other side of his desk.

'No problem whatsoever.' Lydia felt a twinge of irritation as the chair to which she was directed was strewn with assorted papers and she was required to remove the whole pile before she could sit down. Brian didn't seem to notice, but he did graciously hand her a glass of water.

'You well, my dear?' he asked, a huge grin spreading over his broad, sunburnt face. It was impossible to stay irritated with him for long as he was so charming, even though she'd like to at times, particularly as she got to know him more.

'Fine. I'm loving life and loving the kids still.'

'Naturally. You're such a nurturer, Lydia.' Brian smirked while observing her for any hint of a negative reaction; he knew such comments were not best appreciated, especially when expressed as flippantly as he had the tendency to do.

Ignoring this comment with nothing but an imperceptible flinch of the shoulders, Lydia slapped away a mosquito buzzing around her ankles and asked briskly, 'So, I'm assuming you've asked me to your office to discuss Marta.'

'Yes, indeed – Marta, Marta. It wasn't exactly unexpected, was it? But of course it's always sad to see one of our team members go. I just wanted to go through the formalities and find out if you'd like us to help provide you with another flatmate or whether you'd prefer to be on your own?'

Lydia had shared her apartment for two years with Marta from Austria. Marta had also come to Cambodia under the VOA umbrella. She was a trained social worker and had worked with an organisation that sought to provide training opportunities for young orphans. Unfortunately, she had had a long series of health problems and had been struck down with amoebic dysentery three times, meaning that she'd spent almost more time in bed or with her head down the toilet than she'd actually been able to contribute towards work. It didn't help that Marta had eaten out of the market stalls a lot, but to be fair, other expats did the same and they were absolutely fine. Marta had had a bad run of it as far as food poisoning was concerned, and her whole Cambodian experience had been rather negatively coloured by this. She never quite got it into her head to accept responsibility for the things she could change, and she still insisted on eating in the same way fairly frequently, even though the two women had taken on a local girl to cook for them at home.

While some people would have just put up with occasional health problems and got on with things, for Marta this became an overwhelming issue. In the end she had decided it wasn't worth staying, even though she'd come out to Cambodia with high ideals of working for social justice. She had flown back to Europe the day before. In some ways Lydia was quite relieved to see her go, as Marta's growing negativity had started to get her down, and she didn't imagine that they would stay in touch. This was a rather flat end to what had begun as a good friendship.

'Hmm, actually I think I'd be quite happy to stay on my own, at least for a while. Although does that mean that I'd have to move somewhere cheaper in order to save VOA costs?'

'Not necessarily. As you've been with us for two years I think we can be fairly flexible as far as your wishes are concerned, and it shouldn't be a problem as we won't actually be paying out any more upfront costs than we already have been for your place.'

'Thank you. To tell you the truth, that's a relief. I feel like I just need some space for a bit. Marta wasn't the easiest person to live with, especially these past six months. Maybe in a few weeks or months I'll be ready to share again, but not just yet.'

A large gecko scampered across the wall and sat rapidly flicking its tongue in and out above Brian's head. The swelling sound of children's voices and laughter could be heard in the street outside. The *haji* collector – the East-Asian equivalent of a rag-and-bone man – could be heard calling out in a nasal tone, '*Haji, haji,*' as he pushed his cart down the road. Lydia followed the movements of the gecko's tongue, losing herself in its rhythm. Brian drew her attention back by asking her a few customary questions related to her work progress and made some cursory notes on his employee database.

'One last question. Is everything ok now between you and Mike?'

'Yeah, we have a really good working relationship now. He's given up on the heavy-handed approach at trying to convert me and I don't feel he's trying to pressure me in any way. Thanks for having a word with him about that. Sometimes I almost miss him confronting me with words from the Bible, though – it felt like he genuinely cared about me, in a funny sort of way! But I just didn't like the way he made me feel as though I was in the wrong all the time, even though he's the one whose first marriage fell apart because he was having an affair.'

Brian chuckled and commented wryly, 'These born-again types do have their own agenda; there's no getting away from that. They come out here purporting to do development work and caring passionately about the poor, but they're all committed to seeing as many Buddhists as possible become Christians, thereby denying their Cambodian roots and cutting them off in many ways from their own culture. How that contributes to the country's development, I've not quite figured out!'

'They have their reasons, I'm sure,' mused Lydia.

'Dubious reasons, no doubt.' He looked at the clock on the wall and then reached across the table and tapped Lydia on the arm. 'Anyway, my dear, I'm sure you don't need to hear me rambling on and on, and you probably want your tea, don't you? I know I do! Let me know how things go at work. You know I've always got a willing ear if you need to talk to someone. You know, we've loved having you with us in Cambodia and I hope you can stay a few more years.'

Lydia could tell he was being genuine at this point and was touched. 'I've loved being here, too, and at the moment I can't think of any reason why I should go back home, so I guess that's as good a reason as any for staying, wouldn't you say?'

'Excellent! Well, we couldn't ask for more than that, really. Take care of yourself, and keep up the good work with the language learning as well.'

Lydia had worked really hard at learning Khmer during her first six months of being in Cambodia and had continued the process, taking opportunities to practise freely with all the Khmer with whom she came into contact. She was doing much better than many foreigners she knew who had been in the country for the same amount of time. She had a natural feel for languages, and was not afraid to try out in real situations the things she was learning. The learning process for her was grounded in inquisitiveness – she constantly asked questions to push her understanding and levels of vocabulary. She was now able to hold a decent conversation in Khmer about everyday things. It was a struggle to understand work-related or specialist jargon of any sort, but then, in her English-teaching context, that was not really something she had to deal with.

Back at her home, Lydia pushed away her half-eaten bowl of rice and fried vegetables and groaned inwardly as she contemplated years stretching ahead of her filled with the delights and variations of rice dish upon rice dish. She was now used to eating rice at practically every meal but still, if she didn't live in Phnom Penh, where the new supermarkets were selling Western food, she didn't know how she would cope – rice certainly wasn't her favourite food. It never had been, which was ironic considering this was where she felt she was supposed to be. However, she couldn't justify buying supermarket food all the time on her allowance, as it certainly wasn't cheap, so for now she would just have to find lots of creative ways to eat rice. Thankfully, her cook who came three times a week was pretty adept at doing just that. The organisation she worked for paid a fair amount for her accommodation, which gave her an image of wealth, but her day-to-day living funds were not actually that high – maybe around $300 a month. This was enough to live on but certainly not enough to save for the future. Cambodian teachers themselves received a pitiful salary of around $30 to $50 a month, meaning that they were often under

20

motivated, had to take second or even third jobs, or would 'encourage' parents to provide cash for their child's education. This was just one example of the endemic corruption that permeated like yeast throughout Cambodian society.

As Lydia cleared her dishes away with a wry smile, a sudden crash and squeal filled her headspace. At first thought she was only mildly disturbed as Phnom Penh was a noisy city, and you could guarantee that if dogs weren't barking, small businesses weren't working at all hours of the day and night and the ubiquitous all-day wedding parties weren't taking place at that exact point in time, something would be sure to disturb the temporary silence within the next half-hour. It was probably just a catfight outside her window, because it was remarkably close. However, her mind would not hold to this possibility – there was something about that squeal that niggled at her. It wasn't a cat-squall: there had been something half suppressed and even human about it.

Unable to let it go, she picked up her torch in one hand and the heavy wok in the other, cautiously opened the front door and peered into her front yard. Her landlady's gardener, Rith, had left the spade and trowel out overnight, propped up against the shed – something he didn't normally do as he was so meticulous – and the spade had fallen to the ground. She could see a dirt mark against the side of the corrugated shed and a shadow sprawled out to the left of the shed. Her tongue feeling thick in her mouth, she called out, 'Is anyone there?!' as loudly as possible so that her neighbours would be alerted in case of real danger.

Silence answered. A silence that breathed across the darkness with anticipation. Seconds later, the shadow moved, almost imperceptibly, as if trying to edge its way out of sight.

Whoever or whatever it was obviously wasn't dangerous, otherwise they wouldn't be trying to hide from her. Feeling braver, Lydia stepped out of the bungalow and towards the shed. As she moved closer and shone her torch brightly at the intruder, the shadow emitted a whimper. She saw a pair of little hands raise themselves at her defensively. She placed the torch on the ground, reached down and took hold of the upper arm of a small, ragged child. Her face was

21

covered in grime and huge brown eyes stared up at her like a rabbit caught in headlights.

'Whatever are you doing, little one?! Are you trying to scare me?' Lydia spoke this as reassuringly as she could. Her heart was racing, although it was obvious that the girl was much more terrified than she was. The child was beginning to wriggle out of her hold, and in spite of her tiny size she was struggling with the strength of a tethered pony. Lydia glanced at her right hand and realised that her heavy wok was held out threateningly in front of her. She released the wok and said softly, 'I'm not going to hurt you, I promise.'

Suddenly the girl began emitting half-suppressed gulps as if she was trying not to cry. Lydia realised from the scrunched-up look on her face that she was in a lot of pain.

'Where does it hurt?' Lydia said in an urgent voice.

Without saying a word, the child put one hand up to her forehead, where there was a large bruise, and pointed down to her left foot, where dark blood was seeping from the bottom of her foot and mingling with the dirt.

'Ok, I don't make a habit of taking in intruders, but it's obvious you need some care and attention, little one. Please, come inside with me and I'll try and clean you up.' The girl looked at her with a frown on her face, but after a pause she proceeded to hobble towards the front door. Feeling a little ashamed at asking the girl to make her own way there, Lydia picked her up. Although she went stiff in her arms, she was compliant and made no protest as Lydia carried her into the bungalow.

Chapter 3
Cambodia, April 2006

I've no idea what I'm doing; I hope I can do this properly. Lydia sat the girl on her kitchen table and dabbed the blood from her foot with a damp cloth. After cleaning away the blood she could see the wound was not actually very wide or deep so she wouldn't be needing stitches. She wiped some antiseptic on the wound, wrapped a bandage as tightly as she could around the foot and secured the loose end with a safety pin. Then she patted the girl's knee gently and smiled at her.

Without making eye contact with her or raising her head, the girl whispered, 'Thank you,' in Khmer, and then made an incomprehensible sound as if she was trying to say something else but was afraid of giving away too much.

'I'm Lydia. What's your name?'

The child sat silently with her head bowed for what seemed like a long time, and Lydia thought she had misunderstood, so she repeated the question.

'The ugly one,' the girl replied, and suddenly raised her head and made fleeting eye contact with Lydia.

Lydia could not juxtapose the words she had just heard with this grimy but beautiful, fragile creature with her large eyes and heart-shaped face sitting in front of her. Her heart was jolted with a sensation that she couldn't identify and then, as she breathed heavily and turned her head away, the sensation left a lump in her throat and brought tears to her eyes.

'You see,' whispered the child, 'I'm so ugly I make you cry.'

'No!' said Lydia sharply. But despite her Khmer speaking and listening skills having reached a new level and a feeling of breakthrough in communication, she became momentarily inarticulate – all she could do was shake her head and mumble, 'Beautiful, beautiful.' Her body began to tremble with great, angry sobs and she wept for what must have been five minutes, trying unsuccessfully to stop, blowing her nose and wiping her eyes with the one tissue she had in her pocket until it became so soggy that it was useless. All the while the girl sat on the table and stared at her.

Reverberating in her mind's ears was the memory of her mother speaking to her closest friend on the phone when Lydia was seven years old, not realising that Lydia had woken up to go to the toilet and was walking quietly past the stairwell at the point that the lacerating words were spoken: 'I know we're supposed to love our children, Jeannie, and I do, but whenever I see Lydia's unsmiling and plain-looking face I can't help feeling sad and slightly sick.' Lydia's mother had been a loving mother in most respects and was most likely expressing her honest and disturbing feelings in what she thought was utmost privacy, but the imprint of these words had never left. Although outwardly it didn't change Lydia's behaviour towards her mother, she certainly made a more conscious effort to smile more.

After her crying ceased, Lydia took the child into Marta's old bedroom, laid her under the sheet and switched on the fan. She stroked the girl's cheek with a butterfly touch and then turned to go. Just after Lydia turned out the light, the little girl called out, 'My name is Song, Aunty,' and Lydia closed the door softly behind her.

'You have an appointment?' said the young man at the reception desk.

'Yes, I've got an appointment with Dr Duke at 11am.'

'He's currently with a patient. Would you mind waiting over there until he's ready?' asked the receptionist.

'Of course not,' Lydia said sweetly and sat down in the surgery waiting room, while Song slid into the seat beside her, almost as if she was invisible. The receptionist looked over at her with the child, holding her eyes for a moment longer than she considered appropriate, and then smiled distractedly before turning back to his work.

Lydia had been attending Dr Duke's surgery since her arrival in Phnom Penh two years ago, but this was the first time she had seen this particular receptionist. For some reason he was making her feel uncomfortable. Maybe that was because she felt awkward having this child with her who was not her own, and she felt as though she was being investigated for a crime she had not committed.

Song sat silently and looked with wide eyes around the room, then she picked up a magazine lying on the coffee table and began to tear one of the pages out of it. Lydia heard the tearing sound before she

24

saw what the girl was doing and turned around sharply. 'Oh Song, you mustn't do that! I'm sorry,' she said to the receptionist, and could feel herself reddening while she took the damaged magazine from Song's hands.

'It's not a problem, I'm sure,' he said kindly. 'Just don't let her tear up any more magazines otherwise there'll be nothing left for patients to read while they wait.'

Lydia picked up another magazine to read herself and became immersed in a twee story about celebrities' lives. A few minutes later she was disturbed from her reverie by the sound of the receptionist's laughter. Glancing up she realised that he was looking over in her direction again, and felt a twinge of indignation. 'What is so funny?' she asked in a slightly stiff voice.

'Your little daughter has made a paper crow and it's squawking at me!' he replied. Lydia looked down at Song and saw that her head was bowed and she was pulling back and forth the wings of an origami crow that she had made from the magazine page she had torn out, in order to make its beak move. Lydia saw the funny side, patted Song on the knee and said to the young man, 'Well, she's certainly creative – can't fault her in that!' Song looked up at Lydia and smiled – the first smile she'd seen, and it made her face shine with a mischievous beauty.

My daughter? She doesn't look remotely like me, but I'm not going to correct him. It was too complicated to explain, and she also experienced a flush of warmth as she thought of this little, adorable girl and had a vivid impression of her placing her hand in hers.

When she looked up again, the young man was gazing at her, and there was something about the expression in his eyes that caused her heartbeat to speed up, but she rapidly pushed this feeling to the back of her mind. With so much attention from Cambodian men, this didn't mean anything special. It was just because she was white and therefore carried a scent of money and the exotic to them.

'Lydia Philips, please come through if you're ready?' Doctor Duke stepped outside his room and addressed her, as excessively polite as ever.

She pretended not to notice as the receptionist's eyes followed her into the doctor's room.

Doctor Duke stroked his wispy grey beard and focused his piercingly pale eyes on her and said, 'How can I help you today, Lydia?' He was a New Zealander who had been practising in Phnom Penh for around four years now, mainly for the expat community, and he had become a familiar, comforting presence in her life.

'Well, it's not me; it's Song. She needs a tetanus jab as she stepped on a garden tool.'

'Song?' He looked intently at the girl and said in Khmer, 'How are you, my dear?'

Lydia knew that the doctor wouldn't pry too much into the girl's sudden appearance in her life, but she could still feel a hot flush rising in her and a sense of defensiveness, as though she had to justify herself. 'She doesn't have any parents and I'm just taking care of her for a few days, until…' Until when exactly? That was the question that she blatantly hadn't even begun to answer in her own mind.

'Ok, no problem. Let me see the wound.' Lydia marvelled at this man's discretion: it wasn't that he wasn't interested, but he didn't want to pry and make people feel uncomfortable. If you wanted to volunteer information then he'd be more than willing to listen or to answer queries if you had any, but he did not put himself forward, for which Lydia was particularly grateful at this point in time.

Lydia left the doctor's surgery with Song and sat her behind her on her moped and rode home. A thousand and one thoughts ran through her mind. It was a full day and two nights since Song had landed on her doorstep, so to speak, and in that time Lydia had managed to find out that Song was ten years old and that her parents had moved from Vietnam about four years ago, so Song was ethnically Vietnamese. From what Song had conveyed, they had been escaping a rather uncomfortable position of indebtedness in their homeland. For a few years everything seemed to go well; being industrious, her father had quickly set up a small business selling electronic appliances and was even beginning to look happy again. Then just eight months previously, the men to whom her father was in debt showed up and her parents began arguing, although Song didn't understand what about at the time.

'My mother kept saying to my dad, "You've got to get the money from somewhere. You'll have to sell the business," and my dad got angrier and angrier as he'd worked so hard and didn't want to do that. My Uncle Thom told me he must have owed a huge amount of money because they shot him for it. My mother woke up and saw his body lying there in a pool of blood one morning – it was so horrible, Aunty – and she began screaming and screaming, and then she went quiet and hasn't said a word to me or anyone else since. She stopped taking care of me. She doesn't love me any more...'

'No,' Lydia said. 'It sounds like the pressure of the situation was too much for her and something snapped inside her mind. I don't want you to ever imply that you're unlovable again, do you hear me?'

Song glanced at her, unconvinced, and picked at a whorl on the table.

'So who looked after you when your mother got sick?'

'My Uncle Thom. He was born in Cambodia and stayed here and married my Aunty Lena when my grandparents moved back to Vietnam and had my dad. He's a lot older than my dad.'

'Was he good to you?'

'No!' Song's soft voice and demeanour lashed out suddenly like a cat scratching in defence, then retreated again as though shocked by her own reaction. 'Or at least not for as long as I can remember. He hates me, and he was always comparing me to his own children, and accusing me of things I hadn't done, and then he would beat me really hard – sometimes until I would bleed – but always in places where no one could see. One time about three months ago, he hit me for saying hello to an old lady who came past the house every day, saying I was being disrespectful.'

'Song, that's terrible. I'm so sorry.'

'And then I walked past my mother, who was in her usual chair, crying, and she just stared at me with an empty look on her face. I felt so angry and sad I wanted to lash out – but I didn't.'

Song sighed, and all her features screwed up. 'I don't understand why she doesn't love me any more and didn't try to protect me. Not only did Uncle beat me, but he made Aunty give me less food than anyone else in the house and I was getting really hungry.'

'Hence when you ran away, you were looking for food.'

'Yes. I didn't really intend to stay away for ever: I didn't really know what I wanted, other than to get more to eat, and to get away from his horrible hands.'

'I think you had more of a plan than you think; look at where you ended up.'

'Well, I knew there are a lot of foreigners in this area. I hoped someone would have left out lots of food in their rubbish.'

Lydia had been sitting at one side of the table to give the child some space, but she stood up and went round to where Song was sitting, and wrapped her arms around her. 'What am I going to do with you, little one?'

'Don't send me back to him!' said Song, her body tensing under Lydia's arms.

'Of course I won't, if what you're telling me is true, but do you think there's any chance that he and his wife and your mother will be worried about you and start looking for you?'

'Not a chance,' she said with finality. 'I'm sure *he'll* be glad I've gone, and my mother – well, she won't even notice...' Lydia stroked Song's hair. She had a feeling there was something about her mother that Song wasn't telling her, but as she'd been so open thus far, Lydia didn't think now was the time to start prying unnecessarily. When she was ready, the words would seep their way out like juice from an overripe mango.

Song's family lived in a village about two miles from Phnom Penh, so if they did decide to hunt down the missing child, if there was enough of a will there, then a way would surely be found, but from Song's story it really didn't seem like the family would exert themselves to find her. There didn't seem to be any reason to disbelieve her.

Lydia mulled all this over as she negotiated her way past the traffic on the Toul Tom Poung Market and rode onto the dusty and potholed street that she lived on, her moped bumping and juddering over and around the potholes. The local vendors sitting by their stalls all looked at her with the child on the back of her bike, and she could guarantee that they'd all be gossiping about her as soon as she went inside. Soon all the locals would know her business – or think they knew her business – but right now she was determined not to let that bother her.

28

'That wasn't so bad now, was it?' she said to Song as she unlocked the padlock to her front gate and took the bike inside.

'No, not so bad at all. Only a little bit painful,' she said, and smiled again.

While Lydia unpacked the groceries, Song sat swinging her legs and doodling on a piece of paper. She was becoming more comfortable with her already, and certainly wasn't the little mouse that she'd been on the first day.

'So, have you had any schooling at all, little one?'

'I had two years of schooling before my dad was k… died. I liked going to school and learning. I miss it.'

'I can understand that. In my country, England, everyone has to go to school from the age of 5 until 16 – most people attend school until at least 18, in fact. We don't always appreciate it there because we take it for granted, and when we have to go we'd much rather be outside playing. It's only as we get older that we realise what a privilege it is to receive the education that we do. I teach children about your age here in Phnom Penh. Maybe… oh, nothing.' She didn't go any further as she didn't want to give the child any false hope or expectation.

The receptionist had slipped her a leaflet about immunisation when she'd left the doctor's surgery and now Lydia absent-mindedly took it out of her bag and popped it into the bin without even looking at it properly. As she did so, a piece of paper floated to the floor. Song was chattering away about her happy experiences at school. Lydia picked up the piece of paper and was about to throw that away as well – she really didn't like clutter and had the tendency to throw everything away that had no immediate value – when she noticed that it was folded up and had her name on it.

In perfectly formed Roman letters was written, 'You amaze me with your beauty. I would love to see you properly. Please call me on 092 443417. Radha.'

After a brief heart-skipping high, Lydia's first reaction was to wonder whether someone was playing a practical joke on her. 'It's not funny; it's creepy,' she said out loud in English, without thinking.

'You're speaking English. I don't understand,' said Song with a quaver in her voice.

29

'I'm sorry, darling, I wasn't thinking... It's not important. What were you saying?' Lydia felt guilty that she hadn't been paying attention to what Song had been saying, and tried to focus herself completely on Song for the next half-hour or so.

Chapter 4
Cambodia, April 2006

Tears were making inroads down Lydia's carefully made-up cheeks. You've got to stop thinking like this, she said to herself. It happened a long time ago now and you can't walk in fear of abandonment for the rest of your life.

Lydia didn't have very much experience of romantic relationships, but what she did have had been fairly brutal. When she was 27, a newly qualified solicitor called Rob – her 'toy boy', her friends called him in jest, even though he was only three years her junior – had flattered her with his protestations of feelings for her, and whirled her over on a romantic dream of smiles, longing looks, flowers and cheeky text messages. Being naive or simply deeply touched to the soul, she had surrendered herself to him emotionally and sexually too quickly, considering the briefness of their acquaintance. She was not someone to give herself to anyone in a half-hearted or casual sort of way, and she did not make any attempts to guard her heart with Rob, but threw herself onto the path that he had nicely polished and slid down fast into his tunnel. His tunnel turned out to be an extremely shallow one. All Lydia's thoughts were centred on this wonderful young man with whom she hoped to spend the rest of her life. Three months into their intense love affair, with no warning whatsoever, he walked out on the relationship, leaving her a text message that read, 'Sorry Lydia, things weren't working out 4 me and I don't c much point in making things painful by explaining n analysing motives. Good luck in the future and have fun! Rob x'.

This message angered Lydia so much with its cowardice that she picked over the details of it for days, even down to the impertinent kiss at the end. She tried to call Rob several times to plead an explanation from him, but every time his phone would 'mysteriously' be switched off or go straight through to voicemail. In the end, her sense of dignity prevented her from doing any more – emailing him and tracking down his family and friends – and she was left alone with her grief and rejection, a rejection made ten times worse by the complete absence of an explanation. This inexplicability kept her stuck in one place, running around and around the circular treadmill of mental enquiry for a lot longer than was warranted by the length of the relationship.

It was two years before she finally felt that she had moved on from Rob and stopped regretting the words of affection she had spoken to him, and the sexual pandering to a man who had clearly valued her as a dust mite, yet made her believe otherwise.

Radha's note had brought up all these feelings again and, with Song asleep, Lydia was sitting on her bed and standing up and padding around the tiled floor in her bare feet and then sitting down again, trying to get some clarity and put things in perspective. She had taken a shower shortly after arriving home from the surgery but she was becoming so het up with restless energy that with the high humidity she was going to need another one before going to bed.

Exhaling as she stepped under the lukewarm shower again, she wondered why she couldn't just behave as the world expected her to behave and go out and have detached, fun dates with men without her emotions getting in the way, but that was not the way she was wired. 'Don't take it all so seriously, Lydia,' her friend Rhona had said to her. 'Ok, Rob was a complete shit, but why don't you play men at their own game and get what you want out of relationships without being too intense about it all? That way you can walk away scar free if things don't work out. I know, you're too old-fashioned to do that!'

And of course, Cambodian dating mores were very different to Western ones – dating that didn't have the immediate expectation of marriage was still a relatively new thing among the younger generation. Men were used to having their sexual desires met by prostitutes, and respectable women were expected to be modest and virginal. Even after marriage women weren't supposed to be too passionate sexually, perpetuating some men's continuation with prostitutes. When dating did take place, men and women were expected to keep their distance in public; even hand-holding was frowned upon. There was a part of Lydia that yearned for this sort of relational conservatism where the boundaries were clear, although hypocritical at times.

With the benefit of detached self-analysis, Lydia smiled ironically at herself, and by the time she had finished her shower she felt a modicum of peace settle on her heart. There was no way she was going to let Rob ruin the rest of her life, but at the same time there was no harm in being cautious, and she wouldn't let herself settle on a decision about what to do in response to Radha's note straight away.

She settled down to sleep at last, with the ceiling fan whirring comfortingly. Suddenly, at the point of drifting out of consciousness, a wave of thought crashed down on her and she was startled wide awake by something she had not considered. What on earth am I going to do with Song while I go to work tomorrow? After ruminating on this thought for about 20 minutes or so, Lydia settled on going into school tomorrow and asking her manager Mike if he thought his wife would mind looking after her for a temporary period until she'd worked out a longer-term solution. Somehow she couldn't imagine that being a problem. As for tomorrow, she didn't suppose that the child would come to much harm if she was left in the house on her own for one day. She wasn't a baby, after all, and she seemed fairly tough after everything she'd been through.

Even without putting much conscious thought into it, clearly Lydia wasn't conceiving Song as being anything other than a permanent fixture in her life from now on. Somehow the child had inched her way into her heart and life in a way that felt unobtrusive and, in some inexplicable way, meant to be.

'Can anyone tell me what "talented" means?'

A sea of hands thrust their way up in front of her: more than half the class of 30 pupils was attempting to answer the question. Many of them would not actually know the right answer, but they were enthusiastic enough to engage fully with the learning process and loved receiving attention from their kind and beautiful white teacher.

'Yes, Sophor. What do you think?'

Sophor grinned shyly, tucking her hair behind her ears and murmuring something incomprehensible.

'I'm sorry. Can you speak up please, sweetheart?'

'When you are very good at something,' she said, raising her voice enough to be heard.

'Very good, Sophor. Give me an example of something you might be talented at, Phireak?'

Phireak was a lively, lovable boy. She had recognised that he had learning difficulties from her training and experience, even though there was no specific testing or real understanding of learning difficulties in Cambodian schools. He had no problem contributing orally but struggled with reading and writing.

'I can be very talented at riding my bike.'

'Lovely. You've got the right idea. What are you talented at, Khemareth?'

'Nothing.'

'I'm sure you are! How about writing? I think you're talented at writing.'

Many of the children were orphans or came from difficult home situations, and while they were delightful and charming as Cambodian children typically were, they also had extremely low self-esteem. Lydia felt that her job was as much about building up their self-esteem as it was about teaching them English. Khemareth was a tiny, underdeveloped child with a constantly wistful expression on her face. At times she would drift off into her own little world and Lydia would have to grab her attention by repeating her point or question, and the other children would laugh at her for her being fey. Yet Khemareth would write incredibly imaginative stories that made your heart hammer with pride. Even if other people mocked her for her otherworldliness, Lydia was determined to encourage her in the writing talent that she clearly possessed.

'Are you sure you know what you're doing, Lydia?' Mike's wife, Helen, frowned, hitching up little Tom more securely onto her hip. 'You can't just take on all the little waifs and strays of Cambodia as if they were your own. I'm happy to help, but you do need to think about the long-term implications of what you're doing.'

'I know as much as I'll ever know. It sounds so sentimental but I'm really just following my heart here. What else can I do – send her back to her abusive uncle and mentally ill mother? Ok, so it's not the fact that she's mentally ill that's the problem in itself, but rather the lack of care being provided.'

'Don't you think there are other kids in the same situation as her?'

'Of course, but they don't all end up in my front garden like some divinely led appointment. Come on, Helen, surely you must understand that kind of logic?!'

Helen smiled wryly. Tom became fractious and she put him down on the floor, where he promptly began trailing a string which the dog snuffled after. 'You know I want to help you out here, but I just want to be sure you've really thought things through.'

'Some things I'll have to figure out as I go along. I don't have all the answers, but I do have the willingness and commitment to care for her as if she were my own child. Who's to say that if I don't look after her, she won't end up being easy prey for some vicious sex trafficker?'

'That is true...' Helen trailed off, and twirled a loop of her hair thoughtfully. 'Hmm, I could try home schooling her with Amy. They're about the same age, and it'd be good for Amy to have a playmate. There is the language barrier, of course, but I can work with her at her own pace. Mike has already said it wouldn't be possible to take her on at your school, hasn't he?'

'Yeah, which I can understand because of the emotional and boundary complications of me acting as both a mother figure and a teacher. Look, Helen, I know what you're suggesting isn't going to be easy. Are you...'

'Don't worry about it, Lydia,' Helen interrupted, as though she didn't want Lydia to say anything that might shake her sudden resolve. 'I care about you, and believe it or not, I do care about Cambodian children in desperate situations too. I'll figure this out, with the help of God. Like I said, Amy will love having a companion and will have a lot of patience with Song's lack of English language skills. I've seen how she is with our Khmer helper's children.'

Lydia was moved by a compulsion and gave Helen a startlingly fierce hug. 'You're a great friend, Helen. Song is going to love you!'

As Lydia walked back home, past the street market with its usual smell reminiscent of rotting fruit and the old ladies on their haunches in front of their baskets of fruit doing what looked like a brisk business, she was bursting with a spring-like liveliness. '*Som dto!*' she called out penitently after absentmindedly knocking over a pile of pomelos. She helped to re-form the pile, simpering at the seller, knowing a smile covered over a multitude of sins, all the while bubbling inside.

Without hesitating now, Lydia sat on her round wicker chair with the throw-on floppy cushion – a common feature of expat living in Phnom Penh – and typed out the following text message to Radha: 'Thanks 4 ur msg. It was v sweet. If u want 2 get 2 kno me more YOU give me a call! I'm a traditional girl. Lydia.' Lydia pressed send, feeling almost proud of herself for making a move but at the same time putting the ball into the man's court. I've really got nothing to lose after all.

The next minute her phone beeped. It was an incoming message from Radha with nothing but a cheeky face on it. Though bursting with temptation to react, Lydia refused to engage with this game. He can give me a proper call and deal with me like a gentleman or this will not go anywhere, Lydia resolved outwardly, while inwardly she wondered if she'd made a complete fool of herself already. If she hadn't been in such a good mood, this most likely would never have happened.

Five minutes later, her phone rang, and Lydia allowed it to ring a good few times before she picked up as she didn't want to look too eager. Yet as she picked it up, she saw Brian's name on the display, not Radha's, and she was slightly irritated with herself at the trace of disappointment that flushed over her.

'Hi, Brian. How can I help you?'

'Lydia, how are you doing?' Brian asked in a more formal voice than usual.

'I'm doing well thanks, and you?'

'Oh, just a little cold, but nothing to get my knickers in a twist about. How is Song?'

'You've heard, then?'

'Of course, Lydia. Mike has told me the story.'

'Song is doing well. She's...'

'Lydia, you know it's against VOA policy for volunteers to become too personally involved with the locals, especially children.'

'What exactly do you mean by "against VOA policy"?' Lydia felt a sudden chill go through her bones in spite of the warmth of the atmosphere.

'This is serious business, I hope you understand. It's all to do with the understanding between our organisation and the Cambodian government. If one of our volunteers essentially takes on the mothering of a Cambodian child, it would be a breach of that understanding since caring for children is not one of our agreed tasks in Cambodia. Even if it were, what you are doing is as an individual, not as part of VOA.'

'So if what I'm doing is personal and not under the authority of VOA, how does that create a problem? I'm not clear about that.'

'It would set a precedent, Lydia, and risk our position as a well-respected organisation in Cambodia because one of our staff would be breaching our agreed policies with the Cambodian government. This kind of thing does not stay hidden. You know how the Cambodian grapevine works. I'm sorry to be so up front with you as I really respect you, you know, but I'd advise you strongly not to become involved with this girl any more than you already have.'

A cold stone weighed on Lydia's heart. 'What would be the consequences if I do?'

'I would need to discuss that with the VOA international board of directors and let you know what we decide. All I can say again is that I'd advise you strongly to reconsider your decision.'

Lydia had never felt such a clamour of mixed emotions as she did at that moment. She opened her mouth to speak but a dam was blocking her words. All she could muster was a strangled, 'I'll think about it,' then she found herself disconnecting the phone and sitting on the edge of the seat, numb.

Chapter 5
Cambodia, April 2006

He hasn't rung me yet; maybe he never will. Lydia folded up clothes and placed them meticulously in their allocated spots, hung up or folded in the wicker wardrobes in her and Song's rooms. That is the least of my concerns right now so why am I even torturing myself over this?

Song came into the bedroom as Lydia was in her room and sat shyly on the bed. 'I... like... mangoes... and... I... love Aunty... Lydia.' She was testing out the English that she had picked up from Amy, and the painstakingly learnt words touched a raw spot in Lydia.

'Oh, well done! Your English is wonderful.' Lydia leaned over the bed and hugged the child. Lydia was surprised that a child who had gone through the experiences that Song had was able to love so easily, and inside she doubted the veracity of her love. There had been Sodarath, her sweet helper of six months who had barely known her on any level beyond the most basic of communication and who had told her how much she missed her when she went away for a week's holiday while proceeding to hug her tightly. This was during the earliest days of Lydia's Cambodian experience so you could forgive her for her cynicism. Lydia couldn't help holding back her own affections, as in her own culture you would only tell the closest of friends or family that you missed them when they were away.

There was no way Lydia could even consider letting Song go now, despite the strong recommendations of Brian but, in the midst of this uncertain situation, Helen had decided to hold back from actually schooling Song. Nevertheless, Helen did babysit her while Lydia was at work, even though this caused a certain amount of friction between her and her husband. Thankfully, as predicted, bold Amy had fully taken Song under her wing and would use some of their playtime to teach her what she herself knew. As a Third Culture Kid who had lived in Cambodia for five years of her young life, she was able to teach some basic English using her fairly fluent spoken Khmer.

The Baker family were very good friends of Lydia. She and Helen were close, although there had been some tricky boundary issues with

Mike a few months back related to his sharing his religious convictions with her past the point at which she was willing to politely listen. Nevertheless, Mike was a fun and exuberant man who had welcomed Lydia as part of his own family in the early stages. Lydia had forgiven him easily for his heavy-handed approach, and no long-term harm had been done to their friendship or work relationship. She knew from Helen that Mike felt uncomfortable with having Song so much a part of their household due to the VOA stance, but he never treated Lydia personally with anything less than his usual warmth.

Song ran exuberantly round the house, through the front yard and outside the gate chasing an imaginary dog. She had so much energy now that her health was improving that it was hard to keep her still inside. Lydia was happy to let her run and play and keep herself amused in this way. Generally, Song was able to entertain herself and didn't tend to sit listlessly in front of the TV for hours as many kids would. Even relatively poor Khmer families often had a TV, so being a couch potato was not the exclusive realm of the wealthy. Being used to playing alone, she also didn't require someone to play with her, so Lydia was frequently left to her own devices, which suited her desire for space.

Five minutes after this joyful running around began, Song came caterwauling inside to Lydia and wrapped her arms around her waist. Giggling, she raised her eyes towards Lydia and proclaimed in Khmer, 'There's a man outside the gate, says he's looking for a *Lydia*.' Song over-emphasised the 'Lydia' in such an amusing fashion, while shaking her head and rolling her eyes, that Lydia began giggling herself.

'Oh, really, so why doesn't he come in and find her himself?!' Lydia laughed, ruffling Song's hair. With Song trailing after her, she headed to the gate and opened it. She was genuinely surprised to see the young man from Doctor Duke's surgery standing there. He'd obviously heard part of the conversation and was smiling broadly as she walked through the gate. Feeling herself going hot from the top of her head to the tips of her feet, Lydia cleared her throat, and stammered, 'W-ell... s-soo y-you are R-radha?'

'I certainly am. How are you? Surprised to see me?'

'Oh, not at all,' Lydia lied shamelessly as she tried hard to overcome the dryness in her mouth and make her voice sound normal. 'I knew if you were truly interested you'd make every effort to see me.'

'How's Song?' Radha said, directing his words towards the child who was standing quietly at Lydia's side.

'I'm well, thank you.' Song was effortlessly polite and reserved now that there was a stranger in their midst.

'Have you been developing your artistic talents with paper?' He spoke to Song, but raised his eyes briefly while saying this and beamed at Lydia.

'I've made a paper crow, a paper hat, a paper boat, a paper doll, a paper house, a paper... Hmm, what was the last one I made, Aunty?'

'A paper aeroplane!'

There was something about the innocence of her pursuits that was alien to so-called Western sophistication. Back home, if a child was still making paper models at the age of ten, she would be alienated by most of her peers. One of Lydia's friends, who worked in an international school, had told her of a group of Khmer students with an average age of 15 playing clapping games with no shame. Back home it would be all make-up, iPods and boyfriends at that age, with clapping games long left behind by the age of nine or so.

Lydia calculated quickly the advisability of inviting Radha into her house. She didn't feel comfortable just standing out here on the street with the eyes of her neighbours on her every move, and inviting him to a café would mean that she would have to pay for him as well, because in Khmer culture the person doing the inviting was expected to pay for those he invited. Normally, a single woman inviting a man into her house alone would be frowned upon, yet having Song was proving to be a blessing in more than one way: having a child in the house would somehow make the process a lot more culturally palatable. Of course, they wouldn't have complete privacy but that suited Lydia anyway, as she had no intention of getting too close to this young man until she had ascertained his intentions more fully.

'Would you like to come inside for a coffee?' Lydia smiled warmly, determined to be as congenial as possible without giving away too much.

'Sure, I couldn't say anything less than ok!' Radha had switched easily from Khmer to English even though Lydia had asked her question in Khmer. Lydia winced at the cheesiness of his response, but was happy that he seemed to be fluent in English, as this meant they could communicate without Song understanding every word. At the same time, she was not going to exclude Song by spending the whole time talking to him in English.

'You must be wondering how I found your house?' Radha turned his head to face her after stirring his black coffee like he was checking a test tube for a cancer cure. He was disconcertingly direct with his eye contact, different from most Khmer people she knew, and she remembered with a stab of unwanted pleasure the longing gaze he had directed at her while she had been at the surgery.

'Me? No, not at all,' she lied again, playing the coy game. Of course she knew how he'd found her before he even told her.

'I got your details from the patients'notes. Actually, your patient's notes listed only your organisation's address, so I contacted your organisation and...'

'You didn't! Who gave away my dastardly secrets at VOA?!'

'A fat lady with a double chin. I don't know her name.'

Lydia laughed at the description. It was still funny to hear someone being described as fat so openly in Khmer culture. It was not necessarily considered to be an insult as it generally was in the UK. Actually, Tepy was not fat by Western standards, merely what might be called soft around the edges, but Lydia knew at once exactly who he meant. Technically, Tepy should not have given away any VOA staff's private details to a stranger, however well meaning, so Radha must have been very persuasive. Despite her curiosity, Lydia resisted the temptation to pry further; she would find out from Tepy herself on Monday.

Hearing the gate clanking open at the front of the house, Lydia glanced in that direction, thinking that it was most likely someone arriving at the landlord's house immediately behind her own. However, she was surprised to see Brian pulling up on his motorbike. It had been ten days since their telephone conversation, and in all that time Brian had all but ignored her. This was so unlike his usual

41

manner, though understandable in the circumstances, that his coming to visit her now had to mean that something significant had transpired.

'I'm sorry, Radha,' Lydia got out of her chair awkwardly. 'It's my boss. It's really important.'

'Oh, of course. Maybe another time... Soon?' Radha took Lydia's hand and shook it politely, not an ounce of inappropriateness in his touch. Lydia nodded shortly and gave a weak smile, distracted by Brian's presence. Lydia watched Brian stomping heavily off his bike and walking towards her screen door. His normally mobile face gave nothing away. Radha waited respectfully until Brian came into the room, then shook his hand and introduced himself before making himself scarce. Traditionally, Khmer people would greet others with a *sampeah*, a greeting formed by holding the palms together in front of the body like a symbol of prayer and bowing down in accordance with the relative status of the people greeting one another. That Radha had initiated using a handshake was another indication of an easy familiarity with Western culture.

'Ah, Lydia, I'm glad to see you're in,' Brian glanced at Radha as he left but chose not to comment. Normally, he'd be itching to rile Lydia about her 'new boyfriend', but in these less than comfortable circumstances it was a relief that he held his tongue.

'Hi Brian, how can I help you?' Lydia said with more frostiness in her voice than she'd intended, and didn't invite him to sit down as she usually would. She handed him a plastic cup of water from the purified water cooler, and he held it tightly in his hand during the conversation, without taking a sip.

'Is Song in?' he asked, stalling for time.

'Yeah, she's running around somewhere.'

'I guess you'll know why I've come round here, Lydia?'

'Of course.' Lydia's guts were tightening in anticipation of what was to come.

'So I won't make this any more painful than it needs to be. I raised the issue with the VOA board of directors and they were in a good mood that day, as it happens, but...' He was drawing this out as though pulling on a loose thread and Lydia felt frustrated that he wasn't just getting to the point. 'They looked into the legal and foreign relational aspects in careful detail.' A dog barked loudly outside, setting up a chain reaction of other dogs in the vicinity, one barking from one direction and one from another. 'And they decided that in the long run, and in the absence of any other solution that you'd require a severe whipping and to be locked up in a mental institution, but… that it'd be ok for you to keep the child.'

Brian looked at her stony-faced and then broke into a grin, seeing the elongation of her eyes and mouth. 'You bastard, Brian. How could you make me believe you were going to give me bad news in this way?!'

'Sorry, Lydia, I couldn't resist it. I totally disagree with their decision myself, of course, but what could I say against the decision of the mighty ones.'

'Oh shut up, please!' Lydia was not known for rudeness to her seniors, but in this situation she felt perfectly justified, 'Please talk seriously. Explain how this decision came about.'

It turned out that as far as Brian's anxieties were concerned, there was unlikely to be any precedent setting or undermining of VOA's status in Cambodia. If Lydia was serious about taking care of Song, she had the freedom to care for her for two years and then apply for adoption independently of anything that she was doing for VOA. Lydia hadn't even considered the 'A' word until now, but as Brian discussed it with her, it began to seem like the most natural thing in the world to begin pursuing eventually.

Some of the natural warmth that existed in their normal relationship began to reassert itself and, as predicted, Brian began to ask her teasing questions about Radha, while Lydia tried all the time to make the whole scenario as meaningless as possible to draw him off the scent.

'Yeah, yeah, whatever you say, Lydia. We know the real truth!'

'Ok, if that's what your small mind wants to believe, then believe what you like.' Lydia felt a swelling of satisfaction that she had come back with the final dig, and shook his hand warmly, indicating without saying so that it was time for him to leave and also that as far as she was concerned she'd finished with the discussion.

* * *

43

'That's great news, Lydia,' Mike breathed excitedly down the phone. 'Actually, I'll confess that I found this out yesterday but Brian made me promise not to say a word to you. Helen and I have already discussed the situation about Song, and we'd really like to be able to begin schooling her properly from Monday.'

'Thanks so much, Mike!'

'Don't thank me. It'll be Helen doing all the work. I simply twisted her round my little finger to get her to do this. As you know, she's had her doubts.' Of course, it had actually been the other way round, but Lydia knew that by saying this he was in his own little way apologising for making things complicated for Helen previously.

Lydia came away from this phone call exhaling deeply and thanking God that things had worked out satisfactorily. Calling Song in, she gave her a hug and told her that Aunty Helen would begin teaching her on Monday. 'Would you be happy with that?'

'Yes, happy, happy, happy!' Song whirled around like a spinning top so many times that she made herself dizzy. Lydia had not shared with her any of the details of the dispute, nor had she made any promises of education to Song. She had very carefully held back from anything that might turn out to be an empty egg shell, and was pleased now that she'd been restrained since the child's excitement about receiving schooling was fresh because it was so unexpected. An overwhelming sense that the next stage of her life was about to begin flooded her, and combined with this was an underlying and barely conscious hope that Radha would turn out to be the love of her life.

Chapter 6
Cambodia, May 2006

Sitting side-saddle on the back of Radha's Honda as he weaved his way down Mao Tse Toung Boulevard past the wicker furniture shops in the direction of the riverside, Lydia watched with amusement a motorbike that was carrying three adults and two small children plus a vertically placed pane of window glass. The glass was precariously balanced on the knees of the man immediately behind the driver and held secure with spread-eagled arms. It never failed to engage her interest to see the varying and resourceful ways in which Cambodians travelled by motorbike. Cambodian girls traditionally travelled side-saddle if they were on the passenger seat, unless they were travelling with their husbands or another female, and you could see girls wearing the daintiest of heels with one foot balanced on the foot pedal and the other dangling adeptly against an invisible support.

If there was more than one female on the back seat, then it was not uncommon to see three or four women squeezed on together. Lydia had even seen four men together on a moto. Men were generally small compared to their Western counterparts, and were comfortable being in close bodily contact with one another, unlike Westerners with their macho fears of being thought homosexual.

Because of the absence of health and safety laws in Cambodia, at times the items carried on motos bordered on the downright dangerous, such as the previously mentioned pane of glass. Yet after frequent exposure to such sights you would find yourself barely blinking an eye. Businesses did not tend to offer home delivery services, so it was common to see people carrying pieces of furniture in their hands on motos. You would be just as likely to see such items fitted on the other ubiquitous form of transport in Phnom Penh, the tuk-tuk.

Tuk-tuks were named after their Bangkok counterparts but were markedly different. Bangkok tuk-tuks were smaller and noisier with the engine fitted as part of the contraption, and were primarily used by tourists. Phnom Penh tuk-tuks were like a horse-drawn carriage in the sense that a complete motorbike was fitted to and used to draw the contraption. The contraption itself was like an open box with two long seats facing one another, offering comfortable space for three adults on each seat, one with its back to the driver, the other facing forward, together with the option of a plastic covering if it rained.

As with most forms of transport, Cambodians would make as much use of the space on a tuk-tuk as possible. During the November Water Festival when thousands of provincial Cambodians would travel into Phnom Penh for the boat races, you could see hundreds of packed tuk-tuks carrying up to 25 bodies, with legs, arms and backsides hanging off the edge and hands waving cheerfully at any foreign face curiously looking their way.

Radha pulled up outside a small café on a street just off the riverside. This café had more of a Khmer touch to it than most of the establishments along the riverside, which were aimed at the tourists and expats. For a developing nation, Cambodia's economy was largely being built on tourism and NGOs, and in 2006 big international business was in its infancy. Phnom Penh was filled with many NGOs of all types, with both a religious and a secular basis and doing all kinds of work from community development to teaching English and training street kids. This meant that the expat population was relatively high in comparison with many developing nations. As a foreigner living in Phnom Penh, if you chose and had the means you could live a life almost synonymous with the one you had back home, as almost every variety of food could be found, from Indian to Italian and Lebanese. If you were so inclined, you could immerse yourself in the expat bubble and have little need to learn the language.

Lydia hopped off the moto and a guard, who was standing outside the café and keeping an eye on the parked vehicles, winked at Radha as if to show appreciation of his achievement in securing a white woman as his prize. Lydia watched carefully to see how he would respond to this unspoken signal, but there was no noticeable change in Radha's pleasant expression.

This café to which Radha had brought Lydia was decorated in typical Khmer style with Formica tables, plastic chairs and small plastic tissue boxes in the centre of each table, but it wasn't playing loud karaoke music, for which Lydia was extremely grateful. The food

46

and drinks would be about half the price of the cafés that catered for foreigners, and there was unlikely to be a printed menu.

Holding Lydia by the elbow, Radha led her gracefully to the seat that the waiter pointed them towards and, for a moment, he was transformed in her mind's eye into a nineteenth-century British gentleman bowing to her and leading her elegantly into the ballroom. The context and his nationality were completely off kilter, but his manner and gesture were reminiscent of such a world.

Sipping her lime juice and trying to make sure it would last as long as possible, Lydia began the enjoyable process of her first official date with Radha. Long after this moment was over, every detail was sharply imprinted in her memory, including the words spoken, the expression on his mobile, fine features and his intent body language. 'So, finally I can spend uninterrupted time with you and get to know you properly. Who *is* this girl and why has she moved my imagination so swiftly?'

'I don't know why. Can't answer that question. And who *is* this man who has gone out of his way to find *me*?' Lydia mirrored his questioning style.

'My name is Radha, I'm Cambodian, I'm 28 years old, and I'm working as a receptionist. Now you?' He rattled this list off in staccato fashion before pealing out with childlike merriment.

'Ah, no, that's not enough yet,' Lydia was determined to keep up an air of mystery for as long as she could. 'Where did you learn such fluent English and develop such a good understanding of Western customs?'

'That's easy. I've always been good at picking up languages and I've had very good teachers along the way to help. In fact, about eight years ago, I had a young man from New Zealand, Toby, who I met through an NGO friend, to be my personal tutor. During that time my English improved a lot. We had such fun together. Sometimes we would pretend to have phone conversations to practise a new area of language and Toby, completely straight faced, would say something so crazy that he'd have me rolling on the floor laughing – is that the right expression?'

'Yeah, rolling on the floor with laughter. Very natural. I also find it relatively easy to learn new languages,' Lydia offered.

'I've been working at Doctor Duke's surgery for about two years now. As you know, he has a lot of foreign customers, and I've enjoyed making friends with them.'

'Two years – really? I don't remember seeing you there until that time I took Song to have a tetanus jab.'

'That's because I used to work at the other practice near Psar Tmei. I only recently transferred to the Toul Tom Poung practice. Turned out to be the best decision I ever made, or rather I should say, was made for me!' His eyes soaked in her whole face and attempted to linger in an intimate moment, but Lydia lowered her own gaze modestly. She was not about to start making intense eye contact with him just yet. Lydia was also aware of the eyes of the waitress on her – the waitresses tended to stand attentively close – and she didn't want her to start making assumptions about the fast *barang*.[1]

In order to adjust the emotional thermometer to neutral, Lydia swiftly rolled out her next question: 'Have you always lived in Phnom Penh or is your family from one of the provinces?'

'Actually I moved to Phnom Penh when I was offered a scholarship to attend high school here. I stayed with some cousins of mine while my parents stayed in Mondulkiri, which is where I'm from.'

Lydia had vivid memories of her own brief trip to Mondulkiri a year ago, bouncing along on the red-dust road in a pick-up truck and crawling upwards in altitude. She had travelled during the cool, dry season so had not had to contend with getting stuck in the mud, but she had enjoyed a comparatively comfortable trip. However, after returning, her back had ached for a few days because of the jolting of the suspension-less truck over the potholes and ruts. Mondulkiri was forested and hilly in contrast to much of Cambodia, which was flat, and it was also a few degrees cooler, which made for a pleasant stay. 'It's beautiful there; you must miss it!'

'It's beautiful, yes, but I come from a very poor background, and my family life was not much better so I don't have wonderful memories of my time there.' Radha didn't seem keen to talk about his youth, and Lydia felt him skirting around the edges of her questions whenever she tried to probe. 'You've asked more than enough

[1] *Barang* is a derogatory word used to describe white foreigners. It actually means French person. This stems from the fact that Cambodia was a French colony from 1863 to 1953.

questions, for now. I've not learnt anything about you yet,' Radha laughingly dismissed his discomfort. 'Let me see, where should I start... How many men have you slept with?' Radha said this with a poker face, then upon seeing Lydia rise perceptibly as she opened her mouth in transparent shock to rebuke him for his rudeness, he laughed again. 'Don't worry! I'm only joking. I have some sense of what's proper to ask on a first date. I just haven't asked it yet.'

Lydia felt a quiver of distrust under the surface after this question. Though conceding that he was only joking, she couldn't understand why he'd chosen that moment to flay an area of vulnerability and half-wondered if he was going to turn out to be a charming but character-flawed man like Rob had been.

After this one downside in her first date with Radha, everything proceeded as smoothly as cream so that Lydia began to regain her confidence. If she looked back to this time it was as though she could see herself and Radha sitting on soft white cushions on the floor while a servant waved a fan over them, and delicately wispy silk curtains shrouded them in beauty and luxury.

When Radha learnt that Lydia was four years older than he was, he was unperturbed. 'Why should I care about such things? You look the same age as me, and even if you were ten years older than me, you'd still be as beautiful.' Is he just saying what he thinks I want him to say? 'Honestly, I don't know anyone who cares about the woman being older than the man in my culture, and when it's only a small difference it's hardly worth mentioning anyway. My burning question is what led you to come to Cambodia in the first place? Why not stay in England with your family and friends and enjoy a comfortable life there?'

'That's just what I don't want!' Lydia laughed. 'A comfortable life. Or, at least, I don't want a boring, predictable life. I can't say that comfort isn't at all important, though. I'm not sure I could cope living in abject poverty in a tiny, dirty hut with no electricity and poor sanitation as many of the locals do here. The family and friends that are most important to me will always be there.' A breeze stroked her face, providing some welcome relief from the cloying humidity. The ceiling fan had stopped working ten minutes before because of one of the frequent power cuts in the city. She traced her finger along her upper lip to wipe off the sweat, saw Radha watching her and became suddenly self-conscious, aware that her face was probably shiny and her hair would be sticking out at unattractive angles because of the moisture in the air. It didn't matter how well she concentrated on styling her hair in the morning. Owing to its natural waviness, if the humidity levels were high her hair would be all over the place by the end of the day.

'You look gorgeous, Lydia,' he murmured as if reading her mind, eyes twinkling. She knew this could not possibly be true, but she was grateful nonetheless as he said it without a trace of pretension.

'Actually, I had no intention previously of volunteering in a poor country, but then about three years ago I watched a really moving documentary about life in Cambodia, detailing something of the tragic history and how that was impacting on today's generation, and something in me just clicked. A few days later I started researching volunteering opportunities in Cambodia, thinking about the skills I have, and I came across VOA. I agreed with their values and principles and things proceeded from there. What about you? Do you have any desire to work abroad?'

'Of course. If I could obtain some sort of scholarship to study or work overseas that would be a real fulfilment of a dream: I've particularly had my heart set on Japan, Korea or Australia. If I had to choose a European country it would be the UK, though I don't know that I'd ever get the finances or opportunity to work there.'

'Why not? You never know what opportunities are going to come your way.' As soon as she said this, Lydia realised that this statement was loaded and quickly tried to find a way to qualify her meaning so that it couldn't be interpreted to have any connection with her: 'For instance, in the future, once Cambodia is more engaged in international business, you may end up employed by a British company working in Cambodia. If you were to prove yourself to be a valuable employee you might get the opportunity to transfer to a UK branch. Optimistic, maybe, but there's no harm in dreaming big.'

'None whatsoever.' Radha smiled, leaned back in his chair with his hands folded behind his head and stretched his legs out in front of him. It may or may not have been intentional, but as he did this his legs brushed against hers, and Lydia didn't withdraw hers as she didn't want him to think that she was completely frigid or uninterested; there was nothing encroaching about this harmless physical contact. Though fully aware that one simple action was the first step in a chain reaction, she enjoyed the moment without betraying her pleasure by maintaining a nonchalant expression.

'Are you going to marry Uncle Radha?' asked Song, raising her head to look artlessly at Lydia, who was working at getting the knots out of her long hair using a fine-tooth comb.

'Keep your head still, Song,' Lydia said. 'You'll need to start using conditioner on your hair every time you wash it to keep the tangles out of it. Now where did you get that idea from? Song, in my culture a man and woman will get to know each other for a long time before deciding whether or not to get married, and we've not known each other long enough to make that kind of commitment.'

'Oh. Well, he wants to marry you,' replied Song with complete earnestness.

'You don't know that!' Lydia laughed, 'You've only seen him three times yourself. Don't be silly, sweetheart.'

'I'm not being silly.' Song was calmly indignant. 'I just know. I can see it in his eyes and the way he talks to you.' Song left it at that and sat still while Lydia continued with the steady combing process, and Lydia didn't say any more. A memory washed over her of the moment Radha had said goodbye to her after their date only two hours earlier. He had got onto his moto after entering her gate, letting her down, shaking her hand, and annunciating a passionless, 'We'll meet again.' Then on second thoughts, he'd got off his moto again, asked her if he could kiss her – like the true gentleman he was – and pressed his lips warmly on her cheek close to her mouth before withdrawing slowly, inhaling as though savouring her scent, sweat and all.

While Lydia was under no illusion that this meant Radha wanted to marry her, she was certainly clear-eyed enough to see that he was nothing less than in love with her, and her heart sang with gladness at this knowledge.

Chapter 7
Cambodia, August 2006

It was August before Lydia got some clue as to the depth of Song's suffering regarding her relationship with her mother. The overripe mango seeped with the gentlest of squeezing. One rainy afternoon, after riding back from work to pick up Song, with her feet splashing in flood waters, Lydia was surprised to see Helen waiting outside on the porch for her, her forehead knotted with anxiety. 'What's the matter, Helen? Is Song ok?'

'Oh, Lydia. Don't fret yourself. She's ok, but I just wanted to explain the situation to you as soon as I could, without the children listening.'

'What's happened?'

Helen pulled Lydia down onto one of the porch deckchairs without allowing her time to take off her wet poncho. She gripped her wrist so tightly that the skin started to redden. 'Helen, please, you're hurting me.'

'Sorry,' she replied, releasing her grip. 'So, you know that neither Mike nor I drink very much because of our faith, but at the same time we do enjoy the occasional drink?'

'Sure, I know.'

'This morning, Mike came into the house carrying a bottle of red wine and put it on the dining room table. We were planning to have a drink for our evening date time, when the kids stay with Brian and family. Song came out of the schoolroom with Amy a few minutes before me for our mid-morning break, as I was sorting out some laptop problem. I soon came out because I could hear Amy saying repeatedly, "What's wrong Song? Please tell me!" She was so fretful. You know Amy – she's a little optimist, and if she does get upset she returns to her normal happy self before too long. Song really scared her, Lydia. I've never seen her so scared.'

All sorts of garish thoughts ran through Lydia's head in a split second: Song tripping over and cutting her head and falling unconscious; Song eating something that caused an extreme allergic reaction; Song having a severe asthma attack; Song having an epileptic fit. She swallowed hard and waited for Helen to continue, trying to hold on to her reassuring words that she was ok.

It turned out that Song had seen the bottle of wine, stiffened and turned to the wall and then refused to speak to anyone for the next hour or so. Every five minutes or so she would bang her head almost ritualistically against the wall three times. No form of cajoling or reasoning got through to her so, in order to minimise the damage, Helen had placed a cushion against the wall.

'It was horrible as it came so out of the blue, and Amy began crying in agony when she saw Song banging her head against the wall and couldn't do a thing to stop it. I had to send Amy to her room so she couldn't see any more, while I stayed there and simply stroked Song's back and tried to calm her down by speaking to her softly. During this time I called Mike and asked him to pray hard.'

'Helen, please let me in to see Song.' Lydia could feel her heart aching with Song's sadness.

'Hold on, Lydia. I want to finish the story. Trust me.' Helen gripped her hand hard again and looked beseechingly at her. 'After about an hour, Song turned to me and, with the smallest voice, said in Khmer, "Alcohol is bad." She wouldn't say any more than that, but it was like she was some Old Testament prophet preaching words of doom and judgement. I've never seen her like that before.'

'Me neither,' Lydia said, finding it hard to swallow through the barbs in her throat.

'She's not given anything more away but she's stopped banging her head now, she's eaten some lunch and is sitting calmly on the sofa. Amy's still quite upset but she's hiding it and trying her best to cheer her up. I hope you can find out what's going on with her. The alcohol was obviously the trigger, but it was such an innocuous event. It was only sitting on the table; it hadn't even been opened yet. What do you think?'

'I can only guess.' Lydia wouldn't wait any longer.

She got up, still wearing her poncho, and went inside to find Song sitting motionless and slumped low, while Amy moved around the room, picking up one item after another and struggling to attract her interest. 'Look Song, this is your favourite story book. Do you want me to read it for you?' Upon seeing Lydia, Amy cried out cheerfully, 'It's

Aunty Lydia come to take you home!' She was obviously relieved at being able to give up her babysitting role, much as she loved Song.

Song raised her head with a glance of recognition, got up and spoke her first words since her utterance of judgement. 'Ok, it's time to go home. I want to go now,' she said flatly.

Aware that she was acting as a parent figure for Song but not having the faintest idea how to proceed, Lydia smiled stiff-mouthed at Song and opened her arms as an invitation to warmth. With her head hanging to one side and a dejected look on her face, Song came slowly forward and wrapped her arms around Lydia's waist. Lydia could feel the tears rising in her throat, but thrust them down with a falsely positive, 'It's good to see you're yourself again, Song. Let's get you home, then.'

She bundled Song out of the door and onto her moto, mouthing to Helen as she went, 'I'll let you know what happens.'

Helen and Amy called out, 'We'll see you tomorrow!'

The sky opened once more just as they left Helen's, and even though they were both wrapped in lightweight ponchos, the force of the wind caused torrents of rain to gush over their legs and seep through the armholes. After arriving home, Lydia rushed them both out of their wet clothes and insisted that Song have a hot shower. Song stood on the tiled floor with her clothes in a pile around her, as though incapable of action. 'Come on, Song!' Lydia goaded her. 'You're not a baby. You know how to take a shower.' As if suddenly aware that she was standing there naked, Song picked up a towel, wrapped it around her distractedly and trudged into the bathroom. 'I'll just be outside the room, Song. Come and join me when you're ready.'

Lydia raced through her own shower and, without bothering to dry herself properly, stepped out into her towelling robe and went to make hot drinks for herself and Song.

As swiftly as they had come, the rain clouds disappeared again, and by the time Song was ready to talk, the sun was setting, casting a russet glow over the floor tiles. Song flexed her feet and stretched out her little torso upright like a ballerina-in-training. Lydia glanced at the pages of her book, pretending to read. She had begun acting nonchalantly without even consciously making the decision to do so.

Somehow she intuited that probing Song was only going to make her withdraw even further, but her whole self was teetering on a precipice, waiting for any insight that would make sense of what had happened, and Song's movement increased her sharpened sense of awareness.

Unable to handle the anticipation much longer, Lydia got up and began humming an inane Khmer pop song. She was about to go and finish the washing-up in the kitchen when she heard Song's solemn tones piping up, so did a not-so-subtle about turn, almost tripping over her own feet in the process. Song didn't move from her seat on the floor, but the words began pouring out of her as she spoke of her mother's acute alcoholism, which had begun shortly after the death of her father. She had kept it hidden for so long because it shamed her like it was her own weakness. 'My mother was supposed to be taking care of me 'cos that's what mothers do, but all the time that Uncle Thom was calling me bad words and hitting me, she was sitting in a corner gulping down bottles and bottles of drink and vomiting and wetting herself. Nobody apart from me would bother to clean her up.' Song had a distant look in her eyes. 'There was one time when she slipped in her own vomit and fell crashing to the floor, unconscious. I cried and asked for help to get her out of the mess but nobody came to help. In the end the dog came in and began licking up the vomit from both the floor and my mother and I couldn't bear to shoo him out of the house. She never hit me or became violent herself, though...' Here it was apparent that Song was struggling to articulate her thoughts and feelings.

'How did you feel about her at that time?' Lydia enquired.

'I hated her. I couldn't help it. But,' and here her face looked openly confused, 'I loved her too. She is my mother, isn't she?' She spoke this not as a question but as a simple statement of reality. Lydia's heart broke for her ward; not only had her mother been mentally ill but she'd also been an alcoholic – a brutal combination, one that was bound to make a child confused about her place in the world. There was an understandable ambiguity in Song's feelings about her mother. It seemed as if the hatred she had felt stemmed from a frustration that her mother had not taken care of her as a mother was supposed to take care of her child, and this cohabited with a dutiful love that stemmed from indissoluble blood ties and cultural expectations.

As Song opened up for probably the first time in her life, the sweet little girl was no longer there; it was as though a tired and mature older lady had taken residence inside her body. Her face was drawn and cloaked with shame and memory. There was not a single doubt in Lydia's mind that she was doing the right thing in looking after this bruised, vulnerable child, and she knew she'd gained her trust in a way that no one had ever been able to up till now.

In the middle of Song's sharing, Lydia's phone jarred the atmosphere. Upon picking it up and seeing that it was Radha, she spoke rather abruptly to him, something which she regretted afterwards: 'It's not a good time; I'll speak to you later.' And she cut him off without even giving him the chance to say a word. Then, with heart pounding, she sat down again and urged Song to continue.

Song slapped a mosquito that landed on her leg with a viciousness that had no power to surprise Lydia. Her hand came away red with blood, and Lydia wouldn't allow her to proceed until she'd scrubbed her hands clean. Wiping her hands on her lap, Song came and sat down again, throwing a grateful look at Lydia. 'I love you, Aunty,' she said earnestly, and held out her small palm to be held in hers.

'I love you too, little one.' Lydia wrapped her arms around her and gave her a squeeze. 'And I'm really sorry that you've gone through all that you have. No one deserves to live through the kind of situation you have, especially not someone as young as you.'

Song looked at her with hooded eyelids and scrunched up her lips. Lydia spoke vehemently. 'I still find it hard to understand why no one was interested in helping your mother to clean herself when she was dirty, even though I know you're telling me the truth. She clearly couldn't help herself during those times of severe drunkenness.'

Song was quiet; she didn't have the words to explain or justify and didn't want to begin.

'One thing I do want to talk to you about is the difference between the levels of alcohol drunk by your mother and the levels of alcohol drunk by people like Helen and Mike. I can't expect you to understand fully at this stage, but there is a difference. In your mum's case, she's severely addicted and the alcohol has a hold of her life. In the case of people like Helen and Mike, alcohol is simply something that is used socially and harmlessly, without any adverse health consequences. Can you see that?'

Song hung her head and thought for a moment. 'Not really,' she said tentatively, not wanting to offend, but being unable to wrap her mind around this concept when her whole worldview and experience told her that alcohol was evil.

'It's ok. You don't have to understand or even believe that right now. It's just that we don't want to see what happened today happening again, do we? A lot of people were concerned about you.'

Song scratched her mosquito bite and kept her head down. 'I hope I won't see alcohol again,' she said fiercely and shot up as though her word was final and not to be disputed. 'I'm tired. I'm going to bed now.' She looked at Lydia and gave a weak, almost apologetic smile.

'Don't forget to brush your teeth!' she called out after her, while inside Lydia sensed a dark, forbidden attic opening up, all mildewed and rotting. She switched off her phone, feeling unable to call Radha back at this time. How could she explain this to him? How could she begin to lift Song out of the darkness from which she had come? How could she begin to make a difference in her life? How could she feel good about life herself after hearing this story of the miseries of the young child whom she loved?

She sighed and eased her aching bones from the floor – she'd got down to be with Song. Maybe she would be able to answer these questions one day, but right now her head was swimming and she felt nauseous. Lydia filled her glass with water from the mineral water vat and drank deeply, once, then twice, and began to turn off the lights in the bungalow ready for bed.

Chapter 8
Cambodia, December 2006

Lydia lay flat on her back, conscious of the weight and form of her body holding her down and smiled luxuriously as Radha came back into the room. 'Hey, Lydia, I didn't want to wake you,' he said, leaning over and kissing her. His eyes were lit with a healthy shine. 'I just went outside to do my early morning exercises.'

'You didn't wake me. I've already been awake for a few minutes,' she said and gave a cavernous yawn.

'Ooph, you'd better brush your teeth then and freshen up,' he said cheekily, before emitting an exaggerated, 'Ouch!' as Lydia aimed a well-deserved punch at his shoulder.

The cool season had finally come around, when the whole of Cambodia breathed a sigh of relief as the winds picked up, and some were even able to sleep at night with a blanket. Lydia had not rushed into this new part of her relationship with Radha. She had kept him waiting, determined to ascertain the genuineness of his commitment to her and his understanding of Song before giving herself to him. It had only been a couple of weeks since she'd first slept with him, and she felt sure that she'd made the right choice. Radha had been patient, understanding and open with her. Song's acceptance of him had played a large part in her decision. Brian, Helen and Mike had all met him, spent time with him and warmed to him. What more could she ask for?

'Would you like to move in with us?' Lydia broached, having brushed her teeth and tongue thoroughly. 'I've been thinking about it, and Song is so used to having you around that she'd love to have you here, as of course would I, though maybe not quite so much as Song.' She smirked and Radha returned the punch, lightly. As though on cue, Song burst through the bedroom door and flung herself onto Lydia's and Radha's laps, making a trumpeting sound. 'Er, Song, what have I told you about not just bursting into our room without knocking!' Lydia tried to sound stern but her wide grin belied her tone.

'It's Amy's birthday today and I'm supposed to be there for her party in half an hour! They're taking her out to Psar Soriya[2] for lunch.'

'Of course,' Lydia glanced at her watch. 'I'd completely forgotten about that! Radha, would you mind dropping her off as you're already dressed?'

'Yeah, no problem. I have a few things I need to buy near Central Market so I can drop her directly at Soriya. I haven't forgotten your question. I'll let you know when I come back.' He picked up his motorbike helmet, called out after Song to find hers and walked whistling out of the house with Song running after him, fixing her helmet on the move.

Lydia sighed and hopped into the shower. After the alcohol incident with Song, she'd asked Helen and Mike to hide all alcohol from Song, and she worked hard to avoid having any drink at all in her own house, and thankfully, there hadn't been any more incidents. It didn't bother Radha at all as he was actually teetotal, a result of his distaste for his own father's abuse of alcohol. She knew that, in the long run, simply ignoring the problem would not deal with the underlying issue, but for now it was easier to brush the problem with a stiff broom under the nearest cupboard and hope that no one would notice the creeping levels of dust.

'Sorry about the mess in the house,' Lydia apologised as a compact, besuited Khmer lady left her shoes at the porch and came through the screen door. 'You must be Srey Ne.' Lydia brushed her sweaty hair behind her ears, kicked the pile of unwashed clothing behind the couch and came forward smiling and bowing in the traditional way. Srey Ne bowed discreetly and sat down without waiting to be asked.

'Would you like some water?'

'Thank you,' Srey Ne said in her serious, non-flamboyant style, accepting the glass that was offered to her.

'I hope you were able to find the house easily?'

'Yes, no problem. I know this area well.' Srey Ne cleared her throat disinterestedly, took out a file and moved straight to business in a manner that took Lydia a little by surprise: Cambodians were

---

[2] Psar is the Khmer name for market and can be applied equally to a traditional market as well as a supermarket or shopping mall. Soriya was one of the first Phnom Penh shopping malls.

generally known for being relational rather than brisk and businesslike. 'I understand you want to know about the legal situation regarding adopting a Cambodian child.'

'Sure, but Song, although she has some Khmer connections on her uncle's side, is actually Vietnamese. She's been living in Cambodia for more than four years, mind you, first with her uncle's family and then with me for several months.'

'Well, you need to know that technically the British Government does not approve adoptions of Cambodian children who are over eight years old. And, of course, if Song is Vietnamese, that takes the situation out of the Cambodian legal remit completely.'

'Oh, I had no idea her age would be an issue. What are the other options if adoption is not possible?'

'You could foster her in an informal way, as you're effectively doing already, but you must understand that you won't be able to take her to the UK on any legal basis, so you're committed to a life in Cambodia for as long as Song is a minor or until such a time as the law changes, if it ever does. Also, you would have no legal rights over her, so if her family were to decide to claim her back then there would be nothing you can do about it.' Srey Ne turned and looked at Lydia with razor-like directness. 'Only you can decide whether or not you're willing to accept the responsibility of looking after this child when you're on such shaky legal ground.'

'Well, I can almost guarantee that her family, what is left of it, will not be interested in pursuing her. I'll really have to think hard about whether I want to commit to being here for a long time. I guess there's not really much more you can tell me, then?'

'Not really, other than I've seen expats in a similar situation to you do exactly the same thing before. Sometimes there's a happy story, and other times there is great heartbreak.' She seemed unwilling to divulge, but Lydia pressed her for further information.

Srey Ne sighed and, twining her fingers together in an interlocking dance, she elaborated. 'For example, when a relative back home dies and the foster parent is put into a conflict of loyalties, where she may feel torn between wanting to go back home and take care of the grieving relatives and staying here to look after her foster child. Or the child's parents, aunts or uncles who had previously been uninterested in their child, change their mind, maybe for economic reasons, hoping that the child will bring them money. In such cases the foster parent is unable to fight the case because of the lack of legal standing and so has to go through a painful separation from the child.' Her demeanour softened slightly as she said, 'I'm sorry to be the bearer of hard tidings.'

'Hmm, well, to be honest, what you've said has only confirmed what I've already been given hints about, and I had a hunch that legal adoption was going to be difficult or impossible.'

Lydia had been given Srey Ne's details from Tepy at VOA, who had assured her of her qualifications and helpfulness. She'd learnt nothing new from her; simply a confirmation of her already intuited imaginings. Nevertheless, this certainty was reassuring somehow, and she was not disappointed by the visit.

The screen door clicked as Radha strolled in his casual way into the bungalow and found Lydia sitting on the sofa after the lawyer's departure, her head ringing with thoughts. Coming around the chair to sit beside her, he draped his arm around her and squeezed her tenderly, a gesture which never failed to move Lydia. 'Is Song ok?'

'Yeah, I left her with Helen and Mike and managed to get all my chores done. She was so excited to be going to Soriya. You should have seen her face light up as she went up the escalator, like one of those country girls excited at being let loose in the city.'

'I'd forgotten she'd never been in the mall before,' Lydia mused. 'I'd not had the opportunity to take her there until now, and I hadn't thought that of course it'd be something new and exciting for her. What kind of a mother am I?' she said in an ironically reproachful way.

'Well, it's ok as you're not her mother, are you?!'

This innocent comment came as a sharp dig in Lydia's side and she jerked her body away from Radha. He didn't know she'd been planning to see the lawyer today as she'd kept this detail to herself until she knew the outcome, so he couldn't know how poignant this comment was to Lydia right now. Rather than speaking out her pain, Lydia's body twisted, and her sudden quietness alerted Radha that something was wrong. He tried another tack. 'I've been thinking about

61

what you asked me earlier and I'd love to move in with you and Song. It already feels like my natural home. I don't know why I didn't think of it sooner.'

She remained quiet, still torn.

Radha began tickling her in the stomach and she writhed away from him with an irritated grunt. 'Don't!' She stood up and walked over to the kitchen area and began banging pots and pans purposefully.

He sat where he was for a while, rebuffed, and then said, 'You've changed your mind, then?'

Lydia flung out her next words with unintended venom: 'Why would someone who's not a real mother even think about taking a young child into her home? How can I set up house and home with a child and a "father" if I'm not even capable of being a mother?!'

'Where has all this come from, Lydia? I have a right to know that at least!'

Lydia felt incapable of analysing her own reaction. One minute she'd been calmly reassured by the lawyer's words and the next minute she'd felt stabbed in the back by a throwaway comment from the man she loved and had begun attacking him. There was no apparent logic to it. She began chopping some morning glory and sweeping the root ends into a neat pile on the work surface before she would answer him.

As she worked her anger into submission, she knew she had no right to keep this information from Radha any longer. Even though she couldn't justify her reaction, Lydia slowly softened and began to unravel the details of Srey Ne's meeting in a stalling, apologetic manner. 'I'm sorry I kept this from you. You've been so open with me. I don't know what came over me just... You hit a raw nerve when you said I wasn't Song's mother as I know above all knowing that I'm the only real mother she's had for some time.'

Radha came over to the kitchen and stood beside her while she talked. Keeping his eyes lowered, he rolled a knife handle between his palms rather than attempting any more physical contact. 'I don't know what to say, Lydia. You know that right from the beginning I knew as much about Song as I knew about you and I accepted her along with you, as part of the package. If you continue with this fostering process then I'll support you in that.'

'But why, Radha, why? What's in it for you?'

He flinched at these words and raised his head again. 'I love you, Lydia. You know that. And I love Song, too. There's nothing "in it" for me other than a good family that I never had!'

'But if something happens and I have to leave the country, what will happen to Song then? Will you continue to take care of her? Will your sweet words turn into real action or will they turn out to be empty?' Lydia knew she was punishing him needlessly but she couldn't help herself.

'How can I say what I would do at such a… a time?' Radha faltered and chewed his lip. He was pressed into a corner and she knew it. If he said he would take care of Song, then he'd be implying that he'd rather do that than come with her. If he said he would prefer to follow her, then that would imply that he didn't care for Song and her well-being. Turning abruptly and walking away from Lydia in a manner which left her in no doubt about what he thought of her game-playing, he slammed the screen door behind him and began striding up and down on the porch.

Looking after him, Lydia saw a future without Radha and a pang of loss descended into the pit of her stomach. She could also foresee Song's disappointment and felt sure that Song would blame her for pushing him away. Knowing she was largely at fault in this situation, she sidled outside and stood in front of Radha, blocking his angry passage. 'I'm sorry,' rose from her lips, and she poised there feeling vulnerable as she waited for him to respond. When he stood silently with his back half turned from her like a disapproving wall, she tapped him on the shoulder and said, 'I'd love it if you would make a home with us.' The next thing she knew she was being wrapped in a bear hug and feeling the wiry strength of his arms holding her safe. Lydia leaned into Radha's shoulder and breathed hard, trying to keep at bay the lump in her throat. After a wordless few minutes, where the silence snapped shut the circumstance, Lydia raised her head and murmured, 'I'd better go and get Song.'

Chapter 9
Cambodia, February 2007

Song stuck her face excitedly against the window of the coach as it pulled into Siem Reap bus station and watched the horde of tuk-tuk and moto drivers who held up name signs, pressing up against the sides of the latest vehicle from Phnom Penh that they hoped to make some money from. The coach was teeming with tourists, backpackers, expats and middle-class Cambodians, some of whom had boarded the coach along the way and stood in the aisle for most of the journey as there were no more seats available. Lydia was relieved that they'd arrived, as a teenage girl just across the aisle from them had succumbed to motion sickness halfway through the five-hour journey, and the smell of vomit was clinging to her nostrils. She'd been trying in vain to breathe through her mouth for much of the journey to mitigate the smell, and the opening of the coach door sent a blast of much-needed fresh air through the vehicle. Feeling tired and grumpy, she breathed in deeply.

Radha took pains to pick up all their hand luggage but left their rubbish scattered on the seat and floor as they squeezed their way into the aisle. 'You could have picked that up and brought it with us,' moaned Lydia, in no mood to overlook this environmental slight.

'If you're so bothered, why didn't you bring it?!' derided Radha with a frowning smile. 'Anyway, the bus company will clear it up.'

'That's the problem with you... people.' Lydia was about to say 'Cambodians' but resisted the temptation in this public setting. 'You always expect other people to clear up your rubbish for you.' Then, realising that she was being stared at by several older Cambodians, she modified her tone somewhat and lowered her voice. 'At any rate, you could at least have put the rubbish into one plastic bag so that it was neater.'

'Once again, something *you* could have done,' Radha likewise murmured, managing to maintain both his cool and his smile, which irritated Lydia immensely.

Their argument was curtailed as they stepped off the bus to be greeted by a barrage of strident, nasal voices offering their services in clipped English. 'Hold hands,' Radha hissed at Lydia, all the while gripping Song's, 'so that we don't lose each other in this madness.'

'Come Lucky Guesthouse, Sir, only five dollar a night. Beautiful, clean rooms. Good service!'

'How much you want my tuk-tuk? I give you ride hotel and show you round all the temples, very good.'

'I give you best service, come with me, Sir!'

'How much you want, how much you want?' called out a particularly desperate sounding man who leaned right forward and grasped Lydia's arm. The width of his girth and the shine of his features belied any real economic need, and Lydia shook off his hand.

Radha and Lydia ignored the desperados and squeezed round the side of the bus to collect their luggage; then, with backpacks in hand, they sidled away from the tourist trap to where the quieter, less avaricious drivers were waiting.

Lydia and Radha had chosen this long holiday weekend in early February to get away on their first trip together, and they had decided to come to Siem Reap to see the famous Angkor Wat and surrounding temples as neither had visited them before. Bringing Song along with them was all part of the fun, though the holiday wasn't starting off in the best possible way. Lydia had insisted that they sort out where they were going to stay before they arrived in Siem Reap. Many folk would arrive and wander around until they found the best accommodation deal, but as they had Song with them, she felt it was best to be a bit more organised and used all the tourist guides she could lay her hands on to find the best. The best and cheapest deals were actually slightly away from the main town, which meant they would have to travel further to get to the temples. The place they had selected was run by Westerners at a very cheap rate and the guides had promised a 'homely' stay for $5 a room. The only downside was that there was no AC or hot water, but that wasn't a big deal for a couple of nights. Song would share with them, which would also keep the costs down.

'Friendly Guesthouse please, Uncle,' Radha bartered with an alert-looking tuk-tuk driver sitting quietly to one side of the melee of drivers. He knew all the tricks of the trade, having been a tuk-tuk driver himself for a few years, and managed to fix a very reasonable price, which included trips to the temples that evening at sunset and the next day.

Pulling up outside the guesthouse, Lydia was pleased to see greenery growing all around the edge of the building, and she breathed in the intoxicatingly sweet fragrance of the frangipani flowers blooming on the trees near the entrance. 'Whatever time you want to go to Angkor Wat, let me know and I will come back,' Samnang told them in Khmer, while unloading their luggage, eager to please.

'How long does it take to get there from here?' Radha asked.

'No more than 30 minutes.'

Lydia glanced at her watch and answered, 'Hmm, well if we want to get there for the sunset viewing, it would be good if you could come by at 5pm.'

'Certainly, Sir. Certainly, Madam. No problem. I will be there.' He nodded to them, beaming, and with a splutter of his engine he manoeuvred the vehicle round. 'Enjoy the rest of your afternoon.' As he drove off, a peal of laughter rang out behind him.

A little taken aback by his unexpected laughter, Lydia asked Radha, 'Do you think he'll be back?'

'Absolutely. We've not paid him yet! And we won't be paying him until the end of our deal. He'll be here faithfully every time we ask him to. Even if he's not honest through and through, he's a sensible businessman. No doubt about that.'

'He's a good man,' Song pronounced, looking around her with wide eyes, instinctively intuitive.

Radha laughed and rubbed her shoulders. 'That's all there is to it, then. You're the only oracle we need!'

At five minutes to the hour, the tuk-tuk driver was back as he'd promised, faithfully waiting outside the guesthouse. Once the town had been navigated, the last part of the journey to Angkor was a scenic one, and a sea of tuk-tuks and motos drove along a flat, tree-lined, well-manicured boulevard towards the entrance of the main Angkor Wat temple. All three of them were quiet, drinking in the view.

There was an understandable inequality to the way in which the temple authorities managed tickets at this most famous of Cambodian tourist attractions. There was one ticket booth for foreigners and one for Khmer, and while the Khmer were able to enter the temples for free, foreigners had to pay a sizable fee of $25 for a day pass. It was understandable in that this most Khmer of attractions was open for every Khmer national to be able to see their heritage freely, but it seemed unfair that every foreigner, regardless of their own income differentiation, was clumped together as a source of easily tappable income. The reality was that the vast majority of this money would end up in the hands of corrupt, bloated officials, so you couldn't even console yourself that the money would help the country as a whole.

Lydia stood in the foreigners' queue with a studied air of detachment, distancing herself from the nonchalant trails of young Western women wearing culturally inappropriate flesh-exposing vest tops, and the strident American tourists who vocalised every opinion, while Radha and Song stood somewhat sheepishly in the national queue. In spite of Radha's and Lydia's sharing the cost of her ticket, an awkward dynamic had been built between them because of this enforced differentiation. While Song was Vietnamese, she had been in Cambodia long enough to blend into the Khmer culture, and Radha knew she was unlikely to be asked for any form of identification if she was with him.

Passes were available for one day, three days and a week. Lydia and Radha had both agreed to pay for just the one-day pass, although their reasoning was slightly different. Lydia rationalised that one day would be more than enough to get a feel for the most important temples, whereas Radha simply wanted the cheapest option. He wouldn't admit this directly to Lydia since she had been willing to pay the total cost for more days if that was what he wanted. The bonus about the day pass was that it was valid from sunset the night before so you could see the grandest temple silhouetted in the day's glorious final brush strokes. Lydia knew of people who had come when there was too much cloud cover to be able to see a decent sunset, but this evening looked to be a beautiful cloudless evening, and her heart was pulsing in anticipation.

Radha and Song were through the ticket booths quicker than she was and were waiting for her patiently on the other side, Song swinging her legs with a rhythmic bounce against the balustrade they were sitting on.

Lydia gazed straight in the direction of one of the wonders of the world and wondered if she had descended to an alternative plane. She had seen this iconic image in many photos, but looking directly at it drained the heat from her excitement as the building's edges didn't have the sharp clarification that the professional photographers gave them. The five peaks of the temple were without doubt an architectural pinnacle of achievement, but somehow there was a dullness to the stone that gave it, at least to her mind, an understated vacuousness. Turning to Song and Radha, neither wanting to express her initial sense of disappointment nor having the words to explain herself, Lydia smiled broadly and with a forced cheerfulness exclaimed, 'Here at last! Isn't this great?'

Radha looked askew at Lydia and gave her hand a soft squeeze, then addressed his first comment to Song: 'Hey, little one, how many peaks are there on this temple?'

Song's eyes flicked rapidly. 'Five.'

'Well, did you know that its five peaks represent the mythological Mount Meru which sits at the centre of the universe and is the place where the gods live?'

Song had been open mouthed and wide eyed in her appreciation of the temple structure and she enthused to Radha, 'No, I didn't know that. That's amazing! Who designed it so cleverly?'

'King Suryavarman II in the early twelfth century when Cambodia was at its most powerful.'

'Cambodia used to be a powerful country, not a poor country?'

'Oh yes. Cambodia was once an empire which extended as far as modern-day Thailand and parts of Vietnam. Actually, if we get close to the south wall of Angkor Wat we'll be able to see some pictures carved in the stone that narrate the story of King Suryavarman's conquests against the Champa people in Vietnam.'

'I'd like to see them. You can explain the story to me.'

Lydia was glad that Radha had paid enough attention to history to be able to explain such details to Song. She'd not had the patience to read the guides in detail herself and was more interested in just wandering around and getting a flavour of the place.

The temples in the Angkor Wat complex represent two key religions. The earliest temples were Hindu and demonstrated the highest level of architectural design. From the end of the twelfth century with the reign of Jayavarman VII, Mahayana Buddhism became the state religion and a spate of monuments was built in the region within a 40-year period. These are generally considered by historians to be artistically inferior to the earlier monuments in spite of their grandeur. Angkor itself was once a vast city, but all the structures including the palaces have long decayed as they were made of wood. Only the temples were built to last.

It was noon on the second day of their Angkor Wat experience. Lydia pushed back her sunglasses to see Ta Prohm more carefully. Even though it was not yet the hottest season, the atmosphere was close and vibrated with the glare of the midday sun and the sound of crickets. Song had really enjoyed the stories and the historical details that Radha had entranced her with as they explored the main temples. Lydia's personal favourite was this temple which had been left in the state in which it had been first discovered, with the jungle encroaching in on all sides and crumbling walls being overgrown by lithe, whispering trees. As she walked through one of the enclosures she stood back and took a photo of a massive tree root that was pressing down on the enclosure's gallery. There was a fascinating symbolism that appealed to her. Nature was breaking down what was man-made and temporary, and civilisation was being crushed by a rampant wildness.

Out of the corner of her eye, Lydia could see yet another child worker approaching. This particular child was a wan-looking girl with limp hair who looked as though she was about seven or eight, but Lydia guessed she was around the same age as Song as most Cambodian children were a lot less physically developed than their Western counterparts. Dispensing with the usual Cambodian grin, the girl pulled on Lydia's hand rather sharply. 'You want buy books about Cambodia? Very good, yes. Only $1.'

'No thanks,' Lydia replied in Khmer, yanking her hand away. The books were all travel guides about Cambodia and other books of interest to tourists regarding the horrors of the Killing Fields and the Pol Pot era and were extremely cheap because they were photocopies, much like those you could buy in any of the markets in Phnom Penh.

So far, Cambodia had managed to evade all international copyright laws, and this included DVDs and books, and the Westerners who lived in and visited the country tended to support this thriving black market for one of two reasons: either because the products were bottom-of-the-barrel prices or because there was no other option for consumers who wanted these products.

The girl put her hand on her stomach and looked imploringly at Lydia; she wasn't going to give up easily. 'Please, I hungry!' While this stark statement was true of many street kids in Cambodia, Lydia pushed back the pinpricks of guilt. She knew that the sad reality was that this child was being manipulated by adults for their profit. If it were true that she was hungry, it would be better to give her some food rather than money, which would end up in the hands of someone with more power and less concern.

'Would you like to play with me for the rest of the afternoon?' Lydia was startled as she'd not been aware of Song's approach.

It seemed as though the girl was just as surprised, not by her approach but by her suggestion. 'Play?' she said in Khmer. 'I have to sell at least ten books this afternoon or… I haven't got time to play.'

'Oh, come on,' said the irresistible Song, her eyes dancing. 'I'll help you sell the rest of the books, too.'

'*Will* you now?' Lydia wasn't sure that this was such a good idea.

'It's ok, Aunty. I know what to do!' Song wouldn't give up and Lydia decided to throw caution to the wind and let the girls have some fun together. That would probably be better medicine for this waif than anything else.

It turned out that Song's method of playing was actually a way of combining play with work. With Song taking the lead, the two girls, Song and Daneat, accosted potential customers with a rather unusual selling ploy – dancing! Lydia had no idea where Song had picked up this style: she would advance on the tourists and entertain them with a bouncy, leg-intensive dancing style reminiscent of Irish dancing, while Daneat would leave her book tray to one side and sway and swerve around Song. It was not the most choreographically elegant of dances, but the tourists were amused by it as it was so unexpected in this cultural context. Several tourists didn't buy any books from Daneat but they gave generously, from $5 to $20 a dance. Radha and Lydia stayed as far away as possible from the girls, which was for the best as their barely suppressed hysterical laughter would hardly have aided their efforts.

Breathless and giggling, the girls counted their pickings in the corner of Ta Prohm at around five in the afternoon. The total cost was $115 – an absolute fortune for a simple child seller.

'Perhaps you could keep half of your earnings today rather than giving it to your employers?' suggested Radha to Daneat with a sideways glance and a wink. Daneat's default stern expression returned and she cocked her head up from the fistful of notes without saying anything, probably afraid of what might happen if she was found out. Softening like butter at the edges, she responded with an ironic, 'I couldn't!' while clapping her hands in glee.

'Save your money,' Song said, 'and come to Phnom Penh to live.'

Lydia stepped in, uneasy with the way the conversation was going. 'Phnom Penh might not be the best place for her, Song.' She didn't know what the best option was. It seemed pointless the child having all this money if she wasn't going to be able to do anything fruitful with it.

'Please, Aunty, she could live with us!'

Not wanting to seem as though she was rejecting the child, but at the same time annoyed with Song's over-enthusiasm for putting her in this position, Lydia chewed her bottom lip and responded, 'We might love to have Daneat with us, but her father and mother would be sad to see her go.'

'I don't have a mother or father,' said Daneat matter-of-factly.

'Who is taking care of you, then?'

'I take care of myself. I give my earnings to my aunty, but she lets me do what I like.'

Lydia didn't doubt that this was true. It was yet another sad story of Cambodian child poverty that would be repeated all over the country. She felt a hollow kicking inside mixed with an elemental rising-up. There was no way she could take in another 'waif and stray' under the conditions of her organisation, and she didn't even know if she wanted to. She was quite content with her life with Radha and Song, and although some might consider this selfish, she didn't want that to change.

While she was racking her brains about how to proceed, Radha interjected with a helpful deferment. 'We can take your contact details and ask around about organisations and people who can help you. What do *you* want to do with your life? Never mind Song – she's easily excited.' Song's chin twitched and Radha squeezed her hand affectionately.

Never having been asked such a question before, Daneat didn't know how to answer immediately, but when her answer came it was simple and unaffected: 'I want to get a good education and have a nice family.' She looked up, eyes wide and tentative.

'Of course you do; that's what most people want,' Radha responded in an unpatronising tone.

Radha sighed and pulled up a chair opposite Lydia. 'I've finally managed to track down a local NGO willing to help Daneat but they say she would need to approach them first. I can let Daneat know the details tomorrow.' As Daneat didn't have access to a phone, they had told her they would meet her the following morning outside their guesthouse, to let her know what they had managed to find out. Lydia stroked his hand across the table and said with reassurance, 'There's nothing much else we can do. You've done a lot already. I really appreciate your help in all this.'

'It was nothing,' Radha said distractedly. It was 9pm. Song had gone to bed about half an hour earlier and the two of them were sitting with a drink beside the pool. Lydia was taking this opportunity of Song not being around to drink a refreshing pina colada, while Radha drank a cola. Radha sat eyeballing his drink, his shoulders hunched over, without making eye contact with Lydia for what seemed like five long minutes, though in reality it was probably only one or two.

'What's up?' said Lydia. 'I'm not used to you being so quiet!'

'Do I have to chatter all the time?!' he barked, the muscles in his jaw contracting. 'Maybe sometimes I just don't have anything worthwhile to say.'

Lydia didn't say anything in response but tried to encourage him to look at her at least, sliding her toes on the inside of his calf. He responded in the way she wanted and, having studied her face, he began searching for words to unravel the tangle of his thoughts.

'The thing is... I'm seeing myself in Daneat and it doesn't bring back happy memories.' Sensing that Radha was about to open up to her about his past at last, Lydia didn't want to stem the flow by commenting, so she just nodded sympathetically. So far, all Lydia knew about his past was that he'd lived in poverty but that his family had not suffered extreme hardship during the Pol Pot era because they'd been simple farmers living in a rural area, whereas the Khmer Rouge's main axe-grinding had been with the capitalist city-dwellers as they sought to implement a so-called 'Agrarian' ideal in the land. 'You know, from the mid-eighties I was on a treadmill running hard from poverty. My parents managed to get into so much debt – mainly due to my dad's drinking and lack of responsibility – that we always owed two or three times more than we could possibly earn in a year. My mum would borrow money from the local corrupt moneylenders and the interest rates were so ridiculously high that it was a losing game from the start. All I wanted to do was go to school and make a good life for myself, but for a while I was stuck as there were no qualified teachers in the area – they'd all been killed off during Pol Pot's time. We had one so-called teacher but she had only been educated herself until the age of 15 and, although no one said it to her directly, it was known that she frequently taught factual inaccuracies.'

'Like what?' Lydia couldn't resist probing.

'The one I remember best was when she taught us that the boiling point of water was 100 degrees Fahrenheit, not Celsius. No matter how hard we tried to follow her instructions and boil our water, we obviously couldn't. No one would directly contradict her in front of the class even if we had known the truth – it would have made her look a fool. And sadly she was the authority!'

'So how did you find out the truth?' Lydia laughed.

'Oh, I don't remember fully, but there were one or two educated adults in the village who at least knew some basics, and it was obvious to most of us kids that her "fact" was not quite factual as it wasn't working. I think even she realised that she was misinformed, but she wouldn't have wanted to admit that for fear of losing face.'

'Very different from how things are in the UK. She'd have been struck off the teaching register for incompetency and the parents would never have allowed her to get away with teaching such inaccuracies.'

'Yeah, I can imagine. It's not like we had any alternatives, though.'

'Sure, it's easy to take things for granted sometimes,' she said, her face flushing.

'Anyway, I'm getting away from my main track of thought. You're distracting me by asking too many questions!' Lydia was pleased to see Radha's customary casual flippancy returning.

'I never want to go back to that state again,' he said after a pause, shuddering, as though following a line of unspoken thought.

'What state?'

'Of indebtedness. The sense of being trapped in poverty with no way out is my worst nightmare. Last night I woke up sweating after a particularly horrible nightmare, actually.'

'Really? I had no idea. What was it about?'

'It was one of those dreams you can't explain properly. When I woke up the details were already slipping from my memory, but it left me with a level of fear that I could taste, and I knew it had been something to do with trying to get out of debt. What I do remember is a leering face, perhaps of a particularly ruthless moneylender, and a windowless space with cockroaches scuttling up and down all four walls in an endless march.'

'Sounds revolting,' Lydia cringed.

'You know, I'd do anything – absolutely anything – to avoid getting into a position of indebtedness again.'

'Really? Anything?'

'Yes. Particularly if it involved the welfare of my family.' A hardness set itself around Radha's mouth. He fiddled with his watch strap and removed the watch to scratch underneath. 'Tsss, I've got some sort of metal rash and it's really itchy... You know, my dad wasn't always a heavy drinker. He used to be a really respected, hard-working member of our community, and the village chief would turn to him for advice. "Mr Sam-Oeun: moral and wise" could have been written on his forehead and it would have been totally true – once...'

His face contorted fleetingly as though he'd sucked on a lemon – not a green lemon as the Cambodians tended to call limes, but a bright yellow lemon with all its concentrated bitterness.

'So what changed?' Lydia asked hesitantly.

In spite of the fact that Sam-Oeun and his family had not suffered the worst of the atrocities that the Khmer Rouge inflicted on much of the population, he had been adamantly against the Khmer Rouge and its paranoid mentality, which forced family member to turn against family member in desperate bids to save their own lives against a fluctuating ideal that there seemed no sure-fire way of ever living up to. Teachers, lawyers, monks, and even those who wore glasses or had paler skin, were considered to be enemies of the regime. Even some inside the regime such as higher officials were known to have been killed as 'traitors', so there was no way for sure of knowing you were safe. In such a climate, security was a schizophrenic parasite that fed upon itself to prevent itself from being destroyed externally.

Naturally, Sam-Oeun had been happy when the Vietnamese had defeated the regime in 1979 and had freely shared his opinions among the other villagers and farmers from other villages alongside whom he had worked. After the 'liberation' of Cambodia from the Khmer Rouge, a civil war kept the country in a state of turmoil for another 12 years. During the eighties, a range of guerrilla groups representing diverse political parties had plagued the provincial areas, and in 1985 Radha's father became the victim of one of these groups. The party was called the Khmer People's National Liberation Front and was known to be vehemently anti-Vietnamese.

'I'd got up early that morning to help Dad with the birth of several calves and I was feeling really at peace after seeing the amazing process of new life emerging and staggering around falteringly. Have you ever seen it?' Lydia shook her head lightly, knowing that this was not going to be his main topic. 'A tall stranger with an obvious limp and a gun hanging by his hip turned up that same morning, at around ten o'clock, and knocked hard on the door. My mum opened the door and was greeted by the abrupt words, "Where is Sam-Oeun, the farmer? We are looking for him." I had just finished washing my hands and, although I was a little surprised at his abruptness, I was on such a high after the calving that I wasn't thinking straight. So I said, "He's out the back with the cows." My mum looked at me sharply out of the corner of her eye and I felt myself deflate. What an idiot! Feeding my dad straight to the wolves!' Radha shook his head, grimacing, as though trying to shake off a heavy weight. Lydia watched his Adam's apple rise and fall, engrossed.

He exhaled slowly like a woman in labour and continued. 'Most of what I know about what happened to my dad at that time came out bit by bit over the next few years, some of it mumbled while he was drunk and some of it shouted out when he was in a foul mood.'

The tall stranger was the leader of the guerrilla group, whom Sam-Oeun simply referred to as Dop. Dop accosted Sam-Oeun in the barn, where he had just finished placing one of the post-partum cows in her stall. After twisting his arms backwards and tying him to the barn posts, he kept him there for two days, interrogating him. A whole retinue of guerrilla underlings were on hand for Dop to command as he wished, dropping in or out to attend to him at what seemed to be the mere clicking of his fingers.

For the first half-hour or so after being manhandled into the position of prisoner, Sam-Oeun's mind was maze-locked and he was unable to fathom why he was being held prisoner. The only words Dop would let drip to start with were, 'You know why you're here, don't you? You're an animal, aren't you?!'

When Sam-Oeun cried out, 'Please tell me why you've taken me captive!' the only answer he'd receive was a resounding knock round the ears and a repetition of the accusations. It made sense to keep quiet after this to prevent any further abuse, although the fists would get terrifyingly close to his head and the vague accusations continued.

After about half an hour or so Dop suddenly exited the barn, leaving Radha's father even more confused. When he returned later, he was with a shorter, stocky soldier with a lazy eye, whose main role seemed to be to stare him out. Dop's tactic had changed. He was a lot calmer and almost personable, with an easy-going and polite demeanour. 'Ah, sir, sorry for any inconvenience. You must understand that we're deeply concerned about the plight of our nation and we have reason to believe you know something that could be of assistance to us in our fight against the Vietnamese.'

'What on earth could that be?' Sam-Oeun said sarcastically.

Dop refused to be riled and responded, 'I think you know already.'

'Please,' Sam-Oeun tried his own change of tactic. 'I don't even know who you are. Let me know what I can help you with and I can be a lot more useful to you than I am right now.' He tossed his head at his tied-up hands almost apologetically, and Lazy-Eye gave a wry grin. Dop ignored the gesturing and began pacing back and forth, five steps across from Sam-Oeun, and five steps the other way. It was as though he was deliberately drawing out the time of his response in order to emphasise his control over the prisoner. Lazy-Eye stared fiercely at him, willing him to break eye contact, which he soon did. Sam-Oeun wasn't about to compete in these pointless mind games.

Out of the corner of his eye, he saw Cheechaw, one of the mother cows, nudging the edge of her stall hard. The mother wanted to see her calf, which was outside with one of the farm helps, and she was being denied that right. The pitch of her moo reached a frustrated high and, flinching at the sound, Dop stopped in his tracks, swivelled his gun in the direction of the cow and silenced her protests. Sam-Oeun gripped his jaw tight to prevent himself from expressing the anger that rose in his gullet.

At last, Dop spoke, still maintaining his cool. 'Poor cow. She really shouldn't have stood in the way of our very important investigation. I am representing the Khmer People's National Liberation Front and my aim is to flush out those who have betrayed our nation to the Vietnamese.' Sam-Oeun suspected that whichever party he supposedly represented, this man was on his own private mission, a megalomaniac seeking to restore some sort of balance to a world that had been turned upside down. 'Right now, I'd like you to think hard about whether you or anyone you know has been involved in such treachery.' Sam-Oeun opened his mouth to speak but Dop raised his hand stiffly and shook his head. 'Wait, I don't want you to give me an answer now. I want you to take time to revisit all your memories and get as many details for me as you can. I'll be back in the morning. In the meantime, my colleagues will take care of you.'

Dumbfounded, Sam-Oeun slumped back defeated, ready for a long night. Being 'taken care of' by Dop's men was not what one would normally consider to be a caring approach. Over the next 12 hours, a sequence of nameless, blank men passed through the barn, transformed into automatons by the mental state of the prisoner. When looking back later, Lazy-Eye was the only one Sam-Oeun was able to distinguish as an individual since he'd been there from the beginning while he was still coherent. In Radha's father's most cogent moments, the thing that intensified his rage when looking back at this time was the indignity of not being allowed to leave his position to go to the toilet and so gradually finding himself becoming wetter and more soiled as the night progressed. This, more than all the torturing, ate away at his memories in the years to come. Torture is what you did to someone who was your enemy, someone you valued enough to want something from. To Sam-Oeun's mind, leaving someone to urinate and defecate on himself was a way of saying that that person had zero worth or dignity, that he was less valuable than a vegetable or dust mite. The methods of torture he mentioned were almost a sideline to this indignity. One soldier would hold his head so far back against the wall away from his shoulders that he could feel his nerves and sinews stretched so taut that he thought they would snap; another came in and yanked his toenail from his big toe on his right foot; yet another used a grater against the knuckles on both hands.

'I remember hearing a high-pitched, unearthly scream at about midnight that night, and I'm convinced that was dad's toenail being ripped off, though I have no idea what time any of the tortures took place.'

In between the physical torturing, Sam-Oeun was left for 15 minutes or so at a time and he would catch fitful snatches of sleep, but within minutes he would feel another hard blow about the ears from yet another automaton. This was going to be a long, painful and sleepless night. No one spoke a word to him, and if he tried to speak he would receive further knocks. This all seemed to be part of the game they were playing with him – to keep him in the dark about the reason he was being 'interrogated'.

Radha paused suddenly, turned deep wells of sorrow to Lydia and asked her a question which he didn't seem to require her to answer: 'How could anyone treat another human being that way? One thing I've learnt is that violence breeds further violence, especially violence with a hair's breadth of motive. You know what? I know very little about what happened to my dad after that endless night. All I know is that he did eventually find out what Dop was accusing him of and that it was connected with his sharing his opinion with others about the Vietnamese liberation of Cambodia from the Khmer Rouge being a blessing. I can't put my finger on anything more specific than that – Dad was pretty silent about what went on the next morning. The fact that it was so vague an accusation suggests to me that the Khmer People's National Liberation Front, or at least the breakaway part of it that Dop represented, were simply using Dad as a tool to strike fear into the heart of anyone in the local area who might speak in favour of the Vietnamese. Of course, I didn't figure any of this out at the time; it was only later on that I started to put the pieces together...'

A medley of crickets could be heard in the background, striking Lydia with the incongruous thought that it was impossible to locate exactly where their sound was coming from. 'I can't even begin to imagine what you must have gone through.' As soon as she uttered this, Lydia hated herself for its triteness and closed her mouth as if to swallow back the words, then was more annoyed with herself for even thinking that her words were what mattered in this situation.

The manager of Friendly's, a rotund, bulbous-nosed Australian, cleared his throat and said to them in an even tone, 'I'm going to have to ask you to head to your room now. It's almost 1am and I'm closing up shop. You're not making much noise but we do have some families here whose rooms are close to the pool and we don't want them to be disturbed.'

'So sorry!' said Lydia. 'We totally lost track of the time.'

Radha flicked his fingers on the edge of the table, keeping his eyes averted. Then he raised his head and said, 'No problem; we'll go,' in a light tone that belied his body language. Thus, in a moment, the mood was changed and further revelations were put on hold. Lydia stifled her frustration at not hearing the end of Radha's story, and holding him loosely by the hand, she encouraged him up from the table while the manager began switching off the lights.

Chapter 10
Cambodia, February 2007

'Come, Aunty, we've got to get the bus!' Song tapped Lydia hard on the shoulder to emphasise her point. Lydia stood at the gate of Friendly's looking down the street with a sinking sense of hopelessness, like a flailing swimmer knowing that she is about to drown.

'Just one more minute,' she said, her voice sticking in her throat.

Samnang picked up her handbag with a polite grin and placed it on top of their dusty backpack that was already loaded in the tuk-tuk. 'We go now, Madame?' he said with the rising intonation of a question but all the decisiveness of a statement.

'Okaaay,' Lydia flicked away the driver's helping hand and clambered into her seat. She sat wordlessly while the tuk-tuk turned around and headed off, one of the wheels jarring against a protruding stone in the ground. Radha sat beside her, helpfully not saying anything right then. In her mind's eye, Lydia could see Daneat turning up breathlessly five minutes after they'd left, and she could see the look of disappointment on her face. Something rose up in her as they turned the street corner and she was about to call out to the driver to return to the guesthouse so they could wait a little longer, but logic bit down hard and refused to let her speak. She looked at Song, sitting opposite her, gazing nonchalantly at her surroundings as though she'd seen them a hundred times before, and she wondered how she could be so unbothered about the fate of her new friend.

'That was one of her only chances to get herself out of grinding poverty and she's missed out on it.'

'Don't...' Radha said.

'I have to express myself or I'll explode!' Lydia knew histrionics would not get her anywhere but she was irritated with Radha for trying to manage her emotions, and she slapped his thigh with the back of her hand as though the whole situation were his fault.

'Hey, Miss Lydia!' he said with affected horror, and held off her hands with a strong arm.

Song looked at them and said simply, 'If Daneat had really wanted to be there, she could have found a way. I'm pretty sure of that.' She turned her head away from them as though hers was the final word, but Lydia refused to lie down.

'Any number of things could have happened to prevent her from coming today. Her aunt could have found the money the two of you earned yesterday and become suspicious; she could have had an accident on the way here; she... she...'

'What's the point of this, Lydia? We did our best to help her, and the fact is that she didn't come. We all have to make hard choices sometimes, and she made hers. Maybe it was meant to be that way.'

'"Meant to be"! Do you think it was "meant to be" that your dad was interrogated and tortured? Do you think it was "meant to be" that you had an unhappy childhood? How can you be so fatalistic?'

'What does fatalistic mean?' he asked.

'It means that everything that happens is a result of fate, that there is no way to change your circumstances by free will.' As soon as she explained the meaning, guilt hit her with a hammer-like blow. 'I'm sorry, Radha. Of course, *you* managed to change your own childhood situation through hard work and determination. I'm being totally unfair.'

Lydia shifted her position in her seat, and Radha enveloped her hand in his as though it were a small child. 'She did seem as though she really wanted to change her life,' she said wistfully.

'I know – she did.' Rather than fighting with her, Radha was now on her side. After all, he was the one who had put all the effort into finding an NGO willing to help her. He could understand her frustration; he just didn't want to see her beating herself up over something that couldn't be changed.

Several days after arriving back in Phnom Penh from their Angkor Wat trip, Lydia came home from work one evening to find Radha hunched over on the wicker sofa with his shoulders slumped. She discarded her bag on the floor and leaned over to playfully massage his shoulders. 'You're looking a bit tense. What are you studying so intently?'

'It's nothing to do with you.' Lydia was taken aback by the sudden brittleness of his voice. Radha's shoulders recoiled from her touch and he put down the piece of paper he'd been holding. 'I'm sorry,' he said, turning to face her as she came round to the front of the sofa to confront him. 'I'm sorry,' he repeated. 'I don't want to discuss this now, that's all. I'd prefer us to have a nice evening without anything hanging over us.' He beamed at her and stroked her arms with sensuous fingertips, drawing her to himself suggestively, but Lydia could see an aloofness in his eyes that she couldn't quite explain and she held her body tersely from his.

'Radha, that's not the way I work. I'm not going to pretend everything's ok if it's not. I want to know what's going on.'

'Trust me on this one. It's better left unsaid.' His face was hardening and she could sense an invisible wall being erected between them. She was about to raise her voice to argue with him when the futility of such an action struck her and she turned sharply from him.

'If that's the way you want it, you can sleep on the sofa tonight.' Her level voice belied the anguish she felt inside.

'Fine,' he said with all the smoothness of a cat licking its paws. He slouched back into the seat and put his feet up on the sofa.

Lydia was disappointed; she'd expected him to grovel and beg. 'Is that all you're going to say? Wouldn't it be easier just to let me know what's happening?' She tried to reason with him.

'I'm not your tool that you can force me to do what you want.'

'And I'm not your plaything for you to hump without any connectedness!' Her voice hissed out from between clenched teeth as she tried to maintain the control that she was losing.

Radha was silent for a while as he rhythmically flicked the back of the wicker. Pff pff pff. 'Come on, Lydia,' he changed tactic. 'Let's not let this get out of hand. I'll tell you at the right time – I promise you.' The words rang hollow in her ears.

'I don't know you,' she said, one part of her alert to the cliché but unable to resist. 'I've never seen you so cold before.'

'This is going nowhere,' Radha said with sudden decisiveness. 'I'm heading out this evening. I'll let myself in later.'

'Where are you going?' Lydia checked herself and continued with sarcasm, 'Stupid question, little me, why would you answer that one if you won't answer my previous one?'

'Too right.' Radha picked up his helmet and house keys and shoved the offending letter into the back pocket of his jeans. Giving Lydia a cursory glance, he headed out of the door, slamming the mosquito screen behind him.

Song poked her head around her bedroom door where she'd been all this time, and looked at Lydia.

'Don't look at me like that!' Lydia exploded. 'As if it were my fault he's gone!' She felt as though she were watching herself from a distance: this aggressive behaviour was not like her. She'd never raised her voice in this way to Song before. Song retreated swiftly back into the safety of her room like a tortoise retreating into its shell.

Lydia realised her throat was parched and she poured herself two glassfuls of water in rapid succession. Her mind hammered out a barrage of defensive and offensive thoughts. How dare he try to seduce me after refusing to share what was bothering him? He basically accused *me* of being manipulative! What a devil's trick. I bet he's gone out to get a prostitute to spite me. That would be just typical. How could I have allowed myself to get close to another man? He's a liar underneath all his outward charm. I should never have believed him!

A montage sped unbidden into her mind's eye of Radha hugging her gently; Radha playing with Song on his back while she whacked him with an imaginary horsewhip; Radha washing up in his precise, slow manner; Radha's eyes crinkling with laughter after she'd said something funny... She sat down unprotected on the front porch, daring the mosquitoes to bite her, and exhaled hard. Song's right; I did push him away. Why couldn't I have just let him have his little secret? Then he'd still be here now. It might be killing me with curiosity but at least we'd still be together. Has he left me for good? He said he was coming back this evening, but I bet it's just the start of the end. I can't believe I acted in that way towards him and Song. Remorse stung the back of her throat and hot tears began to fall. I've let myself down. I've had an opportunity to make something good out of a relationship and

I've messed it up big time. Lydia wiped away the tears that dripped down her nose and slammed her fist into her thigh. What an idiot!

About five minutes later, Lydia stepped back inside the bungalow and knocked quietly on Song's door. 'I'm so sorry I snapped at you, little one. I had no right.'

'It's ok. I understand,' Song replied, making limited eye contact before flicking her head back down again mournfully.

'Let me get you something to eat. I totally forgot we've not eaten yet. My stomach grumbling like a grizzly bear reminded me.' She smiled, trying to win Song back with humour, but she knew her smiles were forced as though stretched out tight with sticky tape.

They ate their meal in an awkward semi-silence, previously unknown since Song had moved in. 'Pass the salt, please,' and, 'Could I have the water, please,' were the only phrases to pass their lips. Lydia interpreted Song's silence to mean that she was unhappy with her and she didn't have the heart to make small talk to cover the blankness.

As soon as she'd chewed her last mouthful, Song pushed back her plate and said, yawning, 'I'm tired. I'd better go and get some of my English practice done before tomorrow,' even though it was only 7pm and normally she would practise her English *with* Lydia, joking and asking tricky grammatical questions which Lydia had to wrack her brains to answer. Just before entering her room, however, Song turned around to give Lydia a brief, empathetic smile, and her eyes were bottomless lakes of meaning.

Lydia tried to lose herself in her second-hand copy of *Anna Karenina* that evening to distract herself from Radha and his absence, but her mind couldn't stick with her reading and kept wandering down pathways both old and new.

Radha had updated her with more of his story in the past few days. After his dad's torture experience, Sam-Oeun retreated little by little from his family into a haze of alcohol and self-pity. Prior to this experience Radha remembered his dad as being a switched-on man who would engage with his three children and their interests in the little spare time he had, as well as maintain an unusually romantic relationship with his wife. He would kiss his wife, Leda, warmly in front of the children and compliment her freely. Radha felt free to come to him with any questions he had about his homework, and he would always attempt to engage with the process, even if the standard were higher than his own level of education.

After the event, Radha could see his father becoming colder and colder towards his mother. While she sought to draw near to him to meet him in his pain, he pushed her further away. The alcohol never led to him being violent towards his family, but his retreat was freezing their hearts towards him, in particular Radha's mother.

Late one night, about six months after the incident with Dop, Radha woke up to hear his parents having one of the only arguments he'd ever heard them have. Leda was speaking in a tight voice as though her throat was constricted, and Sam-Oeun was shouting, seemingly unaware how much volume his voice had.

'Can you honestly tell me you've not taken any money out of our cash box for drink?'

'What do you want from me, woman?'

'I want you to care about your family like you used to, and not try to hide your pain behind alcohol.'

'Hide my pain! What pain? I just don't like you putting pressure on me. Just leave me be.' His voice slurred unwittingly.

Silence.

Still silence.

A grunt then a squeal like a stuck pig shocked the silence. Radha heard a smash reverberating as a plate hit the wall. 'What are you doing to me, woman?! First you accuse me of stealing and then you try to kill me!'

'Give me back my real husband!' Leda's voice was no longer constricted but had reached a high pitch, released by the passion of her violent action. 'I want him back! I love him and I h-hate what he's doing to himself and us!'

All Radha could hear next was a sequence of muffled words and sounds as Sam-Oeun drew his wife into another room and hushed her, having been stunned into soberness by the sheer intensity of the moment.

Radha told Lydia that it was after this time that his mother began borrowing money at high interest rates from the local usurers. And from that moment, no matter how much money his dad would make from his farming, and how much his mum could make in her local store, there was never enough to cover all their needs. Sam-Oeun's profits went down as his work ethic slipped, and the less he made the more he seemed to throw his money away on drink. Leda retreated into a shadowy protective cocoon – a defence against the loss of her beloved in all but body. Radha's older brother became rebellious and wild, arguing with his elders and living a life of promiscuity, while his younger sister tiptoed around the family circle, trying to please everyone without causing offence to anyone. Radha became determined to make a better life for himself and began a period of soldierly diligence in his studies and in his whole lifestyle. He would get up early each morning to exercise and devour whatever study materials he could get his hands on, which were more freely available in their town than in some places in the country, as it had not been burnt up as 'capitalist' by the Khmer Rouge.

In 1993, when Radha was 16, one of the newly arrived Western NGOs descended into their locality and began making investigations in the village about young people. Their aim was to track down three or four young poor people who had been educated locally and who had the potential to excel in their chosen fields, and to sponsor these chosen few to attend the best high schools in Phnom Penh and eventually through university. Radha was one of the chosen, and this doorway opened up for him as the opportunity of a lifetime. Without a second glance back home, Radha kissed his mother and siblings goodbye, moved to the city and began living with his mum's cousin and their family of six in three rooms in a crowded, stuffy, third-floor flat in central Phnom Penh.

This turned out to be a tarnished opportunity in the sense that the sponsorship only covered his basic living expenses in the city, and the level of education he received was only slightly higher than the education he had received in school in Mondulkiri, and was even marginally behind his self-taught learning. The sponsorship was available up until the end of his time at university, but Radha, unable to be fast-tracked through the system, was frustrated by the speed of his acquisition of knowledge. He also felt stifled by the crowded atmosphere in his cousin's home. He sought to make more money for himself and get out of the house as much as possible by setting himself up as a tuk-tuk driver in his spare time. Radha was able to zip through the assignments set for him by the school in about half the time it took his classmates, so he had more spare time on his hands than he had patience for. Being a tuk-tuk driver gave him the opportunity to get to know the layout of the city like the back of his hand and also gave him the chance to meet some of the foreigners who were already beginning to flock into Cambodia on their do-good mission trips or hippy trailblazing adventures as the country opened up at the end of the civil war. He began trying out his fledgling English skills, and he did good business with his smiles and charm. The main reason for his new resourcefulness was that he had got it into his mind that he wanted to pay back to the NGO as much of the sponsorship money as he could, having decided that he didn't want to be beholden to anyone.

Accelerating several years ahead found Radha still living with his cousin, getting up early six days a week and cycling to a management course at university. The vast majority of students studying management hoped to find senior jobs working for NGOs or somehow ascend the ranks of society through getting a job overseas. Radha's expectations were realistic and he knew that no matter how well he did at university, the job market would be extremely limited in Phnom Penh and he was unlikely to get any kind of high-flying position, even with the backing of his sponsors. He was right in that the first job he was able to secure after university was with an NGO, but it was the humble position of a driver: his English was not good enough at that stage to secure anything more substantial as the vast majority of NGOs were Western managed.

While working for this NGO he met Toby, the New Zealander, who took Radha's disciplined mindset and channelled it into the intensive studying of English. Radha had great fun with Toby, who took him out as a tourist pretending to be a foreigner who only knew how to speak English. Every time he slipped back into speaking Khmer in a public setting, Toby would add an extra 500 riel to his tuition fee,[3] which was a huge incentive for him to work hard at learning not only to speak but to think in English. Within two years of meeting Toby and

---

[3] 500 riel is the equivalent of around 12 US cents.

mixing with the expat community, Radha's English skills had improved a hundredfold, and he found his job working as a receptionist at Doctor Duke's surgery. Radha confessed that while he enjoyed being in this role, it was limited in terms of his management skills and he would love to move on to something more challenging.

Lydia had no doubt that he could succeed at something more challenging, but her heart felt as though it were swimming against quicksand, not knowing how much longer he was going to be a part of her life. She slipped into bed at 10pm, exhausted emotionally and physically, but her mind wouldn't let her sleep and held on to a thread of hope that Radha would come home that night. As she drifted down the road to unconsciousness, she would jolt herself back into alertness at every phb, phb, phb of an engine that she heard outside.

At about 11.15, she heard the soft sound of Radha opening and closing the screen door and her senses vibrated with anticipation. The pad, pad of his bare feet drew nearer to the bedroom door and a ray of light forced Lydia's eyes even more tightly closed. 'Lydia,' he hissed under his breath.

'Mmm,' she murmured, trying to give the impression that she had been deeply sleeping.

'Nothing,' he said as though she'd asked a question. 'I'm just letting you know I'm home. I'll sleep in the lounge area.'

'Mmph,' she replied. The firefly of hope edged around the corner of her mind and sighed out onto the floor.

In the morning, the three of them manoeuvred around each other like polite acquaintances. 'I'll take Song over to Helen's today,' Radha offered. Considering the way things had been left between them the previous evening, Lydia was taken by surprise at his willingness to help.

'Ok, that'd be great,' Lydia replied tight-lipped. 'Song, get yourself ready to go out soon. Don't forget the words you've been learning,' she said with all the flatness of a cardboard cut-out.

'I'll be two minutes!' called out Song through a mouthful of toothpaste.

Radha navigated his way round the room, picking up his socks from one corner, rolling up his sleeping mat and fishing a clean shirt from the fresh laundry pile, while taking mouthfuls of his noodle soup in between.

'I'm ready.' Song appeared in the living space and Lydia wiped the toothpaste smear from the corner of her mouth.

'Have a good day,' Lydia said, smiling down at her.

Song returned the smile loosely, her eyes dull. 'I will.'

Radha nodded his chin in her direction and said out of habit, 'I'll see you later.' Lydia could recognise the lethargy in his demeanour; it was almost as though he were sleepwalking through the day.

'Sure, looking forward to it,' she said coolly, mustering all her strength to avoid the doubt she felt creeping into her voice. Marshalling herself to face the day, Lydia threw her water bottle into her school bag, flung the bag over her shoulder and took a deep breath before walking out the door and padlocking it behind her.

'See you tomorrow!' Lydia crowed in response to her class's habitual cheery farewell. She patted Sophor affectionately on her shoulder as she tripped out of the classroom with a last cheeky glance at her teacher. There was no air conditioning in the classroom, only rather inefficient, badly wired fans, so after a day's work the first thing Lydia wanted was a shower. She exhaled between puffed-out lips, cleared her desk of pens and sorted her papers for marking and filing.

'How's it going with Mr Lover-Lover?' smiled Tepy at Lydia as she stumbled down the stairs past the reception area. Lydia's heart sank. Did she have to choose today of all days to ask me this question?

'Great thanks. We enjoyed our trip to Siem Reap.' She grinned broadly, hoping to muster up a good mood.

'Any good news to tell yet?' Tepy raised her eyes and blinked coyly.

'What? Ha ha, no. I'll be flashing my big rock the day that happens, if he can afford a big rock!' As if to make her point, Lydia waved her fist in front of Tepy's face and began to walk away, hoping her physical movement would curtail any further questioning on the subject. But the nails were being scratched down the chalkboard of her heart even further.

'Well, Pov told me he'd be asking me to marry him soon,' Tepy continued her theme.

'Oh Tepy, don't count your chickens before they're hatched. He may change his mind! I'm sorry, do you know that phrase?' she asked, attempting to turn the conversation away from love to language.

'Yes, I know it. He's already spoken to my parents so I'm sure he's serious.'

'I'm so happy for you,' Lydia took hold of her hands and squeezed them affectionately. 'Now I'm sorry but I really must go. Helen isn't able to keep Song for more than another ten minutes today so I must rush.'

'Ok, enjoy your evening.' Tepy's face shone with the glow of togetherness and Lydia couldn't bear to be around her a minute longer. As much as she normally cared for her she couldn't stand the effect Tepy was having on her. Lies were flushing out of her normally clean mouth.

'Sure, see ya,' she waved her hand absently and walked out, heart thumping. Just as she was about to step on her moped and begin her journey, Lydia felt a pulsing vibration against her thigh. She fished out her phone with a pincer grasp, 'Hi Helen, I'm just coming.'

'I'm not hurrying you, Lydia. I'm calling to tell you something.'

'What's that?'

'Radha came to collect Song about half an hour ago.'

'Really? Oh, that's ok. We didn't really discuss who would do it today but I guess he must have been free.'

There was a pause the other end and an inward breath, 'Well, I'm guessing it's ok. He said he finished work early and was trying to help you out. I didn't even question it at the time, you know, but after they'd gone I began to feel a bit unsettled although I'm not really sure why. Can you tell me why I should be feeling unsettled?'

Helen's question was penetratingly sharp and Lydia laughed, trying to turn this away from her. 'No, how could I possibly tell you why *you're* feeling unsettled?! I'm not you. I'm sure there's nothing to be concerned about.' Even as she built up her defence around her, Lydia was aware of it being knocked down by her own growing sense of inexplicable unease. She drove home, skirting the traffic skilfully, trying not to think and not to feel, her logical mind anticipating seeing them there when she arrived, but not knowing what to expect in the hidden corridors of her consciousness.

Five forty-six pm on 12th February 2007. The emptiness of the bungalow greeted her with an accusatory stare. The gate and the front door were still padlocked and Lydia opened them with clammy, clumsy hands, swearing out loud as it took her three or four rather than the normal one or two minutes to make her way inside. She could sense herself becoming fouler as though the air around her were polluting her thoughts and seeping out through her pores.

Everything inside was exactly as it had been left that morning. Lydia patrolled around, inspecting the place as though she were a detective investigating a crime. The rooms gave her nothing back except the steeliness of reality undisturbed. She opened Song's room and saw her nightwear strewn across her pillow along with several strands of long black hair. Her paper bird sat on the bedside table next to a luminous plastic pen and a half-drunk glass of water. The sheets were rumpled slightly and you could visualise the way in which Song had drawn herself up from the bed. There was a damp smell in the room as the door to the attached bathroom was open and there was a wet patch along the plaster near the shower that would not fully dry during the day. Lydia closed the door behind her to preserve the room in time as though it were an ancient Egyptian's tomb, and stepped out into the main living space, pacing from one side to another, unsure what to do with herself. Every nerve end was buzzing with electric energy.

Helen had called her at 5.15, which meant that Radha had picked Song up at around 4.45. Even given the possibility of a traffic jam they should have been home by now. She fiddled with her phone, resisting the logical action of a phone call to Radha, fearing being labelled a neurotic woman. Looking at the time on her phone she set herself a limit: if they were not back by 7pm, then she would call. In the meantime, she jumped into the shower and washed away the grime of the day and some of the tension in her muscles.

At one minute past seven, Lydia fast-dialled Radha's number twice. The first time she was greeted with the sound of the phone being disconnected. The second time it went straight through to his voicemail. He'd never bothered setting up a personal message so it was an automated voice recording. Images played havoc in her mind of the similar incident with Rob, and the brutal knife of rejection twisted into her again. But the difference was that this time it was not just about her; her sweet ward was involved too. She needed to stay sharp and alert and not descend into self-pity.

Lydia began to feel a pulsating throb of pressure around her throat and across her skull; it was not a physical but an instinctive throb, and it was only as she picked up her keys and stepped back onto her moto that she recognised the feeling as anger. Only later, as she looked back on this time, could she identify the source of her rage. She was angry with Radha, angry with all those who had encouraged her to take a chance on him, and above all angry with herself for being a susceptible fool. All this time there had been barely a hint of anything untoward, but she sifted through the memories, trying to find something that might indicate that Radha was a person of suspect character. The frustration was that she kept coming up against what seemed to be the strength of his character. It would be so much easier if she could point simply at his faults and say, yes, there was the key.

It had begun to rain in the miserable, half-hearted sort of way that it rains in England, which was unusual at this time of year in Cambodia. Lydia pushed on the accelerator and swished through the dark without a raincoat, narrowly avoiding a couple of cyclists who were pedalling on the wrong side of the road without lights, and allowed the rain to soak slowly through to her skin.

Chapter 11
Cambodia, February 2007

'I'm sorry to come by so late. I didn't know where else to go. I didn't know what else to do. Radha hasn't brought Song home and he's not picking up his phone and I...' she swallowed back her words. 'I don't know what my next options are.' The words rushed out in an inarticulate torrent.

'Hey ho! Slow down, Lydia. Come in first of all and calm yourself down.' Mike held out one arm and drew her inside like a mare nudging her foal.

Helen stood just behind him and glanced anxiously from her husband back to Lydia again and didn't say anything, allowing Mike to take the lead. 'And it's not late. It's only eight o'clock, if that. Never think you can't drop by at any time, especially when you're in need. What are you doing to yourself, Lydia, your clothes are wet through?!'

'I didn't have time to put on a raincoat,' she said unconvincingly.

'Come with me,' Helen instructed and led Lydia through to their bedroom.

Ten minutes later, dried and dressed in one of Helen's vest tops and a pair of shorts, Lydia slumped on the Bakers' sofa, holding her hands gratefully round a steaming cup of hot tea.

'I'm so sorry, Lydia. I'd never have let Song go with him if I'd allowed my instincts to lead.' Helen's eyes were filled with guilt.

'Please sit down, Helen. You're making me feel uncomfortable standing there so nervously. It's not your fault. If anything it's mine for allowing myself to get sucked into a relationship with him at all.'

Mike stepped in. 'This is not helping the situation, ladies. None of us could see this coming so we're all culpable to an extent. But at this point we need to start by being level-headed and systematic.' He paused and the two women waited for him to continue. 'First of all, is there any possibility that there could be a reasonable, non-dramatic explanation as to why they didn't come home today?'

'Urm, well, I've thought about this since arriving home, but none of the options seem viable now.'

'Ok, just run through them and we can rule them out if they're not possible.' Mike sat opposite Lydia, pen and notebook at the ready.

'What's the point,' said Lydia irritated, 'if those options are already done with?'

Mike sighed, letting that be his answer, and waited patiently for her to begin.

Lydia kicked her heel on the edge of the sofa with a show of rebelliousness and leaned forward. 'Radha's moto could have broken down and he could have lost his mobile phone or had it stolen.'

'What would his options have been if his vehicle had broken down?'

'He could have had it fixed at a garage, in which case he'd already be home, or he might have dropped in on some nearby friends or relatives to wait till the morning. If his phone was snatched, that would explain why he's not answering it.'

'And that, of course, is a real possibility in this city.'

'Yeah, but it doesn't add up for me any more 'cos he should have been able to borrow someone else's phone and call me to let me know what's going on. He knows my number off by heart.'

'But if no one else was around?' Helen put in.

'There's always someone around,' Lydia said impatiently, 'especially on the route he would have taken to get from here to our place. And he's Khmer so it's easier for him to approach Khmer strangers, even in their houses.'

'That's true,' mused Mike. 'He's an intelligent guy so he could have found a way to make contact if he'd wanted to.'

The three of them sat thoughtfully for some time, struggling to get to grips with the shifting sands of reality around their feet.

'Either they've been attacked or had an accident and are unable to contact us, or Radha has abducted Song, in which case he doesn't want to be found!' Lydia blurted out, expressing the dramatic possibilities that none of them wanted to believe, simply because she couldn't bear not to any longer. Neither option bore thinking about. The first option meant that their loved ones were suffering, or worse, somewhere. The second option meant that Radha had betrayed everything Lydia had believed about him and their relationship, which was in many ways harder for her to accept. Nevertheless, this was closer to the truth that pulsed around her heart.

Helen drew near to her and wrapped her arms around her shoulders in sympathy. Mike said, 'We can't be sure that either of those possibilities are what has happened but, ruling out the non-dramatic options, I guess we need to start taking some serious action.' His face was hard to read though Lydia could see a muscle twitching near his right eye.

'Can I take the day off work tomorrow so I can be involved?' Lydia asked.

'Without question you can. I'll arrange for your classes to be covered, either from among the casual volunteers or from the Khmer staff at the school.' Mike looked at his watch and in a businesslike, colourless manner said, 'Whatever we decide to do, there's nothing we can do until tomorrow, so I suggest we go to bed soon and start afresh in the morning. Of course, you're welcome to crash out here overnight, Lydia.'

'Thanks. I don't think I could face going back to the empty house tonight.'

After ten minutes' further discussion about some of the investigations they would be conducting the next day, Mike put down his pen and paper and insisted that they head to bed.

After a restless night, Lydia padded into the main living area the next day at the belated hour of 8am, in comparison to her normal waking time of 6am. Helen, swollen-eyed, was pouring milk over her breakfast cereal. Little Amy was bouncing around puppy-like as normal, but seeing Lydia enter the room, Helen took her to one side and whispered in her ear and she sobered up instantly without asking any questions. Lydia felt suddenly awkward around Amy and glanced at her with a shy wordless smile before sitting down at the dining table.

'What would you like for breakfast? I'm too lazy to do anything but cornflakes for myself but we do have some bread and jam or some fruit and yoghurt if you like.'

'Bread and jam will be fine for me,' Lydia responded listlessly. 'Where's Mike?'

'He's making some phone calls already. He'll be through in a second. Did you sleep well?' Helen raised her eyes sympathetically at Lydia. 'Stupid question, really,' she said, shaking her head.

'Ummm,' Lydia replied ambiguously and gratefully accepted the plate that Helen handed to her.

Radha's handsome, chiselled face appeared unbidden in her mind's eye and Lydia stifled a groan. How could she even be dwelling on him when the main issue was that he'd most likely snatched Song away from her? The bread tasted like sawdust in her mouth but she continued chewing laboriously.

A reticent throat-clearing sound could be heard at the top of the steps leading up to the Bakers' second floor and, a moment later, Mike's sandalled feet appeared on the steps. He clambered down, turned around and smiled weakly at Lydia before taking a deep inward breath. 'I called the surgery and it turns out that Radha didn't go back to work after his lunch break yesterday. The doctor I spoke to was quite free in telling me this because he wasn't at all happy as other key staff had to cover the reception instead, which meant they weren't able to offer as good a service as normal. So ...' the tone of his voice lifted significantly on "so", '... whatever he was doing yesterday was at least premeditated to some extent and ...'

'... he obviously didn't want people to know what he was up to,' Lydia finished Mike's train of thought. 'Damn it!' she said with sudden vehemence. 'Why am I such a sucker for the charming ones who turn out to be bastards?! Why, why, why?!'

'For God's sake, Lydia. We were all taken in by him! It's not as though you were or are alone in this.' Mike's hand came down hard on the table and Helen raised her eyes at him quizzically.

'He's right, Lydia. We're totally here with you on this one. I cared for him and I still do. Whatever he's done, he's done it out of character. I fully believe that.'

Forgotten in the midst of the revelations, Amy sat, her neglected cornflakes sodden, gazing wide-eyed from one to the other.

'How can you be so Christian and forgiving at a time like this?' Lydia's voice was cynical but under control. Helen and Mike were silent for a moment and Helen busied herself wiping the surface of the table.

'Don't get us wrong, Lydia. We can't really talk about forgiveness yet as we don't have the facts, but please understand that we do want justice to be done.' The way Mike spoke on behalf of both of them both touched and irritated her at the same time.

'So what's next, then?' Amy piped up and the adults turned to her.

'Oh, Amy. You shouldn't be hearing all this.' Helen was anguished.

'Well, I am,' she said matter-of-factly. 'Song is my friend and I want to know what you're all going to do to bring her back.'

Lydia hid her face behind her hands, her elbows resting on the table, and waited for one of the others to respond for her, to put a stamp of truth and justice in front of her and to carry a lamp of moral certainty ahead of her.

'Welcome on board our Air Asia flight.' Upon seeing Lydia's skin colour the smiling flight attendant spoke in English, but Lydia automatically responded to her in Khmer. 'Your seat is to the right.' The compact, perfectly proportioned attendant checked Lydia's boarding pass and continued in English as though dismissing her attempts to converse in her native tongue.

Lydia trundled her hand trolley down the right-hand aisle and found her seat. It was a window seat and she was relieved as not only could she turn her head to the window to avoid conversation with overly friendly or earnest passengers but she could also bid her final farewell to the country from the air. A young Cambodian wearing a smart pinstriped shirt sat next to her, his face all aglow as though he'd been scrubbed hard and polished. Lydia tried to avoid making eye contact but the young man's legs were bouncing with such excited energy and he kept glancing over at her that she knew it wouldn't be long before he was trying to make conversation. Just what I didn't want, she sighed imperceptibly. I'll get this over with as quickly as I can.

'It's my first time to leave Cambodia,' he ventured bravely.

'Really?' said Lydia as if she couldn't have guessed. 'Where are you going?'

'I'm going to India for study computer engineering. I'm so happy and my family are so happy for me.'

'Of course they would be. That's great. Where are you from?' She leaned back against the window of the plane to maintain a cool distance from the man, who was inching his way towards her.

'I'm from Kandal province. How long you were in Cambodia?'

'Two and a half years. I've been teaching English with VOA. I'm sad to be leaving.'

'So why are you leaving then?'

'Oh, you know, it's time to move on. I've got a life back home, too,' she said as vaguely as she could.

'A boyfriend?' he asked.

'No,' she replied trying to stymie all further enquiries on that subject.

'But why not?' he said as though it were entirely a matter of choice. 'You so beautiful.'

Ha, Lydia thought cynically. I've heard that one before. She made no reply but manufactured a sweetly grateful smile.

The plane began an urgent juddering as the engine started up and Lydia landed on a brainwave to end further conversation. 'You know what? I'm really scared of flying, especially on these smaller planes. It gets worse and worse each time even though I've done it several times, and I find it helps me to overcome my fear if I concentrate hard on alternative thoughts. In order to do that I need to avoid talking so I'm sorry if I seem rude. Lovely to meet you and I wish you all the best.'

'Ok, no problem,' said the young man, rather taken aback and disappointed at the loss of his conversing opportunity. He picked up the safety card from the pocket in front of him and began to read it. Lydia turned her head gratefully to the window with only the slightest twinge of guilt. About a minute later he piped up again, 'I think it helps your fear if talking to distract, not thinking.'

'Nnnoooo, it really wouldn't help,' she said with great deliberation, irritated that her foolproof idea hadn't worked, but also slightly amused at his persistence. 'Trust me: I've been here before and it's not a good place to be.'

'Just an idea,' he said lightly.

Lydia was silent. Realising that his attempts were not going to work, he went back to studying the safety card.

Lydia's eyes were dry as she watched the undulations of the Mekong River and the smatterings of sugar palm trees tilting and dropping away beneath her as the plane rose and gradually circled in the direction of Bangkok. She had already cried so many tears that her emotions had somewhat shrivelled up at the source. It was two months since Radha and Song had disappeared. She and the Bakers had come up against brick wall after brick wall in their investigations. Every time they seemed to be making some headway, another door would close in their faces while they would try to pry the door open futilely with their fingers.

Lydia turned down the corridors of her mind and came up against the mask-like faces of the tuk-tuk drivers on her street. Sakoeun had listened to her with his eyes lowered when she asked him, 'What was the last you saw of Song and Radha?'

He chewed his bottom lip before lifting his eyebrows and replying in English, 'Not seen girl or gentleman.'

'Did you see them two days ago?', 'Did Radha tell you anything about where he was going?', 'How did Song look?' She probed with question after related question, but each time he came back with the same response like a brainwashed POW. She resisted the urge to growl at him in frustration. She had tried the same tactic with all the other drivers she knew on different occasions and had been met with a similar emotionless response.

For Lydia, the most painful memory was when she personally went to see the superintendent of police in Phnom Penh. After having gone through what seemed to be a never-ending chain of administrative form-filling, where she would be directed to see yet one more officer to fill in and sign yet another document detailing what had happened, she finally walked into the hallowed ground of the superintendent's office. She had taken her shoes off at the entrance to his office and kowtowed low (she winced now at the thought) as she entered his sanctuary. The first thing she noticed was how flat his head was; she'd never seen anyone with such a tabletop head in her life, and it mesmerised her throughout the whole of her interaction with him. Even though she knew he was called Superintendent Samedy, forever afterwards she thought of him as Flathead, which helped to dehumanise him in the way she felt he ought to be. She had tried to address him in formal Khmer to show her respect but her attempts were obviously so unsuccessful that he bulldozed her attempts by replying with immaculate English.

'Yes, I have read the documents you filled in,' he responded coolly. 'We will do our best to investigate the whereabouts of Sen Radha and your ward Lee Song, but let me tell you now that we are extremely unlikely to be successful.'

'With all due respect, Sir, isn't it your responsibility to bring the perpetrators of crimes to justice at all cost, without assuming that you're going to fail right from the start?'

Flathead stared at her blankly. 'Madame, you are obviously unfamiliar with the way the justice system works in Cambodia. Lee Song is Vietnamese by birth and has never claimed the right to citizenship in this country. She is thus not legally entitled to protection by the Cambodian state.'

'Isn't it your right and responsibility to take care of all people living within the boundaries of your country regardless of their nationalities?!' Lydia was flabbergasted by his response.

He leaned back in his chair and flicked his pen rhythmically on the table. 'You'd like to think so, wouldn't you, but that's not how it works in practice, I'm afraid.'

'How does it work in practice, then?! Would it speed things up and make them more efficient if I were to hand you a few thousand dollars under the table?!' Lydia knew she had gone too far as soon as the words came out of her mouth. Her heart was throbbing at the base of her throat.

'Madame, I suggest you exercise a little self-control,' he said with enough ice to freeze the Caribbean. 'If you want to get your loved ones back you may be waiting a long time. Even with the best will in the world, there is only so much we can do.'

'So tell me what I should do then?' Lydia said in a lower voice, despair sweating from her pores. 'I have contacted the senior police. Do you want me to speak to Prime Minister Hun Sen himself?'

Flathead laughed wryly. 'Have you contacted the British Embassy?'

'Yes, and they suggested that we work through the Cambodian channels where possible.'

Seeming to soften, he tapped Lydia's hand where it rested on the table. 'Look, we have taken all the particulars related to Sen Radha and Lee Song's disappearance that we can from you. Leave it in our hands and we will do our absolute best to bring the perpetrators to justice.'

Lydia looked him in the eye and knew without a doubt that he was lying, that he was trying to butter her up and leave her with a positive message after their rather difficult confrontation. She also knew that she was right and that only an extensive bribe would make a difference in this case. In fact, she had a hunch that a pay-off had already been made by some malevolent source, which would explain the dead end that she was facing now.

'Thank you. I appreciate it,' she said dully, stepping out of the inner court, her hopes splintering like breaking glass. All the effort she had made to get into the senior policeman's presence had come to nothing. She felt wrung dry as if she'd gone through a tumble dryer several times.

That night, Lydia sat in the Bakers' kitchen after they'd gone to bed and suppressed the sound of her frustrated weeping. She felt a claustrophobic sensation as though the walls were closing in on her, and she blinked at a bottle of wine in front of her on the shelf. It swam in front of her eyes, seducing her with thoughts of blissful oblivion. Then, unbidden, Song's doom-like voice called out in the recesses of her mind: 'Alcohol is bad,' and her hands shook visibly as she placed the bottle in a cupboard under the sink.

'Is there anything we can do to persuade you to stay?' Brian had listened to her story with a loyal but weary concern. 'As you say, it does sound as though Radha has abducted Song and probably sold her for a vast sum of money to pimps. There doesn't seem to be any other reasonable explanation for what has happened. I'm so sorry that the police have been no help whatsoever, though sadly it doesn't surprise me at all. Tch, if Song had been your adopted child then you might have had more legal grounds for pushing for justice, but as things stand... I'm sorry, I don't seem to have anything positive to say. However, you've done some great work over the past couple of years and we'd love it if you would continue, in spite of all that's happened

101

over the past few months.' He rifled through some papers on his desk melancholically.

'How can I stay, Brian? My whole life was tied up in Song and Radha towards the end, and you know it. I can't be happy again here, especially knowing that the police system is probably working with rather than against the perpetrators.'

He sighed with resignation. 'I knew that's what you'd say, and I'd feel the same as you under the same circumstances.' Brian came around the desk and said solemnly with his face downcast and his hands clasped together, 'Do I have permission to give you a goodbye hug?'

Lydia smiled in spite of herself and punched him playfully on the shoulder, 'You don't have to ask permission!' He gave her a broad grin and clamped her to his chest. Lydia choked back the salt tears that threatened to return and hugged him back hard. 'The only thing I will ask is that you don't attempt to send a farewell delegation to the airport with me when I leave. I *hate* group goodbyes!'

'I promise you that, though I can't promise we won't try to win you back to us by some devious methods.' His eyes twinkled.

If saying goodbye to Brian was hard, saying goodbye to Mike and Helen was even harder, especially after all their care and practical support. 'I know I've got trust issues after what happened with Radha, but I genuinely do respect and trust you guys. It's not because of anything you've done or not done that I'm leaving – I want you to know that.'

Helen squeezed her hand and, glancing at Mike, said, 'The thing we regret most in all this was that you didn't ever get to know Jesus in a way that would have put all of this pain into perspective.'

Lydia laughed. She loved them both for their honesty and earnestness. 'To be fair, I don't know how "knowing Jesus" could have put this hell into any sort of perspective, but I love you guys for your faith and generosity. I mean that.' She could see from their faces that there was more that they wanted to say on the subject but they kept quiet, and for that also she loved them.

* * *

Lydia's students were sad to see her go, but they were used to foreign teachers coming and going so were half expecting it. Knowing that didn't make it any easier for her and she waited until the last possible moment before she told them that she would be going home to England and not coming back again.

'What about your boyfriend that you were going to marry?' asked Phireak. Lydia hadn't mentioned anything about Radha directly to her students but word had got around, as gossip generally does.

Lydia smiled sadly and said, 'Sometimes things don't work out the way we would like them to,' knowing that her kids would take this to mean that he had simply left her and nothing more, a far better belief than the truth. 'Keep studying hard and pursuing your dreams, and if you face disappointment know that there'll always be more to life even after your disappointments.' Lydia was spouting a philosophy that she didn't quite believe herself at that time; a stone weighed on her heart, dragging it down and rendering her incapable of joy.

As Lydia mulled over all that had happened in the past six months or so she knew that she was going to have to make a choice. Was she going to allow her whole life to be coloured by this haunting experience? It would be tempting to do that as it would make her feel that she was a victim who had been wronged, thereby mitigating her own part in the affair. But at the same time Lydia knew enough about psychology to know that the resulting bitterness would not harm anyone else as much as it would harm her, so that option was becoming less and less appealing. The only other option she could see was to put this whole situation to the back of her mind and move forward from this point, older and wiser but none the worse a person for what had happened. You might call it denial, but to Lydia it was survival. By the time the wheels of the plane screeched to a standstill in Bangkok to end the first leg of her journey to the UK, Lydia had made up her mind. She would choose survival.

Part 2
Song's melody

Chapter 12
England, November 2036

Song shifted her backside in her seat, plumping the cushions around her carefully, and contemplated the soft furnishings and the dim lighting with an artist's eye for detail.

'Oh, thanks,' she said with heartfelt warmth as Lydia placed a cup of green tea on the coffee table near her knees, 'I've never got used to the taste of breakfast tea so I'm happy to see you've got Cambodian style tea.'

'Well, all anyone ever drank there was bland and flavourless so it's hardly surprising you never got much of a taste for it.'

'Things have moved on since then,' Song said jauntily, 'but you can't win me to it all the same!'

'I have to say your English is almost flawless now. A lot has changed since...'

'Thank you. I've spent around 20 years moving in art and business circles internationally, which would explain it.'

'Oh really, what is it that you do now?' Lydia felt a small stirring of pride in the accomplishment of her former ward, which came up against the whisperings of the accuser.

Song's answer was to reach into her handbag and pick out a beautifully bound album and hand it to Lydia with shy reticence. Lydia began turning the pages and was confronted with a subtly shaded black and white photograph of a young Cambodian girl leaning over a wall with a cheerful smile on her face that didn't hide the sadness in her eyes. 'This is amazing, Song, you've got real talent. Is she someone you know?' asked Lydia.

'Yes, I know her very well: she's one of my daughter's friends at the home for vulnerable children we support.'

'You have a daughter?'

'Yes, I have two: Sara and Leda. Sara is 12 and Leda is 8.'

'Did you marry, then?'

'I did, although sadly he died two years ago,' Song cleared her throat and pursed her lips.

'May I ask what happened?'

'He was martyred for sharing his Christian faith in a staunchly Buddhist area.'

Lydia took a sharp intake of breath. Here was something that ran counter to all her expectations: Song's husband a Christian evangelist, and peace-loving Buddhists being involved in violent persecution. 'My goodness! Does that mean…? I mean, who would do such a thing?'

'Yes, it does. I am.' Song read between the garbled lines. 'And those who killed Sovann were manipulated by village leaders who believed that everything that they stood for was being challenged.'

'I can't believe…' Lydia stood up in a bubble of confusion, clumsily knocking her cup of coffee onto the floor, where it began seeping into the dark floorboards that were heated from underneath. Lydia could feel her blood pumping through her arteries harder than she'd felt in a long time. There was going to be so much to take in; so much ground to cover; so much unchartered territory to expose, and they had barely even scratched the surface. She didn't know if she could take it all in without mentally and almost physically combusting.

Song crouched down to pick up the coffee cup. As she did so, she reached out and touched Lydia's hand with a comforting gesture. Almost at once an unfathomable sense of peace veiled itself over Lydia's stirring heart. Her heart continued to beat hard but it no longer seemed as though it was going to overwhelm her. With a vehemence that surprised her, Lydia heard herself spitting out words that vomited themselves up from some unbidden place: 'How can you be so nice to me after what I allowed to happen to you?'

She realised what she'd said as soon as she'd said it and began turning the pages of the photograph album, looking intently at each one to cover up the embarrassment that was spreading from her hairline to her toes. 'You are such a talented photographer, Song. I'm proud of you. You must tell me how you got into photography,' she babbled.

Song walked over to a painting on the wall which showed a silhouetted young man looking up at the sky at a subtly rendered sunset. After some time she turned around, came back and sat down again. She was agitated, but an inner strength showed itself in the way she held her chin up, a gesture Lydia remembered from all those years back. 'We've clearly got a lot of catching up to do,' Song said. 'It could take a long time. Shall we begin now or do you prefer to sleep first?'

'I should be the one asking you that,' Lydia responded.

'It doesn't really matter, does it? So what do you prefer?'

Lydia glanced at the clock above the mantelpiece. 'It's not even 7.30 yet. We can start now.' Drained as she felt, there was no way she could go to sleep while so many unanswered questions were sloshing around, and with the adrenaline that was pumping through her body. 'Do you want another cup of tea?'

'No thanks, I've barely started this one,' Song half-suppressed a chortle. 'It's true what they say, then, about English people and their insatiable tea-drinking habits?'

Lydia sighed, barely registering Song's comment, and sat as far back into her seat as she could, settling herself down for what promised to be a long story.

Cambodia, February 2007

I'll never forget that day – 12th February 2007. It's indelibly marked in my mind like a deep flesh scar. I never blamed you, you know. As much as I liked Uncle Radha, a part of me had my reservations about him; I could never put my finger on why and I could never have communicated that to you as there didn't seem to be any logical reason. When you had that argument with him the night before – of which I could hear almost every word, I'm sorry to say – I was more upset with him than anything else. Why wouldn't he just tell you what was in that letter? I wanted to show you my support but I didn't know how to express that to you.

When Radha came to pick me up from Helen's, I did wonder why he had come instead of you, considering the argument you had had, but I just assumed this meant that the two of you had made it up in the meantime. However, he said much less to me than usual when we got on his bike. After a few minutes I became aware that we weren't going the way we usually went, towards the Toul Tom Poung area, but we were heading out to the touristy area close to the Independence Monument. 'Where are we going?' I called out over the judder of the engine.

'We've just got to do some business,' Uncle called back to me in a tone that seemed almost too light.

'What sort of business?' I asked, having no reason to doubt his intentions towards me, but merely having a childish curiosity.

'Oh, wait and see. It's difficult to explain.'

'You can try. I'm not a baby!'

I could feel his back muscles tensing under my grip and he flashed back at me, 'Just wait, will you!' We swerved around a few bends in the road and skidded to a halt outside a smart-looking hotel down a backstreet. I noticed an alleyway off to the side of the hotel and saw a man waiting there with a clipboard, all very official looking. My nose was assaulted by the distinct smell of frying garlic mixed with an acrid aroma that hit the back of my throat, and which could well have been burning rubber. When we got off the bike the man didn't bow to Uncle as I would have expected but shook his hand instead, and my sharp eyes noticed a small bundle passing from the stranger to Radha's hand. His face was pockmarked and weather beaten and he must have been about 45 to 50. He smiled down at me and I shivered – the look in his eyes was like that of a lion about to devour his prey.

'So, this is Song, is it?' he said, placing his hand on my shoulder. I didn't shake my body away in actuality but inside I recoiled.

'Yes, *bpoo*,'[4] replied Radha, avoiding looking at me. He touched his nose then rubbed his hands against the leather on his jeans pocket – a gesture I'd never seen him make before.

'Well, little one, we've got a treat in store for you!' I kept my eyes respectfully lowered, but my palms were sweating with fearful anticipation. Something told me that this 'treat' was not going to be my idea of a treat.

'We know how much little girls like to dress up and make themselves beautiful. Inside this hotel we've got the opportunity of a lifetime for you to get dressed up and be part of a modelling competition for a famous clothing brand! Your uncle has been kind enough to arrange this treat for you as a surprise.' As you know, I really wasn't that interested in making myself up but a part of me lifted at this news, and I raised my head and looked up at Mr

---

[4] *Bpoo* means 'uncle' and is used to address men who are a generation older than the speaker.

Pockmark cautiously, hoping that the voracious look in his eyes would have turned into something a bit more genial. In fact, he was unreadable; it was as though a mist had covered his eyes and his mind was away somewhere else, drifting on thoughts that I couldn't even begin to imagine.

'Are you happy with that?' he said, as though I had a choice in the matter.

'Yes,' I said dumbly. 'Will Aunty Lydia be able to come and see me when I perform in the competition?'

'I don't see why not,' Uncle Radha said vaguely.

Mr Pockmark laughed, an open-mouthed laugh exposing the red meatiness inside and said, 'Of course, of course!' at which Uncle flinched imperceptibly. Noticing Radha's discomfort, my own anxieties floated up again and I wished I could take back my rather too eager assent.

As if reading my mind, Mr Pockmark turned his face into a well-practised look of concern and said, 'You've got absolutely nothing to worry about; one of our lovely ladies will be taking care of you for the rest of the day. Once you're all dolled up and ready you can join the rest of the girls in the dining room ready for the modelling fun to begin. Your friends and family can then join you as they watch you shine in your modelling debut!'

While I was listening to Mr Pockmark, whose real name I never found out, I sensed an emptiness behind me and looked behind me to see Radha discreetly slipping onto the back of his moto and foot pedalling till he was far enough away to rev the engine without me being able to reach him. 'Please, wait!' I said, my voice choking as it hit me that he was not going to wait and was not going to come back, but he had already roared away down the road without a backwards glance. From that moment I knew without a doubt that something untoward was happening. Up until that point I'd had some hopes of being reunited with you, but it hit me like a battering ram that there was no hope: I'd been unequivocally abandoned. I didn't know what lay in store for me but I knew it wasn't going to be for my good.

'Come on in, little one,' Mr Pockmark said. 'I need to introduce you to the lovely lady who will be making you up. You'll get along with her just fine.'

I blinked as my eyes adjusted to the dimness inside the hotel lobby. The receptionist avoided looking at me. I noticed this as I kept looking over at him as he reminded me so much of my Uncle Thom, down to the shape of his jaw and the lines on his face. He glanced at Mr Pockmark and nodded to him and then allowed his eyes to glaze over when they looked in my direction. Since I rapidly wanted to disappear, his ignoring of me only confirmed my budding sense of absence from myself.

Mr Pockmark took me to a top-floor bedroom where the 'lovely lady' was waiting for me. The room was carpeted, which as you know is unusual in Cambodia, and my feet sunk deliciously into the red pile as I walked in. The room was air-conditioned so the warmth was pleasant on my feet rather than sweltering. The bed was overlaid with a gold-coloured spread and embroidered in delicate red beading. I couldn't take my eyes off the curvaceous and gold-embossed chandeliers with their six drooping arms that seductively drew me in, causing my heart to leap with an unbidden sense of hope again.

The bed creaked as a short, fat woman got up from her seat on the bed and came to greet me with a shiny beam of a smile. Her face was oily in spite of the powder she had put on it and it glowed dully. She introduced herself as Channary, but I'm not sure whether this was her real name or an assumed one.

'Make sure she's ready by eight and give her something light to eat before the big event,' were all the instructions given by Mr Pockmark as he handed me over and left the room.

Channary clicked her tongue against the roof of her mouth – a habit she repeated quite frequently, much to my irritation – and looked me up and down. 'Sweet,' she said tersely, as if she was talking about me to someone else in the room, even though there was no one else there. 'They always are.'

She busied herself taking make-up out of a case and sorting it on the bed, and it was a couple of minutes before she spoke again. 'The first thing you'll want to do is have a really nice warm shower. Use this oil on your body when you come out to make yourself smell amazing. It's frangipani.' I have never been able to smell frangipani flowers since without being reminded of that day. They're tainted by association.

I said nothing but picked up the towel she threw at me and closed the bathroom door. I wasn't used to having hot showers. It felt too humid and stifling to me. My breath felt compressed and narrow so I washed as quickly as I could and switched off the shower head, gasping.

After drying off, I lathered the oil over my arms and legs. Channary called through the door, 'Make sure you put the oil on your belly and buttocks, too!' I had no idea why this would be necessary but I complied.

I realised I didn't have a fresh pair of knickers to wear so I poked my head around the door and asked what I should wear. 'Come out here and let me look at you before you put anything on.' A sudden rush of shame buzzed like a swarm of bees through my ears as I stepped out obediently into the open. 'You have very small hips,' was the only comment she made about my appearance, before throwing out an unexpected question: 'I don't suppose you've started your monthly bleeding yet, have you?' You had told me something about periods so I knew what they were but I was still very much pre-pubescent.

'Not yet,' I said quietly with my head down.

'Well, that makes things a little easier,' she said, talking again to her unseen audience. I was bewildered by her comments and wished she would give me some underwear to help mitigate the overwhelming fog of vulnerability I felt that I was under. Instead of responding quickly, however, it seemed as though Channary had no sense of urgency whatsoever and she pottered around, searching through piles of knickers. 'Just trying to find a pair suitable for your size,' she explained. Eventually she threw a pair over to me. I held them up in my fingers and shuddered. They were black, made from a synthetic material, and horrifyingly translucent.

'I can't wear these,' I said, with my first attempt that evening at resistance.

'You've got no choice, Lady Lee,' she said in a sing-song voice. 'This is the only pair I've got that'll fit you.

'But does it matter if I wear a pair that's too big? No one will see them, will they?'

Channary laughed and retorted, 'Quit your whining, Lady Lee. You'll understand soon enough.'

Giving up, I sighed and put them on, feeling just as naked as I had before.

'Well, one thing's for certain – you won't need to wear a bra.' She clicked her tongue again and again while searching through piles of clothes that she'd taken out of the hotel cupboard. 'Anyway, even Madame won't complain when she sees the dress I've chosen for her.' She was right. In spite of myself, I fell in love with that dress the minute she laid it in front of me. It was a deep blue dress designed for an adult woman. It had lace all around the edges and beading at the hem and around the waist. The neckline was heart shaped, designed to show a hint of cleavage, although I had none. Channary helped me into it. Her hands chafed against my skin and I shivered. She looked me over in the dress and pinned it in a few places, before taking it off again and deftly sewing it up by hand to improve the fit. The dress came to just below my knees. As you know, Cambodian women are usually very modest in their dressing but tend to show more flesh when attending weddings or other special functions, and that dress was exactly like a dress designed for a wedding.

Channary wouldn't let me look in the mirror at first and said I'd better wait until she'd done my make-up. In spite of myself, I was jittery with anticipation to see the finished result.

As she rummaged through the pile of make-up which was now strewn on the bed, I was taken back to a time before my mum became an alcoholic. 'Little one,' she said, as she smiled gently into the dressing mirror while holding me on her lap, 'never forget the golden rule for East Asian women. The paler your skin, the more beautiful you are considered to be. Now I know that you are beautiful no matter what your colour, but if you want to make something of yourself, this is what you should remember.' I listened to her and played with the kohl pencil on the dressing table and daydreamed of fluffy white dresses and twirling parasols. As I remembered this, a sudden deep yearning gripped me around my core and I made a simple request to Channary, not knowing what this was setting me up for: 'Please make me look as pale skinned as possible.'

'Of course. That was my intention.'

114

Having caked my face with a thick layer of cream foundation, she allowed my skin to dry and then applied layer upon layer of heavy powder. It felt as though if I smiled, my face would crack in two, so I kept my face as serious as possible. The crowning touch was the kohl eyeliner and mascara which she applied thickly around my eyes. My eyes were watering as I blinked hard at the touch of the fine point, and Channary berated me for messing up her work, tush-tushing as she used a cotton bud dipped in water to clean the blurred edges. To avoid further distress, I developed a firm-eyed gaze which enabled me to cope with the touch of the eyeliner.

The whole process took a good 30 minutes or so, much longer than I've ever spent on making myself up ever since. Even when I got married, I refused to spend more than 15 minutes on my make-up and kept it as simple and pure as possible to avoid reliving that moment.

To finish off my look she piled my hair on my head, applying many clips in the process, and touched off with a deep red lipstick. When she finally allowed me to look at myself in the mirror, a startled, clown-faced stranger stared back at me. I was undeniably beautiful, but it was a fragile beauty like a frightened rabbit dazzled by the headlights of a car. I didn't know what to say. Channary tidied up her accessories without offering a hint of a response to my appearance, before calling room service for a light dish of noodles for me.

Throughout my meal, all I could think about was making you and the uncorrupted version of my mum proud. I so wanted you to be there to see me looking like this, even though a part of me knew that was a pipe dream. After laying down my plate, I was startled by a transparent bullet-shaped bottle that landed on my lap without warning. I twisted open the lid and frowned at Channary's back, while gulping down the water as though it were my last.

'Watch it,' she tutted, looking hawk-like at the red rim around the bottle top, 'I'll need to redo your lip gloss.' While reapplying the gloss with one hand and holding my chin with the other, she kept her phone pinched between her shoulder and ear to make a call. 'Yes, she's ready. Do we have any customers? ... Just the one? ... No need to bring her downstairs then. He can come straight up here so long as he's paid up.'

He could come straight up here? Well they certainly weren't talking about Uncle Radha. My skin began tightening in a million different places and I could feel myself shaking inwardly. Even though I had no idea what was awaiting me, I knew it couldn't be good. All pretence of a beauty contest was over. Now there was nothing but men and money.

Any speaking would only give away how petrified I was, so I just sat there on the edge of the bed bolt upright, with a plastered smile on my face. Channary's final act was to lay a large white towel on top of the bed and haphazardly throw the rest of the make-up and clothes into her bag. 'Whatever you do,' she said just before leaving the room, 'Don't talk and do not, I repeat, do not take the towel off the bed.'

The white zone. I retreated into the white space between my ears and dreamed of angels floating around me, smiling and blessing me with good gifts like fairy-tale godmothers. The pain inside as his manhood stretched and violated me was so excruciating that it caused a mental numbness and half-delirium. I ignored the weight on top of me and the laboured, exaggerated breathing and lay passively, absent to myself, until he was done.

The minute he walked into the room and saw me sitting on the edge of the bed, he pushed me down hard and clambered on top of me with no warning. Terrified, my first reaction had been to scream out, 'Aunty Lydia's coming!' Instantly, a clammy hand clamped down on my mouth and an irresistible snake of inevitability coiled around me, hissing lies in my ears: 'You had this coming all along. How could you have believed your life was going to get better?'

Thankfully, knowing what I knew afterwards, he hadn't even attempted to arouse me; he was hard as soon as he saw me. The pain was worse than it might have been, but I was able to retain some modicum of emotional dignity at least. When he had spent himself, I couldn't even look in his face, couldn't even pretend to smile, but lay there shaking all over, the pain rolling in waves through me. To this day I have no idea and no desire to know what his face looked like. I only remember his weight – he was a bulky man – his smart polished shoes and the sour smell of his breath. Plus he wasn't a foreigner: he was unequivocally Cambodian.

The beautiful dress lay around my waist and I yanked it down around myself as an act of modesty before realising that blood was seeping all over the white towel and was now leaking onto the edge of the dress. He surreptitiously wiped himself while I yelped at the sight of the blood. 'Most definitely a virgin,' he said triumphantly, without a hint of compassion. Then he fumbled into his trousers, put on his smart shoes and left the room.

Time had distorted itself. I lay there for what felt like hours, crying as the numbness unfolded itself from me and the physical and emotional pain set in. The physical pain was not only in my genitals but throughout my muscles, which had tensed in fear and now ached uncontrollably. I also realised that the inside of my mouth was bleeding – I'd bitten it to distract myself from the rape, in the same way that picking a scab is less painful than the cut that caused the scab.

In reality, I couldn't have cried for long, as Channary slithered back into the room, whisked me into the shower again and scurried away all material traces of my violation into the laundry – it says a lot about the hotel's complicity that the materials were not completely destroyed.

That was only the beginning.

Chapter 13
Cambodia, February 2007

Now began a new season in my life, a brutal but increasingly numb one. For about a week after my deflowering, I stayed in that same hotel room, being repeatedly raped each night by the same man, who had paid a high price to have sex with me, a virgin. Perversely, despite the intense dirtiness and widely considered immorality of having sex with a young girl, there was a pervading belief that having sex with a virgin was life enhancing and strengthening, and that it could even prevent diseases. Aunt Channary was my *meebon*, a woman whose role it was to deal in prostitutes, provide for all our physical needs and rent out our bodies. She told me quite bluntly that Client Number 1 had paid US $2,000 to sleep with me. I have no reason to doubt this, especially as he was with me for seven days.

I had made a covenant with myself that I would never look this particular man in the face, though in the days to come I did look other men in the face, sometimes surreptitiously. Once the pain had subsided and I began to get used to it, I started to become curious about these men who would take so much pleasure in something so perverse.

My eleventh birthday passed without significance in that hotel room. I remembered it suddenly while I was gritting my teeth and lying flat on my back on the 18th February. I thought of you, and remembered with poignancy that you had said we would go out and have a pampering session together on my birthday. Well, I thought, if this was being pampered…

I saw nobody that week other than my putrid anonymous client and Aunt Channary. She came in at least twice a day to give me food and to make sure I was keeping myself clean.

Every morning I woke up with the smell of his sour breath in my nostrils, and the remembered odour was so intense that I had to rush to the bathroom to vomit. Each day I began healing over, but each night the wounds would open up again and I ached as though I'd been stung by wasps 50 times over. Aunty forced me to use salt water down there, which was needed to prevent infection, but it made the stinging

118

so much worse and for a while I could hardly bear it. By the end of the week, however, I had stretched a little and was no longer in quite so much agony. This was my body's way of adjusting and making my horrendous situation a little more bearable.

Having spent some time with you talking about right and wrong behaviour, a part of me kept hoping that all of this would be righted, that the police would come banging on the door one night and Mr Pockmark, Channary and Client Number 1 would be made to pay for their injustice and cruelty, and I would be taken to a safe place and even reunited with you. In order to survive I needed to walk a fine line between hoping for a saviour and using various coping mechanisms to manage the reality of my situation. As time went on and the hoped-for rescue did not take place, a part of me began to die a small death. Yet God had His good hand upon me, and a paradoxical light burned inside of me, inspiring me to live in spite of it all.

At the end of the week, Aunt Channary came to have a talk with me. 'We need to move you on from here. Do you know why?' She didn't really care to hear my answer but was relishing the opportunity to tell me.

'No,' I mumbled, with my eyes fixed to the floor.

'Sadly, you're no longer considered virgin goods, so we won't be able to make such a large amount of money from you.'

We? Since when had 'we' been in the business of making money? I knew only that she was making money from me. I kept silent.

'I'm afraid we can't risk you trying to run away so we're going to have to blindfold you when we take you to your next base. It won't be quite as luxurious as this place, but there'll be other girls there for you to make friends with so you'll have more company than here, which will be nice, won't it? I'll be passing you on into the care of another aunty but I will visit every now and then.' She said this as though it was supposed to be of some comfort to me.

A narrow-walled comfort.

'Wake up, wake up!' I could feel Channary shaking me roughly and I emerged from a deep sleep, like a drowning man coming out of the water. It was 3am on 20th February and I'd been asleep for four hours. Three o'clock was a good time for travelling secretly as everyone was in bed by this time and it would still be another hour or so before the early risers would get up. My meagre possessions were already packed up in a small backpack and all I had to do was slip out of bed and follow Channary down the stairs into the lobby.

Surprisingly, my first feeling was one of excitement. For the first time in a week I was getting out of that hotel room, where I'd experienced one of the worst weeks of my life, and there was a sense of breathing in fresh air and looking forward to something new. That feeling was swiftly overridden, though, by the sinking sensation that life was not actually going to get any better. The hotel doorman didn't give us a second glance as we walked straight past him to the motodop driver who was waiting just outside the door.

'This one's got milky-white skin. Is she Vietnamese?' A filthy smile cracked the weather-beaten face of the driver, and I could feel his eyes taking me in from top to bottom.

'Yes, I think she is,' said Aunt Channary. 'You keep your hands off her,' she vociferated, suddenly and surprisingly protective.

'Would I dare?' the driver said with mock innocence, taking out of his pocket a long, thin strip of material. Before I knew what was happening, my arms had been grappled from behind and the strip had been wrapped tightly around my eyes.

'Hey, no need to be so rough; she's not going anywhere.' There was a new note of gentleness that I'd not heard in her voice before, and I had a sudden pang of attachment to my captor. Better the devil you know than the devil you don't, as they say.

I sat side-saddle behind my new captor and gripped on to the seat, feeling more vulnerable than normal due to my enforced blindness. I felt my backpack being hoisted between us and, without a word of farewell, I heard the rev of the engine and began to feel the breeze against my cheek.

There was very little noise at that time of night, so the only way I could differentiate locations was by the changing smells and the varying road surfaces. This was a couple of years before they began the widespread concretisation of the smaller roads in Phnom Penh, so the main variations I could feel were the sharp revs, the stops, the bumps of potholed roads, and the gentle judder of the smoother if more dusty roads. The driver was avoiding the tarmacked ring roads in order to minimise the risk of detection by any interfering busybodies or do-gooders, who might rightly be suspicious of a blindfolded young girl on the back of a moto. Because I was blindfolded, my other senses were on high alert; nevertheless, I was unable to pinpoint exactly where we were going as we swerved around bends to the left, to the right and to the left again, and my usually good sense of direction was befuddled.

We must have been on the road for about 20 minutes when we began stopping and starting, and my whole body was jarring as we rode on what must have been a badly potholed road. I crinkled my nostrils at the unmistakable stench of a nearby sewer combined with the smell of body odour. Then I heard the ting ting of a bicycle bell, and I guessed that we were almost at our destination.

The motodop juddered to a halt and my eyes, blurry after the pressure of the cloth, were freed as the driver removed my blindfold. I blinked hard to bring my eyes back to normal vision and saw in front of me a motherly looking lady with a flop of wavy hair pulled back loosely from her face. She was grinning like a Cheshire cat. 'Welcome, Song, to our little community,' she crooned.

A gaggle of girls stood around her, one of whom looked to be around the same age as me; the rest I guessed to be between 12 and 15 years old. One of the girls, with wide-set eyes and a tiny snub nose, looked intently at me and offered a heartfelt smile of welcome, although her eyes were hollow with sadness. This was Sodarath. She was 13 years old and became my best friend and confidante in that place.

The aunty was known as Kalliyan, and she was one of the most confusing character mixtures I've ever come across. Even though she was the *meebon* of a brothel, at times you might be forgiven for imagining that she was running an orphanage because of the loving, maternal way she spoke to us. All was well when we did what she wanted us to do. When we didn't do as she wanted, then the full force of her other side would be unleashed, and we would experience the whirlwind lash of her tongue, her icy aloofness and the piercing cruelty of her leather whip.

As I got off the bike, I took in my surroundings. The building was a typical Khmer wooden shack, raised on stilts to minimise the risk of flooding, and was only slightly larger than an average family house. There were eight girls in this particular brothel including me. There were two rooms for the prostitutes, and each room had been divided into four by roughly made plywood dividers. A loosely flung, shabby, musty cloth acted as a curtain in front of each cubicle. We each had our own cubicle, which was both our personal living space and space for servicing clients. Each cubicle was scarcely bigger than a single bed, and each bed was nothing more than a stained mattress on the floor. Any privacy we had was nominal; you could hear every sordid sound and breathe in every smell, yet despite how squalid it was, there was a strange sense of comfort in knowing we were so close to one another and that nothing could be hidden.

Aunty Kalliyan lived in the room on the ground floor, which was made of concrete, and the open space as you came upstairs before entering the cubicles was the viewing room. Here we would parade before clients and they would choose which one of us pleased them the most.

The driver whispered something to the aunty, and she smiled at me and said with a dulcet tone, 'He's paying for your services. After driving you all the way here, it's the least you can do in return.'

I was repulsed and wanted to scream and scream, 'Nooooo, I didn't ask for any of this! I was quite happy living with Aunty Lydia and Uncle Radha in Phnom Penh, and I want to go back there right now!' But of course I submitted. I gritted my teeth and took the full horror, lying woodenly, trying not to feel anything.

Having lasted a week with the same man who had not demanded anything of me, I was surprised to learn that this was not enough any longer. The aunty berated me sharply afterwards because the driver had been displeased that I'd been so unresponsive. I felt the metal bite of her belt against my arm for a week after that, and soon was trained in the art of pleasing the clients through writhing and moaning, plus more that I don't want to share as I'm so ashamed even now. At the time, I had to suppress the shame in order to survive, but afterwards, when I was out of prostitution and had space to think and feel, the full tsunami of shame hit me.

Within a month, my breasts began to bud and my periods started. They may have been going to start at that time anyway, but I believe they came prematurely because of the hormones triggered by the sexual activity.

Aunty Kalliyan was relatively enlightened as far as *meebons* were concerned, and she did encourage her clients to use condoms, recognising that if all her prostitutes were to get Aids then she'd no longer have much of a business. Nevertheless, some of the men chose to ignore her. We were at least exempt from intercourse when we were having our monthlies, though we still had to provide other sexual favours which were no less sordid.

Between 3am and 9am was our usual sleep time in the brothel since there were very rarely any customers at that hour. Night time was spent servicing clients and after 9am it was too hot to sleep. Occasionally the flow of customers would dry up early, especially in the rainy season, and then we girls would get together and gossip, giggle and talk about our hopes and dreams, like any teenage girls. We got used to having only six hours sleep at night and would catch up on sleep after lunch – at least when business was slow. It's strange to say, but it really was like a community. The girls in that brothel made my life worth living at that time. Most of us were not competitive, apart from one, and that is the bend in the road we will take now.

Chapter 14
Cambodia, April 2007

Mau, Mau. I shall never forget her. Her name means 'dark skin', which is apt as she did have darker skin than the rest of us. It was a beautiful bronze colour, although she was unable to see it as an asset; most of the men were looking for paler-skinned beauties, so she was frequently overlooked for one of us. In fact, the trouble first began when I came along, as I had the palest skin of all and was chosen more frequently than any of them. This didn't exactly make me happy as I'd much rather have been left alone, but it began to grate with Mau as she was aware that she was making less money for herself now and was unable to pay off her debt as quickly as she'd like. Mau was the oldest of us. She was 15 and had been in the brothel for three years.

Around 11am one sweltering morning in April, Sodarath and I were relaxing in the shade in the viewing room, trying to capture the minimal breeze from the open window as well as the flow of air that was circulating from the ceiling fan. We'd switched it on for five minutes. Even though Aunty preferred the fans to be off during the day to save electricity, we knew she wouldn't punish us for it, especially when it was as hot as it was. Four of the others were servicing clients, so we knew we might not have long before one of us was in demand too.

'Look at the leaves up there,' I murmured dreamily. 'They're so still.'

'Like our lives,' whispered Sodarath.

'What do you mean?' I raised myself off the floorboards and propped my head against my cupped hand, my elbow grazing the floor, and looked searchingly into her face.

'You know, we're still. Stuck. Can't go anywhere, going in and out every day with this man and the next. Will it be like this forever?' She pursed her lips.

I sighed. 'It wasn't like this before I was sold. At least I had hope for a season.'

'Tell me about it.'

Although I'd raised the topic, a part of me felt reluctant to share it, as though it would open Pandora's box and unleash a power that we couldn't control. When I opened my mouth next, though the words were simple, I felt a rush in the nape of my neck.

'Well, there was a white lady, a British volunteer, and she had me in her home for a while.'

'Really? How did that happen?'

Our conversation was curtailed as a police motorbike pulled up outside the brothel and we glanced down warily. A stockily built man with official stripes on his shoulders got off and looked around. He disappeared from our view under the floorboards, and we knew he was headed for Kalliyan's room. We recognised him as Sophoan, Aunty's lover, and we soon lost interest. Kalliyan was not married, but Sophoan was her favourite lover: she had a few regulars. Sophoan was off limits to us. That was not our decision and we couldn't have cared less, but Kalliyan insisted upon it as a way of keeping something sacred for herself. Sophoan was one of several authority figures, both policemen and military officers, who would attend our brothel. They mostly came in the dead of the night if they were senior, although many came quite freely and openly at any time of the day.

Just as we heard the door close behind Sophoan, a frowning face came up the stairs with a sarong wrapped around her body and her hair gleaming after having a shower.

'I don't see why Aunty has to keep Sophoan to herself,' Mau grumbled, rubbing her hair vigorously with a colourful cloth.

'Why do you care?' queried Sodarath.

'Because he's unobtainable, and that's tempting for me.'

'Tempting for you?' Sodarath teased. 'You can't pretend you actually enjoy what we do?'

Mau sat down next to us on the floor and twisted her toes in the gaps between the floorboards. She didn't answer immediately but sat there for some time, coyly. 'Most of the time I don't, but occasionally you get one who treats you like you're something special, you know?'

'It's not real, though, is it? You only represent something for them; you're not actually special, otherwise they'd take you away, out of this life into a better one.' I studied Sodarath's face as she spoke with a wisdom and a cynicism that were incongruous with her youthfulness and her chocolate-box sweetness.

None of us quite knew where to take that topic next.

'If I were you, I'd get dressed quickly – a new customer might come at any time,' I said, impatient with Mau.

'Why should I? If he sees me like this I can show off my assets more easily, which is one thing you haven't got, sweet pea!' She laughingly fondled her breast, and at that time I felt like slapping her, though now I just feel sorry for her as she was so desperate.

'Don't you have any sense of dignity, Mau?!' Sodarath said to the older girl as if she were the younger. 'We may have to do this job, but we don't have to lower ourselves more than necessary.'

The juddering hum of an engine stopping alerted us that a customer was here. Two clients stumbled out of cubicles consecutively with flushed faces. One stumbled down the steps half drunk, while the other flashed a beaming look at us and walked down with his back straight and head held high. The new customer was yet another police officer, one that we'd not seen before. He was scrawny and serious looking. He knocked on the door below. Kalliyan answered from inside, 'Just one second – I'm coming,' and came out to negotiate with the police officer. Sophoan stayed inside out of view, just in case.

'The lovely ladies are upstairs. We have only the youngest and the freshest here. No, they're not virgins, but they'll give you your youth and vigour back, all the same.' She plied her usual sales talk in a lively and engaging manner as though she were selling chicks rather than young girls. 'There is a fixed price of 2,000 riel,[5] though I add an extra 1,000 for our youngest, and extras for unusual sexual favours.'

'We have the cleanest girls here, and we like to make sure they stay that way,' she added with a chuckle, presumably holding out a condom.

'No, I couldn't possibly use one of those,' Officer Morose replied. While she was talking we knew we were expected to ready ourselves for viewing. Mau refused to change so I stood, embarrassed, waiting for the latest customer to come up the stairs. Sodarath and the other girls who were free stood in line with Mau on the edge. Officer Morose

---

[5] At that time 2,000 riel was approximately half a US dollar.

hawked and spat loudly as he came up the stairs and we grimaced at one another with a secret coded signal, making sure our faces were ready to smile elaborately when his head appeared over the steps.

Mau kept her sarong tied but her left breast was almost completely exposed, and as Officer Morose appeared his eyes were drawn to her, especially as she curved her hips around languidly and put her finger in her mouth in a blatant ploy to seduce him. I curled up inwardly, though outwardly I smiled as normal, knowing what the outcome would be if I did not. Not surprisingly, Mr Morose chose to sleep with Mau, and as she went into the cubicle with him, she threw me a triumphant look. As if I cared.

To cover up the sound of exaggerated moaning that was soon emanating from the cubicle, we gathered in a huddle to express our disapproval of Mau's tactics. 'She's just jealous of you,' Chenda said. Chenda was the most fragile of the girls; you felt that if you were simply to touch her legs they would break like pieces of china. 'I wouldn't worry about it.'

'Oh, I don't care about her getting the man, but I do care about her attitude. It makes me cringe.'

'You know what? She needs to know that the rest of us don't think much of her attitude. We should freeze her out for a few days,' said Sodarath with sudden vehemence.

None of us even thought about telling Aunt Kalliyan what had happened because of course we would shy away from any direct confrontation, and ignoring Mau seemed like the best way of letting her know what we thought. However, as it turned out, Kalliyan found out anyway. Officer Morose apparently gloated to her about her state of undress and how pleased he was with her when he left.

'Really? How charming of her,' we heard her say sweetly, her voice coming into gradual range as she walked out of her room.

We knew that Aunty was not best pleased. Mau was called downstairs and returned afterwards with a sour and red face after receiving a severe biting from the Belt. We had to surmise the reasoning behind her beating, and I think it was that Kalliyan was scrupulously fair and would not allow one of her prostitutes to have an advantage over the others in terms of her market value, especially as I could have made more money for her. Knowing what the consequences would be, Mau never pulled that same trick again. Seeing as she had received her punishment already we tacitly decided her debt had already been paid and didn't subject her to a total freeze-out, just a partial cold-shouldering for the rest of that day.

If there was one thing Mau couldn't stand, it was being ignored, so by the end of the day she was reduced to slavishness to get back into our good books. 'Can I brush your hair, sister? It's so soft.'

'Hmm,' I murmured non-committedly, with my back towards her.

'Would you like to borrow my turquoise tight-fitting T-shirt, Soda?' she asked the girl who was closest to her own body size. Soda didn't reply and just hummed to herself with a quiet dignity while pulling and rubbing her wet clothes vigorously in and out, back and forth on the slatted wooden washtub.

Mau exhaled horsily between puffed-out lips, knowing that her only chance of escaping this temporary freeze would be to service as many clients as she could that day. There was nowhere for us to go and nothing for us to do outside the confines of the brothel. For a start, we'd all been brought here blindfolded so we didn't know where we were in relation to the rest of the city. Secondly, we were forbidden to leave, and thirdly, all our resources – toiletries, food and condoms, and occasional medical supplies – were brought to us by a daily stream of two or three ever-faithful motodop drivers, so we had no 'need' to leave our little community.

December 2007

Most of our clients were done in five to ten minutes if sober, and a little bit slower if drunk, and they treated us as reasonably as could be expected given the circumstances. However, there was the odd atrocity, and there was one during the 14 months I was there.

One cool night in early December, when we were in the middle of servicing an increasing number of clients, we were all stopped in our tracks by a loud furore outside the brothel. There was an escalation of men's voices deep in an argument a few metres down the street, and a sudden cracking sound. Most of us came out of our cubicles, startled, the momentum lost for our clients, and looked as discreetly as we could over the railings on the edge of the viewing area. I could see two legs lying on the left-hand side and a dark trickle of blood pooling in our direction. Two legs were standing closer to us and the man's back was hunched over, the outline of every taut muscle displayed through his shirt. His back gyrated and we could see a gun in his hand.

'What are you looking at?' the man roared up at us. 'Have you never seen a play fight before?' We didn't say anything, not quite knowing what to say, but smiled down at him as best as we could. To try to defuse any potential violence, Kalliyan began plying her trade.

'Play fighting? Of course we've seen play fighting. If you'd like to play with one of our girls you might begin to feel a bit better. We can see you're a bit tense and it might help you relax.' We all stiffened at this suggestion, understandably anxious about being with a man like this, and wondered if Aunty was employing the wisest tactic at this point.

He stood there absently for one moment, looking back and forth between his victim and us girls standing above him, and he let out a wild whoop, raised his hands and began stomping up the stairs. 'I *like* that idea!' Kalliyan had to pull him back slightly to negotiate business with him.

My existing client, an extremely young and sheepish man, poked me under the ribs and said, 'Can we get back to it?' I was relieved, knowing that this meant I would not have to face the Wild Cat, whereas some of the other clients drifted off as unobtrusively as they could.

Within ten minutes Master Sheepish was done and I came back out into the cool air. Sodarath came over to me, gripped my hand and whispered, 'We should pray to God for Chenda. She's in there with HIM.' I shivered, afraid for her.

Now I thank God that Chenda survived what happened next. We heard a sudden yelp of protestation, a loud thud and a muffled and pained gasping for breath. We called out shakily, 'Aunty Kalliyan, please come!' and at the same time Wild Cat stumbled out of the cubicle, head down, and ploughed off and down the steps as quickly and wordlessly as he could. Sodarath and I pushed back the curtains to Chenda's cubicle, all decorum gone in the bid to protect our sister. Chenda lay half-conscious on her mattress, wheezing, and her eyes glazed up at the ceiling. She'd taken a severe blow to the stomach and her legs were curled up in a foetal position, both in defence and for comfort.

'Oh God, Aunty, what shall we do? Do we need to take her to the hospital?'

'Let me get to her first,' she said capably, no hint of the slick saleswoman left. We let her squeeze past us and she squatted down next to Chenda, felt her forehead and her pulse and gently rubbed her stomach, which elicited a sharp intake of breath. She was struggling for breath and her eyes rolled with the physical effort, seeming to beat against the pain.

'I think that's our answer, girls. We'll have to get some medical help. I'll get Sovath to run for the doctor.

The seven of us girls who were left – me, Mau, Soda and the others whose names I've not mentioned yet, Navy, Champey, Pich and Samnang – stood around stamping our feet and crying. The shock caused us to feel the cold more than normal. We couldn't even begin to think about sleeping while Chenda's fate was unknown, and there was no way we could conduct any business at this time. Aunty wisely kept away any clients.

'You'll have to get her to the hospital,' Doctor Boupha said, taking off her gloves and coming out of the cubicle. 'She's dehydrated and needs to be put on a drip.'

I was the companion chosen to assist Chenda to hospital. 'You'd better be prepared for a long wait,' warned Doctor Boupha. 'You're prostitutes and won't be seen as high priority.' She never said how they would know we were prostitutes, and in hindsight this seems rather odd. She was unfortunately right.

I held on to Chenda carefully as we travelled on the back of Sovath's moto. Her head was lolling to one side and she seemed somewhat light-headed with the pain. I did my best to support her neck without losing balance. I don't remember the name of the hospital we were taken to as I was focused on Chenda and not paying attention to those sorts of details, but I do know it was on the outskirts of Phnom Penh and was a typically yellowed two-storey building, with rows of wide windows and long, empty, echoing corridors. Sovath dropped us off at the entrance to the hospital and said nonchalantly, 'You'll be some time. I'll wait outside until you've finished. Kalliyan kindly gave me extra cash to compensate for the inevitable waiting time.'

We were ushered through to a wide, empty reception area by a surly-looking porter, and when I stammered out to the lady at the desk what the problem was, she didn't even look at us, but just wrote Chenda's name in a book and said curtly, 'Sit and wait.' I looked at the long rows of patients waiting on hard wooden benches and found a corner where we could both squeeze in. Poor Chenda slouched against my shoulder, breathing shallowly.

Five minutes after sitting down I saw a doctor I distinctly recognised as one of our clients. He'd not been with me but with one of the other girls, but I remembered the purple splodged birthmark on his right temple. Doctor Purple Splodge glanced over the patients waiting and I'm sure he recognised us, too, as he leaned over the receptionist's shoulder and murmured something in her ear and she gazed in our direction blankly. We waited. And we waited. The busy hum of the hospital continued around us, as did the varying pitched moans of patients in pain.

We must have arrived at around 11.30 at night. By the time we were seen, it must have been about 4am. I tried to keep Chenda as comfortable as possible on the hard seats, but eventually my shoulder and whole right arm went numb with the weight and I shifted her head to my lap. Sporadically she murmured things to me such as, 'You're such a good sister to me,' or, 'My stomach hurts.' I murmured assent to her and tried to keep her quiet while I drifted in and out of sleep, losing consciousness and then jerking myself awake for fear of what might happen if I slept for too long.

I didn't dare go and ask when we would be seen. My whole sense of being was locked in shame so I cowered inside myself and awaited our turn. In the meantime I saw at least four or five patients who had arrived after us being called in to the doctor, and my heart clenched with the injustice of it all. The only reason we were even seen at 4am was that I felt an absence of weight as Chenda suddenly rolled off my lap onto the floor in a dead faint, and since no one responded or seemed to have even noticed, I called out frantically, 'She's fainted! Please help!' As I knelt down on the floor beside her, half-dizzy with exhaustion, eventually a medic came running and Chenda was picked up off the floor and carried into another room. I tried to run after her but the curt receptionist said, 'You wait here still.'

I couldn't sit down again so I paced up and down while people looked at me with varying degrees of pity and contempt. Ten minutes later Chenda was wheeled out into the reception area in a wheelchair, and Doctor Purple Splodge approached me to say a few words. He wouldn't look me in the face but looked over me at a distant spot on the wall while I looked down at his feet the whole time he talked. 'I've put your friend on an intravenous drip which includes nutritional fluids and a strong painkiller. She's clearly dehydrated and she'll need bed rest for a couple of days. She has received a heavy blow to the abdominal area but she hasn't sustained any internal injuries as her stomach muscles are strong, so she's very lucky that she received injury there and not in a more sensitive area such as the liver or kidney.'

He didn't ask any questions about how she'd received this heavy blow, and I'm glad he didn't. I have no idea if he asked Chenda herself as she remained quiet about the whole event, and none of us asked her any questions, respecting her desire for privacy. Five hours after arriving at the hospital we were taken back to the brothel in a tuk-tuk, Sovath riding alongside on his moto, with Chenda strapped to her drip and me holding the contraption that fed the drip into her arm. Two days later, we removed the drip ourselves and sent the contraption back to the hospital with Sovath, and that was that. End of story. No medical follow-up. Chenda was safe and alive and we were all relieved that nothing worse had happened.

Some of our day-to-day challenges were no less painful, although less dramatic. Whenever a man refused to use a condom or any of us missed a period, Aunty Kalliyan would dole out morning-after pills like they were sweeties. She was a shrewd business woman and didn't want to deal with the fallout of any of us falling pregnant. We all caught sexually transmitted diseases at least once, if not two or three times, during our time as prostitutes. About three months after my initiation into the adult world of sex, I spent one very uncomfortable night going back and forth to the toilet with a burning pain when I passed urine. I tried not to wake up the others by screaming, but that's how bad it felt – it was so bad I thought I would faint a few times. When I discovered some untimely discharge I went and knocked on Aunty Kalliyan's door rather sheepishly. She took one look at me and listened to my tale, and quickly diagnosed gonorrhoea.

'Take this pill and you'll soon be well again,' she said matter-of-factly, yawning at me. She was used to this sort of thing. And she was right: it didn't take long for me to return to good health. After a bout of STD Kalliyan would let us have from a day to a week off work, depending on the severity of the symptoms. She was wise enough to know that a sick girl would be of no appeal to the clients, and wouldn't do her reputation any good either.

As for the big bad wolf STD – HIV – well, you'll just have to wait to hear my story about that.

Chapter 15
Cambodia, May 2008

I knew there was something different about him as soon as I saw him. It wasn't his physical appearance. He was as slim, dark and lithe as most Cambodians. He was probably about 35 years old and had come on a motorbike like most clients. If it wasn't his physical appearance and it wasn't his mode of transport, then what was it? There was something about his eyes, an ingenuity and a lack of the shiftiness that resided with most of our clients. Perhaps I'm only saying this in retrospect, basing it on what I knew of him after my first impressions, but as you know I always was very good at getting the measure of a person.

'It's my nephew's birthday soon and we're hoping to surprise him with a young girl to initiate him into the pleasures of sex. He's turning 16 but he's a little bit shy, and I think he'd value a younger girl who wouldn't be quite so intimidating for him as someone older.'

Aunty Kalliyan listened with her head tilted to one side, withholding all judgement until he'd finished his spiel: '... and we were hoping we could take a girl to a hotel for him to receive his initiation.'

'I must say,' she said cautiously, 'that this is outside our remit. We don't normally let the girls off this property. It's not worth our while because of the risks involved.'

'Not even if we were to agree a larger sum of money?' he said, his voice jaunty and coaxing, waving in front of her what I later discovered to have been the equivalent of $200. 'And you could send your guard with us to keep an eye on the girl.'

I can visualise Kalliyan mentally calculating the financial benefits of this transaction and wavering in her resolve. Still, a note of caution held her back. 'If you've got this much money to spend, why didn't you go to a more reputable establishment?'

He laughed flatteringly. 'Oh, I've heard very good things about this place, and like I said, the more, as you say, "reputable" places are likely to have older girls who would be intimidating for my nephew.'

Those of us who were free were listening carefully to this conversation, all senses alert to this new and unusual venture.

'Well, we may be able to agree something...' Her voice tailed off as she popped inside her room to pick up a sheet of paper to record the details.

We looked at each other, eyes widening in interest, and prepared ourselves to be viewed. Mau was in bed with flu and Navy and Pich were already with clients, but the rest of us arranged ourselves as glamorously as we could.

Kalliyan followed the man up the stairs to view us. I for one felt keen to be chosen this time as this man represented something different – a change, a way out of this homely prison, at least temporarily. I can't vouch for the other girls.

Kalliyan began telling him a little bit about each of us, which was also rather unusual. 'This girl here, Sodarath, is well seasoned and pleases the customers. I've never had any complaints about her. She's good with virgins – those who admit they are, anyway!' When she came to me she surprised me when she said, 'This is our most popular girl, Song. She's of Vietnamese origin and has been with us for just over a year. Her skills in giving pleasure have been enhanced over time and she's now a real expert.' When she'd finished doing the rounds she said with a modest flourish, 'I can't possibly seek to recommend any of these lovely girls over and above any of the others; I'll have to let you decide, of course.'

He took longer than most clients, his eyes perusing us and retreating to his own thoughts, mulling this decision as carefully as if it were the most important decision of his life. Finally, he pursed his lips, flexed his fingers as though preparing to play the piano and said, 'I've decided on Song. I think she'll be the best present for my nephew, and I want him to have the best.'

My heart leaped in unbidden hope. Logically this was a risk, as I had no idea where he was going to take me and there'd be no safety in numbers. I'm sure this was the overriding thought of many of the girls. Nevertheless, my intuition about him ushered me into an inner court of future focus that I'd not felt since I'd been with you.

I smiled broadly and made a submissive *sampeah* to show that I felt honoured. The other girls looked at me questioningly as it was not

135

usual to do this in a brothel transaction, but I think some understood that this occasion warranted something a little different, especially as there'd be no retreat into the cubicle at this time.

I was not privy to the more detailed arrangements about this deal as they were made behind closed doors. Kalliyan simply told me to be ready at 11.45pm on Saturday 10th May, which was only three days away.

I couldn't suppress my simmering sense of excitement. Mau was irritated as she would have loved to have been chosen, but she hadn't even been on display because of her sickness, and there was no suggestion of offering me any of her clothes for the occasion. She avoided talking to me about it, and when I passed her on the steps or in the showering area she would grimace, sigh or roll her eyes as though I was a perpetually exhausting and demanding little madam. Chenda was anxious for me. 'Are you sure it's safe, sister? Perhaps he wants to take you to a hotel to kill you.'

'Now, why would he go to all that trouble and pay so much money to do that? For absolutely no reason?' I said trying to calm her overactive imagination.

'Well, I don't know, but people do the craziest things, don't they?'

Sodarath was all ears and all sympathy for me. She would have loved to have been chosen for the change in scene, but she was genuinely happy for me too.

'Listen, sister. If you get the chance to escape out of all this, somehow and somewhere, don't forget about me, will you?'

'Of course I won't forget you,' I said, wrapping my arms around her, 'but I'm sure I'll be right back here with you all on Sunday morning.'

'Would you like to borrow my pretty beige vest top?'

'Yeah, if you like...' I said tentatively, while she showed her appreciation of me by slipping her favourite shimmery pink lip gloss into the back pocket of my jeans and whispering, 'Keep it.'

On Saturday morning, after a restless night, I woke up with a bunged-up nose and a heavy head and a sinking feeling that if he found out I was ill, I wouldn't be going after all.

'I want you to spend the whole day resting,' said Kalliyan, for as soon as she heard me speak, she knew I was sick. I hadn't been going to tell her but I couldn't completely avoid speaking to her when she spoke to me. I was already bringing in $200 so she could afford to give me a day off. Plus she wanted to make sure he would go through with it too and not demand his money back, so the more time I had to rest, the more likely I was to be presented to him as fresh and at least semi-healthy.

The problem was that bed-rest also meant more time to think. By about 7pm my heart was in turmoil and I was twisted up in convoluted and confused thoughts and feelings about my mum, Uncle Thom, you and Uncle Radha, and Mr Soulful Eyes was appearing as two opposing personas in my mind: the devil incarnate on the one hand and my secret saviour on the other. As my head pounded with a slight fever and too much mental activity, I came out into the cooler evening air and found Sodarath perched on the edge of the viewing platform, her legs swinging back and forth as she gazed out at the darkened sky. She took one look at my face and rushed to get a glass of water for me. 'Drink up, please,' she said. 'Have two or three glasses, not just one.'

I drank rapidly as if it were my last. I hadn't realised how thirsty I was until I began to drink. After the first glass my head felt a little clearer, and I sipped the next one when Soda handed it to me.

'What happens if this man is out to do me harm?' I expressed my deepest fears to my best friend.

'Harm? Don't all the men who come here harm us in some way? They keep us trapped in this situation. They keep needing us to be prostitutes.'

'You know what I mean,' I said, kicking Soda with my bare foot. 'I mean harm like Uncle Radha did to me or like that Wild Cat did to Chenda.'

'Oh, man,' she called out in a crazed whisper, 'we're too young for all this! We should be out there going to school and playing games and dreaming of our futures, not giving our bodies away.' It scared me to hear her talk like this, as if we had any choice over our futures, but I could see where such thoughts had come from.

Soda had told me her story over time, in the same way that I had told her mine. She had been born into one of the hard-working rising middle-income families in Phnom Penh. They started off running a

137

small retail outlet which had flourished and grown, and she had gone to school. When she was ten years old, both her parents died tragically in a motorbike accident, at a time when wearing helmets was not compulsory. Soda and her brother were sent off to live with poorer relations in a village in one of the nearby provinces. Her relations were roaringly jealous of the material resources that her parents had amassed as a result of their hard work and success and, not having any emotional investment in Soda, they saw nothing wrong in selling her into prostitution to the first trafficker who came along as a way of matching – TV for TV and Toyota for Toyota – the material success of her parents. This happened when she was almost 12 years old.

I was quiet. I, not she, was the one being given the chance for something new, an adventure, and I didn't want to brag about it, nor did I feel inclined to anyway, seeing as I was so ambivalent about what the outcome would be. Shortly afterwards a client came up and whisked Soda into her cubicle, and I was left alone again.

At 11.35, Soda was putting the last touches to my lip gloss and Chenda sprayed some of her inexpensively sweet perfume over my chest and the edges of Soda's stylish top. My heart was stiff, tired out and drained after oscillating between elation and fear and trying to contain both emotions. I was 12 years old but felt more like 42. 'You go get 'em, girl,' Soda breathed. 'You look amazing.'

'Thanks,' I murmured unconvincingly. 'Is this skirt short enough?'

'Yes, it's just right,' Soda said. 'Perfect for a night with a shy virgin. Short enough to be tempting, but soft and floaty enough to be girlish.'

'Song!' Aunty Kalliyan called up the stairs, 'Are you ready? Sovath is here and you need to be blindfolded again ready for this new journey.'

'Good luck!' the girls called out to me, squeezing my hands and rubbing my shoulders so that a lump came unbidden to my throat.

This time the blindfolded journey on the motorbike was very different. I knew what to expect yet paradoxically was completely unaware at the same time. I experienced the same contrasts in the road surface and speed as I'd experienced the first time, but my mood was impenetrable.

When my blindfold was finally taken off, I was sickened but not shocked to see that this was exactly the same hotel where I'd been deflowered all those months ago. There was a sense of things coming full circle. Mr Soulful Eyes stood there smiling at me. He shook hands with Sovath saying, 'We'll bring her back to you by 11am tomorrow morning. Do whatever you have to do.' Sovath's job was to stand guard outside and keep an eye on my whereabouts.

I followed Mr Soulful Eyes' back as he walked inside, and saw the same Uncle Thom-like receptionist I'd seen the first time, though I don't think he recognised me. The room he took me to was not exactly the same room, but it had a similar plush carpet and a similar bedspread and I felt that my life was being replayed like a worn-out record.

That's when everything changed.

Mr Soulful Eyes locked the door behind us and waved at the chair in one corner. 'Have a seat,' he said almost absently. 'This might take some time. Would you like something to eat or drink? A packet of crisps, perhaps or a chocolate bar, a soft drink?'

'No thanks. I'm not hungry,' I said submissively, 'though I'd appreciate a tissue, if you don't mind?' The wind on the back of the motorbike had made my nose run overtime and it was impossible to control with the handkerchief I had.

'Feel free to use the bathroom.' He waved politely at the bathroom door as though he was the host and I was a guest.

Upon my return into the bedroom, Mr Soulful Eyes was glancing out of the window into the distance, and he smiled at me a little nervously, it seemed to me.

'Phew, I've been doing this for some time, but it doesn't get any easier,' he said. Something about the timbre of his voice reminded me of Uncle Radha's charm so forcefully that I couldn't quite believe anything he was saying when he began to speak.

'Well, let's begin.' He fiddled with the watch on his wrist, clicking the clasp several times. 'You're not going to be servicing any young men tonight. Now, how's that for a starter?' he said trying to crack a joke with me.

I stared at him blankly, without making any direct eye contact.

'You're not going to be servicing me, or anyone else again if you choose not. My name is Dara and I work as a freelance rescuer to help girls get out of prostitution. I work independently but in collaboration with advocacy organisations and NGOs that run after-care facilities to take care of girls such as you who've been sold into sexual slavery.' What was he talking about? I understood the meaning of the words he was saying but their impact was coming up against a muffled wall of unreality, confusion and doubt that had been built up around me. 'If you choose, tonight could be your first night of freedom.'

The word 'freedom' beckoned to me from a hidden, half-suppressed place inside my mind. I looked around the room cautiously, fearing that something or someone was going to appear out of nowhere and mock me with a display of his sexual organs. Gradually, my mind remembered the taste of the word 'freedom' and I started to listen with owl-like alertness, incapable of forming my mouth around any words.

'Do you want to be free?'

I opened my mouth but the words would not come.

'It's ok, we have several hours here to give you time to think, if you need that much time to make a decision.' I could hear a faint pff, pff, pat outside the window, signalling the familiar sound of a baker making bread through the night in readiness for business in the morning. 'I know it's hard for some girls to let go. Hard to let go of their lifestyle in the brothel and the "family" they've made. Hard for them to see any future for themselves beyond prostitution. I was the same in some ways when it came to making a decision for Jesus: it was hard for me to let go of my old ways of living and easier to hold on to what was familiar.'

Jesus? That name was familiar to me from my time in Aunty Helen's house, though my English was not good enough at that time to have understood the full nuances of what was being said.

He had his face turned to the window, and for the second time I looked at him properly. His face was handsome, in many ways like Radha's, though he had a small amount of clipped and neat facial hair which was unusual for a Cambodian. Looking at his face I began to understand one thing: that physical attractiveness is irrelevant to the quality of someone's character. This might not seem like any great

140

revelation, but it was to me at that time as I had almost begun to see beauty as a curse, as a sign of character corruption. Being beautiful had resulted in our lives being laid in the dirt and trampled upon. We could have been sold into prostitution if we were not beautiful, but our beauty was a tool that naturally increased our market value and concurrently cheapened our social and moral value.

Dara cleared his throat before speaking again. 'If you want to, I can arrange for you to be taken to a home run by an NGO. It's called Safe Hands and you would be with other girls like yourself. You'd be given the opportunity to receive counselling to help you with your healing process, and you'd have the chance to learn some new skills to help make you employable outside of the sex industry.' Healing? At the time I didn't even think of myself as needing healing, I was so numb inside.

A cog was churning in my mind; it was so stiff that only time would oil the wheels. I couldn't wrap my thoughts around this new revelation in any meaningful way and I sat there blankly staring at the floor. The sexualised part of me imagined that if only I could get him into me and out again then all this confusion would be over, and I shudder now to remember that, even while sitting in the chair, I slowly began to wriggle out of my knickers, curving my hips suggestively. Dara stood up with a red face looming over me. 'No, no! Don't *do* that!' he vociferated, his jaw clenching with the tension. Then in a more studied tone, with his eyes averted to the bed covering, he said, 'That is *not* what I want. I thought I'd made that clear.'

His response snapped me into a new sphere, a reality where all men did not want to have sex with little girls, and the words he had spoken began to solidify into veracity rather than sliding away down the slippery pipe of falsehood.

Chastened, I pulled up my knickers, shuffled back and sat hunched over, my head bowed in humiliation. 'Look,' he said moderately, 'if this is all too much for you I can leave you alone for a while and give you time to think. I assure you that I am telling you the truth. You can get out of prostitution if you like. It's up to you.' He turned the door handle.

'No, please don't go,' I called out, my voice released by a sudden sense of fear. I pulled out another ream of toilet paper and blew my nose as discreetly as I could. The woolliness in my head as a result of my cold was not helping me to think clearly. 'Could I please have that soft drink you offered earlier?' I whispered, with as much subservience as I could muster.

'Of course,' he said, and there was a pause while he opened his bag and pulled open the tag on the can, which let out a reassuring hiss.

I drank from the can in small gulps, trying to avoid too much build-up of gas. 'How will we get away from here without being seen by Kalliyan's man?' I raised my head from its default submission.

'So you do want to leave, then?' Dara's face cracked into the most genuine warm-hearted smile I'd ever seen.

'Mmhmm,' I murmured. 'Can you help my friends to get out from the same brothel? I don't want to leave them behind.'

He puffed out between his lips, 'Phew, there're two questions there. I'll start with your second question. You're a smart girl and you must understand that it'd be extremely difficult and possibly dangerous to try the same method again in your brothel. They couldn't help being suspicious as you'll already have left, and they're much less likely to allow any of the other girls to leave. The only other option would be a raid, and that is a big operation which we cannot attempt without a lot of preparation and planning. Please just assume that, at this stage, if you want to go free, it'll be a long time before you see your friends again.'

My mind playing with memories of Sodarath and Chenda, I stared at the wall. Some of Soda's last words to me played in my mind: 'Listen, sister. If you get the chance to escape out of all this, somehow and somewhere, don't forget about me, will you?' I knew she would be cheering me on right now, even without the chance to escape herself. She wouldn't want me to go back to the brothel knowing that I'd turned down the chance of freedom. My heart began pounding again with hope for myself, even while weighed down with sadness for my friends. 'I understand,' I sighed.

'It's ok. Even if you're not completely sure, you can always change your mind. No one is going to be imprisoning you at Safe Hands. You can choose to return to your life as a prostitute if you want to. In answer to your first question...' Dara removed a sealed pack of white tablets from his bag, raised his eyebrows and grinned conspiratorially.

'Sleeping tablets used in a rather large dosage – not enough to harm him, but enough to make him sleep very heavily until we're well away. How will we get him to take them?' he asked rhetorically. 'I'll invite him to celebrate with us the deflowering of my "nephew" with this one innocent can of Angkor beer – half empty so it looks like I've already drunk some. And this will have the tablets in. It's the oldest trick in the book.'

'What happens if he won't take the can, seeing as it's already been opened?' I asked.

He laughed. 'Oh, I know a trick or two in reverse psychology, and I'm good at acting drunk.'

'Reverse psychology?'

'It'll work, never you mind.'

It was around 2am when Dara went downstairs and I, too excited to sleep, paced up and down the room, checking out the phone, reading the hotel instructions regarding room service and bouncing on the bed giddily, my head whirling with possibilities.

At 2.46 Dara bounded back into the room. 'It worked,' he hissed exuberantly. '*Bpoo* Sovath is snoring out there on the back of his moto. I'm pretty sure he'll be fast asleep for another eight hours at least – more than enough time for us to get away. He took a bit of persuading to join me in celebrating, but once I nailed it, the can was finished in less than a minute!'

'We don't want to look like we're in a rush, so we'll just walk out of the back door as quietly as possible. Try not to look like you're running away. The guards changed duty about half an hour ago so they won't have seen you going in, which helps. The back door heads out past the swimming pool to a small car parking area where our vehicle is parked. If anyone asks, we're just going for a late-night swim. In fact, we should probably take a quick swim to avert any suspicion. Can you swim?'

'Yes,' I said. I'd learnt when I lived in Vietnam and you never lose the instinct to swim, even though it had been a long time. We took a couple of towels from the room as we headed downstairs. The only sound that could be heard was the tinny buzzing of the poorly circuited electric lights. Even the late-night drinkers from the hotel bar had headed to bed by this time.

The man sitting at the reception desk was no longer the Uncle Thom lookalike, but a more solidly built, perpetually smiley-faced man. He raised his eyebrows with all the collusion of a partner in crime as Dara called over to him, 'Just going to cool off in the pool after a rather hot late-night session.' He emphasised the word 'hot' in a tone designed to frustrate the man. The fact that most of the staff were complicit in the trafficking of young girls was actually turning out to be an aide in getting away.

We walked out of the door to the pool area, which was just behind the reception, and let the door swing behind us. I took off my shoes and Dara took off his shirt and jumped into the pool, laughing and fully getting into the swing of things. The guard came and lingered at the screen door, presumably getting a quick eyeful as my skirt lifted in the water, and then strolled nonchalantly back to his post. Dara dived under the water and surfaced again, spitting out a few droplets of water. He whispered to me, 'He's gone out of sight. Let's go. Pick up your towel and wrap yourself with it, then follow me.'

I shivered as I stepped out. The atmosphere felt cool against my wet body. Grabbing my towel, I wrapped it around me, held my shoes in my hand and padded around the courtyard following Dara in the direction of a door in the wall at the far side from the one we'd entered. The temptation was to run, and adrenaline was pounding in my ears to spur me on, but I had to resist. A polished blue Honda lay just behind the door. Dara opened the passenger door and beckoned me in. I'd never been in a car before, and I breathed in the combination of petrol and leather seats as I clambered in.

It wasn't like the films. There was no last-minute chase and heart-pounding escape. Just a subtle engine splutter as Dara started the car, a titillated man sitting bouncing his leg at the hotel reception and a drugged-up driver lying senseless on his moto. By 3.15 we were on our way. The doors of the car were tinted so no one could see in. I ensconced myself in the car seat next to Dara, gazing out at the city wordlessly, and looked inwards.

Chapter 16
Cambodia, May 2008

The car door opened just inside the secure gates of a typical Phnom Penh compound. The walls were beautifully plastered with a subtle shade of cream, and there were overhanging porches with gold-embossed railings, burnished wooden doors and window details. There was a sign board just above the outside wall with the words 'Safe Hands' embossed in a childlike font, and a drawing of two hands holding each other – one large and one small.

A tiny lady with crow's feet and a twinkle in her eyes greeted us and held my hand as I stepped out of the car. 'You must be Song,' she said, and gave me a warm, heartfelt hug. 'We've been looking forward to your arrival.' I held myself back a little stiffly, but the strength of her embrace was difficult to resist.

'Thank you so much for your stellar efforts, Dara,' the lady said, touching him on the shoulder as he got out of the car, looking worn but pleased. 'God bless you. We'll have to debrief as soon as possible but please go and get some sleep. I'll see you sometime late tomorrow morning.'

'Sleep well, Song,' Dara winked at me. 'I'm sure Aunty Visal and her team will take good care of you. But whatever you do, don't let her bully you with her kindness,' he said, giving her a playful punch on the upper arm. Aunty Visal laughed. That infectious melody was to cheer me up on a regular basis during the dark moments ahead.

With all the excitement of the night, I hadn't realised quite how tired I was until I stopped completely. A leaden weight took hold of me and I was rooted to the ground, almost unable to move. As Dara backed out of the compound in his Honda and I waved goodbye, the aunty turned to me and asked, 'Is there anything you would like to do before sleeping: have a shower, eat something or drink something? We can talk in the morning. There's plenty of time for talking.'

'No thank you,' I mouthed gratefully through the great yawn that took hold of me. 'Sleeping would be just fine.'

I followed her through one set of stairs to a first-floor corridor that ran the length of the building, which was built in the rough shape of a horseshoe. She showed me a door on the left-hand side, just past the stairs, which she indicated was a communal bathroom, and then she poked her head into a darkened room on the right-hand side which had the number 28 written on it. She stood outside and said to me in a whisper, 'Number 28 will be your room. You're sharing with Thida. Please take the bed on the left. She's sleeping on the right. I won't detain you any longer. Just take this package to make your stay a little more comfortable. Goodnight. I'll see you in the morning. If you're not awake for breakfast, which is usually between 6.30 and 8, I'll ask the cook to leave you some food, so feel free to sleep as long as you like, at least on your first day!'

Upon entering the room I saw a bulk under the sheet on the right-hand side. I couldn't see her face as she was turned to the wall and partially covered by the sheet. I was curious about my faceless room-mate but would have to suspend my curiosity till the next day.

I undid the package, which was wrapped in a sarong. Inside was a pair of pyjamas with ducks on them, a toothbrush, some toothpaste, a small bottle of shampoo and a bar of soap. There was also a clean T-shirt with the Safe Hands logo on it and a clean pair of knickers. I felt immensely grateful for all this as I had nothing other than the clothes I was wearing at the time. After brushing my teeth and washing my face I changed into my new pyjamas, clambered into bed and drifted off into a much-needed deep sleep.

I woke up to the murmur of voices, some way above my head, and a suffocating heat. It seemed as though the sun was pouring directly into the room and hitting my bed, which gave me a hint as to the time of day. 'Should we wake her up?' I could hear one feminine voice asking.

'No, Aunty Visal said we should let her sleep in. She only arrived at about four o'clock this morning.' The second voice was asserting its authority yet spoke with an undercurrent of timidity. I felt a sudden flush of anxiety about getting out of bed and facing these unknown people and a new institution, and was hit with a pang of longing for companionship with Soda and Chenda. The bed creaked as I climbed out, giving away the fact that I was awake. I'd not slept so well in a long time, sleeping solidly for around seven hours in a comfortable bed without fear of being woken up by clients.

I padded out to the bathroom past the two girls I'd heard talking. I smiled over at them. The bigger of the two girls approached me. She did not smile but gave me a nod and said flatly, 'I'm Thida, your room-mate. This is Vanna. I think Aunty Visal wants to see you downstairs when you're ready.'

After using the toilet and taking a shower I followed Thida downstairs to a working area where a few offices branched off the main hallway. Visal sat just inside one, with her legs curled up casually around her on her chair, facing another woman with whom she was deep in discussion. This other woman looked to be European and had a pink and grey scarf tied loosely around her light brown hair.

When she saw me, Visal got up from her chair and came towards me, hands open in greeting. 'My dear,' she said, 'I hope you slept well on your first night of freedom. It'll take you a while to get used to the way everything works around here, but please feel free to ask any questions and we'll answer them. Your breakfast is here if you're hungry.' She gestured to a tray resting on the nearby cupboard where there were several pieces of white toast, a small carton of jam and a tiny container of butter. My throat felt slightly compressed and no words would come out, but I nodded and grinned politely. 'This is Helga,' Aunty said, gesticulating in the direction of the European woman. 'She will be your case worker. She bakes very good cakes and I hope you'll soon get the chance to try some!'

She winked at Helga and Helga smiled softly. 'Nice to meet you, Song,' she said in a sweetly accented Khmer.

I finished my mouthful of toast and responded, 'You too.'

I felt even more exposed than I'd ever felt as a prostitute, as if I were laid out like a piece of raw meat on a table ready for cutting. Knowing that these were affable people who most likely had the best of motives somehow made me feel more vulnerable. It was as though all the worst of human nature that had been enforced upon me was clinging to me like ivy, and I was afraid of having that ivy stripped away in case it was discovered that underneath my walls were coated in filth. A crushing fear gripped my windpipe even as I chewed with seeming calm on my breakfast. This fear was all the more confusing to me as you would have expected that, having been released from

147

prostitution and now being in a safe house, I'd actually feel more at peace than before.

'We'll be working together,' said Helga kindly, 'so you'll see a lot of me over the next few months. I'll act as your counsellor and hold your hand as you come to terms with your trauma, and give you guidance about building up some skills to help you make a better life for yourself outside the institution.'

I looked at her blankly, her words meaning nothing to me. Sensing my confusion, Helga tried to reassure me: 'Don't worry if you don't understand what I'm talking about at the moment. It's your first day and you're bound to be a little bit confused and uncertain about what you've let yourself in for.' I dipped my head to indicate my acknowledgement of her words, unsure whether to be relieved or intimidated that she recognised my trepidation.

'You'll have plenty of time to ask questions and to find your bearings here, so don't feel like you have to figure out everything all at once,' Aunty Visal interjected. 'You couldn't be in better hands than with Helga, so feel at ease. Dara is on his way to see me for a debrief, which means he'll be telling me the details about last night, including your responses. You don't have to be there if you don't want to. But of course you're welcome to if you like, as nothing will be shared that you're not already aware of.'

My face flushed as the memory of my attempt to seduce Dara came unbidden to my mind, and I said with certainty, 'No thanks. I don't want to be there.'

'That's absolutely fine. Well, I'll be busy for the next half an hour or so with Dara, but I'll let Helga show you around before lunch and introduce you to our extended family. You've just had breakfast so you may not feel like eating much lunch, but I'd encourage you to at least have a bite so you get your body clock into our routine as soon as you can.'

There was a light knock on the office door and Dara poked his head in. 'Hey there, Song. I hope you slept well after all the excitement last night. Have you eaten yet?'

'Yes, thank you.'

'Will you be hanging around while I debrief Visal?' he said, walking in and plonking himself comfortably on a free chair.

I looked sheepishly over at the Aunty, not wanting to say no to Dara in case he took it as a personal snub, and she intervened with, 'No she won't, Dara. Helga is going to show her around.'

Helga took this as her cue, stood up and smiled personably at the other adults, holding out her hand to me, 'Come on, Song. Let's leave them to it.'

'See you later!' Visal chirped, robin-like in her enthusiasm.

'You might be thinking you've escaped from one form of institution only to land yourself in another, but let me tell you that this place is structured like it is to ensure that you girls get the best support and care possible, and the routines really help with that.'

We walked into a room filled with the noise of pots clattering and knives working hard against chopping boards, and steam. 'This is where the girls learn professional cooking,' Helga said. Four girls were working in different areas around the room, and a man was walking between them giving them the occasional piece of advice. 'Give that fish a little more salt, Makaria. It'll make the biggest difference to the overall taste.' Concentrating on their work, the girls didn't register our entrance into the kitchen. Helga smiled at me, signalling that we could leave the room.

'I suppose cooking is fairly familiar to you already. Did you see much cooking before you were sold into prostitution?'

'Yes, I saw both Khmer and Western style.'

'Western style? Really? How come?' Helga sounded genuinely surprised and interested.

'It's a long story.' Wanting to hold back from talking about my life at this point, I used this as a stalling tactic, but at the same time I knew I was the one who'd opened up the door to further communication by mentioning Western-style cooking. I wanted to share my life, but I wanted to do it my way so that I was in control of what was revealed and when.

'Ok...' her voice tailed off with an uplifted, questioning tone. 'Well, there'll be plenty of time to talk in the days to come.'

Helga showed me the different skills classes that the girls were taking at that time. As well as cooking there was jewellery making, sewing, hairdressing, crocheting and ICT. She indicated that the girls

149

had a choice regarding which skills they wanted to learn and develop, but in the first year with Safe Hands they were required to try at least three different skills. Then in the second year they would commit to train more rigorously in one. 'We teach you a trade so that when you eventually leave us you have a way of providing an income for yourself that will negate any economic compulsion for you to go back into sex work. You're only 12 years old and the youngest you can leave us is 16. We're not going to force you to stay if you really want to return to your old way of life, but we are here to protect you, and we're assuming that most girls, especially the younger ones like yourself, don't want to return to sex work.'

I shook my head as that seemed to be what Helga expected. Of course I didn't want to go back to sex work, but at the same time, assenting to being there for four years on day one was difficult to comprehend, and I knew I was going to miss my 'sisters', no matter what.

It was twelve o'clock, lunchtime at Safe Hands, so Helga led me towards the dining hall. 'We'll meet again after lunch for our first counselling session. Counselling sessions, both group and individual, take place from 2pm. There is a siesta time immediately after lunch, during which time you can sleep or do some relaxing activity that won't disturb other people.'

'Like what?' I asked, worried that this was a stupid question, but genuinely not knowing what I could do.

'Any craft activity, reading (we have a small library of both Khmer and English books), puzzles or quiet games that you can play on your own, such as patience.' She saw the disconcertion on my face. 'I know you're not used to having this sort of free time. To be honest, if I were you, I'd just sleep. You'll need as much as you can get for the emotional challenges that lie ahead.'

'I used to...' I let my sentence tail off unfinished as I knew I wasn't ready to talk about you yet.

A sea of eyes greeted me as I walked into the dining hall. The sea quietly flowed and then ebbed as many of the girls realised that they'd already seen me walking around that morning. I tried to keep my own eyes averted, but I let them discreetly wander, searching for familiar faces. There were about 25 girls in that room, ranging from one tiny girl who can't have been more than 9 or 10, up to about 16 years old. The dining hall was open on three sides to the elements and, as well as the girls, there were ten or so adults there, Cambodians and foreigners, all of whom were staff at the centre in various roles.

Helga queued up with me to receive food from a serving lady who had a couple of bowls piled with food in front of her. My mouth began to water as I realised that the food on offer that day was my favourite dish, Amok – you remember, the fish, rice and coconut dish we ate out sometimes? I'd not had it since before that fateful day when I was sold into prostitution. This lifted my spirits and gave me a hint that life was going to be accommodating and good here.

My room-mate, Thida, waved to me from one of the long tables as I took my plate and looked nervously around. I glanced at Helga for some sort of direction, and she nodded to me, 'Please, go ahead. Make friends. Enjoy yourself.'

Still unsmiling and monotoned like the first time we met, Thida was nevertheless friendly. 'I've been here just over a year. Vanna here has been with us for six or seven months. We're all at different stages here in the centre, but we're all in the same boat, which makes us equals.' Thida was a large-boned girl of 14. She was somewhat masculine in her demeanour and it made me wonder what her experience as a prostitute had been like. What type of customers had she appealed to? Vanna, her sidekick, was 12 like me, and shy, though with a penetratingly sharp wit, which never failed to take me by surprise.

Thida leaned over the table and said in a low voice, 'Aunty Visal is truly wonderful. She really is like everyone's mother and we love her. Some of the counsellors are not so great, mentioning no names, but Helga is fine. You're in good hands.'

I dredged my mind for some conversation to make, not sure what types of things people talked about in this context. 'What skills are you learning?'

'I'm specialising in computing. Last year I tried out crocheting, sewing and cooking, but I was never that good at any of them. Too fiddly for me. I'm a bit clumsy with my hands.'

'I'm trying out lots of different skills,' said Vanna in her quiet voice, 'to give me as wide an experience as possible. I really like photography.'

'Photography? I didn't know that that was one of the skills on offer.'

'Well, technically it's part of the creative programme rather than a skill for trade, but it's still fun.'

I sat there quietly and savoured the taste of my Amok. 'Does everything happen at fixed times around here?'

'Yes,' said Thida, rolling her eyes, 'and it doesn't suit me, though I can see that it's needed. Haven't you been told yet?'

I shook my head, 'Not fully, no.'

'Well, I'm sure you'll be given a schedule, but to give you an idea: breakfast is between 6.30 and 8am. You can come and get it whenever you like during that time as it's self-service. From 8am till 10am it's school classes, though we only have two – Khmer and English. Then we have a break till 10.15. After that it's skills classes till lunch, and counselling or life skills from 2pm till 4pm. Then we have an hour's free time until dinner at 5. You'll soon get the hang of it. This place is run by Christians so after dinner we tend to have an hour's devotion and worship time. It's not my sort of thing but I go anyway to toe the line. We don't have to go, but they encourage us to.'

'What does devotion and worship mean?'

'Oh, you know. The staff lead us in a time of singing songs about Jesus and God, and share some thoughts about the Bible.' I didn't know, but there it was again, that name, Jesus.

Nobody had said anything about their personal experiences in the brothels, but I was soon to learn that that was an area of conversation that was off limits: unless someone volunteered information, you didn't ask. We all had more than enough time to offload in the counselling sessions, and that was as much as most of us could take.

I wasn't able to sleep properly during that first siesta time as my mind was buzzing with myriad first impressions, and I'd only just woken from a long sleep a couple of hours before, but I lay there dozing, giving the impression of being asleep to avoid conversation. Thida lay in the other bed, tackling a crossword and slapping away mosquitoes. My stomach was doing somersaults and I was swallowing away the taste of bile as I prepared myself mentally for my first unveiling. I had no idea what to expect from my first counselling session, but I was prepared for an emotional hammering.

I'd become so used to not thinking and not feeling, shoring up a protective wall around me to prevent myself from being sucked into a cesspool of shame, that this was the first time I'd been given any space to feel. I lay as still as possible in the bed to avoid giving away my inner turmoil to Thida by tossing and turning.

At exactly 2pm, Helga gave a tap on the bedroom door and said in a voice just above a whisper, 'Hey, Song, are you ready? I'll just wait outside and we can go down to the counselling room together.'

Murmuring my assent, I clambered out of my sweaty sheets and headed for the door. 'Good luck,' said Thida, as though aware that I needed a little boost.

Helga gave me a warm smile as I came out of the room. 'There's nothing to be worried about. I'm not going to be forcing you to reveal anything you don't want to share. A little bit of anxiety is perfectly normal though.'

Without saying anything I smiled weakly in response and followed Helga down the stairs to the floor below the bedrooms. There were a few offices clustered in one corner, all of which had signs on the door in both Khmer and English saying, 'Private. Counselling.'

Helga unlocked one of the doors and beckoned me inside. The room was small, with a couple of low, soft-backed chairs facing one another at a slight angle, a coffee table with a Bible on the bottom shelf, a box of tissues and two coasters. The window opened to a shaded area where bushes grew right up against the window, and you could see the wall of an adjacent building running along one side.

'Ok, Song. We always start with a short prayer as we want to commit our time to God and ensure that everything that is said within these walls is said in a spirit of love and truth. That doesn't mean you can't express negative feelings, because that wouldn't be truth if that's what you're feeling. I hope that's ok with you. If at any time you feel uncomfortable or want to stop, please just say.'

I looked at her and waited for her leading, my throat tightening.

She closed her eyes and began: 'Heavenly Father, who knows all things, we commit this time into your hands and ask that you would guide us and lead us as we talk. Give Song peace in the midst of any fear or anxiety that she might be feeling, and give me wisdom in asking the right questions. In Jesus' name, Amen.' Helga opened her eyes and smiled at me. 'That wasn't so bad, was it?' I shook my head, keeping my eyes averted.

'By the way, I should let you know that at 4.15 today you're scheduled to meet the doctor for a physical check-up. This is all part of Safe Hands' procedures for entry. We want to know if you need any extra support as far as your health is concerned, and we test for HIV. Now superficially you seem healthy enough, but it's best for us and for you to know if there are any medical concerns so that we can provide the best care for you.

'Also, you might be wondering: am I going to be having these scary, one-to-one sessions every day? The answer is no. We give new girls quite a bit of support in the early days but there will also be times when you work together in a group with other girls to learn life skills such as saying no, making choices, handling money and conflict. Sometimes you might feel like you just need a break from it all, which is fair enough, but we do encourage you to keep attending your scheduled sessions and persevering through the challenges if you can. However, if you really need a day away from it all, let either me or Visal know and we can give you some space and free time in the afternoons instead.'

Not knowing how to respond to this, I gave an anaemic smile. I could feel Helga's eyes on me and began to feel pinned. She lowered her gaze, sensing my unease, and picked up her bag in a businesslike fashion, taking out a notebook and pen and plumping them on her lap.

'Tell me about the last time that you were really happy,' she began without any further preamble. 'I'm not talking about a brief moment of happiness. I'm talking about a time when you were mostly happy for a good period of time.'

Relieved that she hadn't begun with the most recent history, I felt the tightness in my throat ease a little, tilted my head to the ceiling and pondered my answer. 'When I was living with Aunty Lydia.' I didn't mention Radha because of his responsibility in selling me, although, to be fair, he was a part of the happiness I experienced at that time.

'Who is Aunty Lydia?' Helga probed gently.

154

'She is a white British lady who helped to take care of me for almost a year.'

'Interesting. How did you come to know her?'

Over the next 30 minutes or so my story with you unfolded like a delicately woven garment which could easily tear. I revealed details about the way we met, what life was like with you and what it was that made me happy. As she prompted me, my responses began to flow effortlessly and I lost track of time. Throughout my whole story I purposely left a gaping hole where Radha had stood.

'Ok, let me get this straight. During that time in your life, the people who helped to make you happiest were Lydia, Helen and Amy. Is that right?'

'Yes,' I said.

'So, then, how did you get from wonderful life there to sex slavery?'

I swallowed, attempting to stem the rising bile churning from within, and I couldn't open my mouth. My eyes lifted to Helga with a helpless look.

'It's ok, take your time. You don't have to share any of this right now if you don't want to. I just can't see any obvious connection between your life with Lydia and your life since, and naturally I'm trying to make connections to make sense of all this.'

I glimpsed at the walls on either side of me and suddenly had the distinct impression that they were narrowing in around me, and Helga's face loomed massively into my visual perspective. Standing up with a start, I said, 'I've got to get out of here, sorry,' opened the door and went out into the courtyard where the fresh air and the sunlight were in glaring contrast to the confines of the room.

'Come and find me whenever you're comfortable, Song! I won't go anywhere,' Helga called from inside.

Not knowing where to go as I didn't want to be inside, I wandered around the shaded areas near the building and avoided looking at the various people passing, pausing, considering and giving me space.

The blue zone. My life was laid out before me like a running track. I was running and running, with my heart pounding like a bass beat, but I was getting nowhere. The faster I ran, the further the track ahead of me stretched out into the distance. In my mind's eye I could see someone coming alongside me and, when I allowed them to hold my hand, my running synchronised with the track. As much as I didn't want to trust again, didn't want to let anyone see what was inside, I knew that if I wanted to get anywhere in life I needed to let go of the temptation to go it alone. The walls were going to have to be stripped of ivy, as painful as that would be.

After ten minutes of wandering and thinking and exhaling hard, I stilled my nerves and went back into the counselling room. Helga was reading a book and raised her head when I came in. 'Good to see you again, Song.' Her voice and words sounded genuine.

'Sorry, I had to…'

'I know, it's perfectly normal. Don't ever worry about needing to get out every now and then.'

I sat down again and shifted my backside into a comfortable position on the chair. Once I'd made up my mind, my voice went into action as though released by the popping of a cork. 'His name was Radha, and he was Lydia's boyfriend.'

'Wooaah! Are you sure you want to rush in like that?!' Helga leaned back in her seat with a theatrical movement so unlike her normal demeanour that I laughed. The laughter poured oil on the flow of words, a deliberately chosen ploy by Helga, I'm sure.

'I thought… I wanted Lydia to marry him.'

'He was Cambodian, right?'

'Yes.'

'How did they meet?'

'I think, yes I'm sure, he was a receptionist at the doctor's surgery we went to. It was love at first sight for Radha. Then he chased her.'

'Very romantic,' Helga said with a wry smile, guessing that the story wasn't going to end with a happy ever after. 'How did *you* feel about him?'

'You know what? I liked him and he was always kind and helpful towards me, but a part of me wasn't sure about him…'

'Perhaps you're just saying that because of what happened later on?'

'No,' I said firmly. 'I remember thinking that.'

'Can you give me an example of something that made you unsure about him?'

I could only remember one specific thing and it was difficult to articulate to her then. 'One time, when Uncle Radha came to pick me up from a mall after a birthday party, I told him I'd had a great time and asked him if he'd had any fun times himself as a child. His voice went colder than I'd ever heard it before and he said, "Childhood's not all about fun, you know. There are times when sacrifices need to be made." It was such a strange thing for him to say, especially as I already knew from experience that childhood was not all fun. It unsettled me somehow.'

'So if you weren't sure about him, why did you want Lydia to marry him?'

Screwing up my lips, I thought about this. 'I could see how much he made Lydia happy and I wanted ...' - not having the articulacy to express this well I said what I could - '... a family.'

'A family? But what about your birth family?'

'My mum was sick and not able to care for me well and my dad had... died. I wasn't living with them 'cos I'd escaped from home. Things weren't great there...' More and more layers were peeling away. We spoke for some time more and I told her about my home life, including my mum's alcoholism and Uncle Thom's violence. I compared it to how settled and secure my life with you and Radha had been.

I lost track of time until Helga looked at her watch and said, 'It's 3.45. I think we'll stop there. There's no need to let everything come out in our first session together, and you've done really well today. You're going to have your medical in half an hour so give yourself some time to rest, go to the toilet and so on before that. We'll meet again tomorrow.'

It was only as we finished that I realised how drained I felt, as though I'd been through a spin dryer, but at the same time there was a sense of relief that the truth was finally being made known.

157

Chapter 17
Cambodia, May 2008

I lay on a table with my legs wide open while the doctor peered and poked inside me with a surgical instrument. You'd have thought I'd have been used to keeping my legs wide open, but all my muscles had tensed up, and the doctor had had to work hard to get me to relax.

'Fine,' she said, signalling to me that I could put my clothes back on and return to the chair. 'You received some cuts and abrasions in the earlier stages of your prostitution but all those have healed up, and everything looks to be in healthy working order. You'll hopefully have no problems, should you want to, in conceiving children.'

Having children couldn't have been further from my mind. Nevertheless, I breathed a sigh of relief that I was healthy. Dr Anchaly had also checked my blood pressure and weighed me. I was slightly below the weight expected of a girl my age, but she told me that this was nothing unusual and I was sure to put it on with the good routine and nourishing food at the centre.

'Now, the last thing we need to do is take a blood test to check for HIV. This is completely routine and nothing to be scared of. Did most of the men you had sex with use condoms?'

'Yes, but there were some that didn't.'

Dr Anchaly made a record in her notes, 'Well that's not a great sign, but it's to be expected. Some of the girls who come here have only ever had unprotected sex and even then they occasionally come away HIV free.' She peeled gloves onto her hands and prepared the surgical needle. 'Have you ever had an injection before?'

'Just the one time.'

'Do you know what it was for?'

'Yes, it was a tetanus jab a couple of years ago.'

'Well, this will be a bit different as we're using a needle to take blood from you rather than inject you with a vaccination. Were you ok with it?'

'Yes, I think I was rather fascinated by it all, to be honest!' I laughed at the memory, looking back on myself as though I was so much older and wiser than I had been then, which, sad to say, I probably was.

I turned away as she suggested while she numbed the area inside my arm and slid in the needle. Rhythmically opening and closing my fist, I couldn't resist looking at what she was doing as she began drawing out a small vial of dark red fluid.

When the vial was full, she drew out the needle and wiped the spot with cotton wool, before smiling at me. 'That'll be all, Song. We'll have to send off the sample but we should find out the test results tomorrow so I'll have another chat with you at the same time then.'

'Ok, thanks then,' I said, presuming that I was allowed to go. I took this all very matter-of-factly. You must understand that being a prostitute for more than a year had hardened me somewhat as far as sickness was concerned, so I was prepared to face this. Nonetheless, I knew from talk in the brothel that being an Aids carrier effectively put an end to a girl's money-making abilities as far as sex work was concerned, but all that seemed vague and meaningless to me at the time as I didn't even really know the difference between HIV and Aids. I thought it would just be like any other STD and I could just take a couple of pills to sort me out and that would be it. And at that moment I was totally indifferent to having less money-making potential since, as of early that morning, I was no longer a prostitute.

After dinner, I sat at a table with Thida and Vanna while a few adults began setting up the cafeteria for devotion time. Not having anything else to do, and being curious as to what it was all about, I stayed around. A square-jawed Westerner called Bob, who worked as the computing teacher along with miscellaneous other jobs, took out a guitar and began tuning it.

'Is it going to be like a concert?' I whispered naively to Thida.

'Not exactly,' she responded. 'There'll be some singing led by Bob, which everyone can join in with. Don't worry if you don't know the words. They're easy enough to pick up. Then one of the staff will talk to us about God and Jesus and they sometimes give us the opportunity to respond.'

Aunty Visal stood on her tiptoes to reach up to a rather high-standing microphone, and signalled with a giggle that it should be lowered. One of the Khmer male staff ran forward and complied with her request.

'She's so cute,' said Vanna under her breath.

I was a bit taken aback by this comment, never having thought of an older lady as 'cute' before.

Within minutes, a few well-thumbed booklets in Khmer script were being passed around. It appeared that the songs we were going to sing were all listed in this booklet. I don't remember much about the songs we sang that day, though we sang three or four, but I do remember the lines, 'Worthy is the lamb / Seated on the throne', because I didn't understand them at the time, and I kept visualising a pitiful mewling lamb scrabbling around on a throne that was much too big for it, and the incongruity of this image was a distraction for me.

The moment that imprinted itself on my memory came when the singing stopped. Aunty Visal came forward with a Bible and a few notes in her hand and stood at the mic, her face glowing with an unfathomable something.

'I'm going to talk to you today about Jesus meeting an unrespectable, outcast lady. You might think you know how a holy man would respond to someone like her, but you will be surprised.' She then proceeded to read the chapter in the Bible from the book of John which told the story.

Jesus, a Jew, stopped on His travels in a town in Samaria, where the people were as different from His people as the Khmer and the Thai – in other words, they had a similar heritage but didn't mix well with each other. The woman in question came to the well in the middle of the day to get water. Putting this into context, Aunty explained that this demonstrated her outcast position in society, as most women would have collected water in the cool morning before the sun had much heat. As a way into conversation with her, Jesus asked her for a drink of water, and she answered with a comment that showed that she expected people to reject her. 'You are a Jew and I am a Samaritan woman. How can You ask me for a drink?' Jesus then began to talk about living water and springs of water welling up to eternal life. I was lost, but the words that grabbed my attention at this point were, 'Whoever drinks the water I give him will never thirst.' Clearly He wasn't talking about physical water, and as Visal talked I began to feel a stirring inside me, which I quickly suppressed.

The detail that most caught my attention was the fact that Jesus knew without asking that this woman was an unrespectable woman, that she was living with a man who wasn't her husband and that she'd already been married five times, but He didn't condemn or accuse her; He simply stated it as a fact.

'Are you surprised that Jesus, a holy man, sought out and engaged in conversation with a woman like this? Didn't He care what other people would think about Him?' Aunty Visal paused when she said this and looked around at us. All of a sudden her voice began to quiver with emotion and she pleaded with us, 'Don't ever feel that because you've been a prostitute nobody is going to look at you as anything but trash any more. They may think what they like, but Jesus is in the business of forgiveness and transformation. He knows exactly who we are, and what we've done, and what people have done to us and He says, "Come to me all who are weary and heavy-laden." He doesn't excuse us and say, "Everything will be fine." But He sees the pit that we're in, accepts us as we are and asks us to walk with Him on an exciting journey of faith.

'More than a few years ago – hey watch it, I'm not that old!' she frowned and laughed as she caught the eye of someone else in the room, 'I was a prostitute myself. This is the first time I've revealed this to any of you but I felt it was important tonight to make my point.' She told us a harrowing story of how she was chained in a brothel room during the day and only released at night when the clients came. It sounded much worse than anything I'd experienced. Being in a position as the lowest of the low and having been treated appallingly by several of the clients, Visal had come away from her experience hardened outwardly, bristly and defensive, but shattered and bruised inwardly. I couldn't square this bristly and defensive character with the warm, effervescent one I saw in front of me now, and I understood that something dramatic had taken place within her. Time ticked on as Visal talked and talked, but no one wanted to leave as we were all caught up in the drama of her story.

Visal's story was unusual in that she'd actually escaped from prostitution herself rather than being rescued. She'd taken the opportunity of a really drunk client who fell asleep on her to make her getaway, amazingly without being noticed. She'd walked right past the eyes of the guard, quivering all over, but the guard had looked right through her as though she wasn't there at all. Clearly, this had required a huge amount of courage, but it was only later when she read the story of the Apostle Peter escaping from prison in the Bible that she'd understood that God had blinded the guard's eyes to her. 'This happened in 1981. I was 18 years old, which is older than all of you here today.' I did a quick calculation in my head to work out how old she was. She wasn't as old as the crow's feet suggested. Perhaps this was a sign of the physical toll her harrowing experience had had on her.

'This was a time when Cambodia was in a mess politically with the demise of the Khmer Rouge, and the Vietnamese Communists were in power. For a while I didn't know what to do as I had no idea where my family were, so I lived with the rats near the sewers and starved, other than when I could get hold of the odd beetle or spider. It was not like Phnom Penh now. The city had been virtually emptied during the Pol Pot regime, and people were only just beginning to move back in from the countryside. There was killing and looting as people tried to stake their claim on land that had been lived in prior to the purging of the city in 1975. You might be asking how this sort of a life could have been better than being in the brothel, but strangely it was, simply because I was free.

'After three weeks of living this way, and running like a headless chicken whenever I saw anyone who looked remotely like they might have designs on young women, I met a monk. I was wandering around Wat Phnom when I bumped into an old man.'

Visal looked down at her watch. 'I've just realised this is taking a lot longer than I'd planned. Feel free to leave if you're tired.' None of us took up her offer; we were rooted.

'He was sitting serenely near the bottom of the east entrance to the Wat, with its rather grand steps leading up to a pagoda, flanked by statues depicting various deities. As I walked by in my constant search for food, he looked at me and smiled. "You look as lost as I felt a few months ago. Would you like to come with me on a journey? Many are leaving Phnom Penh to escape the madness here, and they're going to the Thai borders where there are some refugee camps. In those camps, so I've heard, is the opportunity to get good food, learn English and even be sent overseas to a better life."

'I have no idea why he landed on me, and my first reaction was a prickly response of, "I've got a good life here, thanks. Who are you? Get lost," or something of that ilk. But clearly, this was all bluster and I had no life worth speaking of.

'After a day of avoiding the monk and wandering around the narrow roads and alleyways near the river, I came to the conclusion that I'd nothing to lose by going with him, so I bit my pride and came back, hoping he'd still be there. He was. To cut a long story short, we began a two-month-long trek across the country towards the Thai border, dodging bands of guerrillas and landmines.

'It was certainly an intrepid adventure, although the thing that struck me the most during that time was not the adventure itself but knowing Chamrouen, the monk. Although he was dressed in the garb of a Buddhist monk, he'd had some sort of encounter with Jesus, the details of which I don't remember now, and he was more of a Christ-follower than a Buddhist. He was hardly a typically orthodox Christian as he'd not had much teaching so his understanding of the faith was limited. Nevertheless, his attitude and behaviour towards me were markedly different and more respectful than any other man I'd ever met, so I began to trust him and let my defences down a little.

'After two months we arrived, leaner and fitter but no healthier, at a refugee camp called Nong Chan. While in the camp we got used to waiting and queuing and endless flies, but at least we had good food and medical attention and gradually began to build ourselves up again physically. It wasn't particularly safe there, though, as the camp was a target for the Vietnamese army because of its strategic importance, and we experienced occasional danger from shells and missiles.

'The key for me at that time was encountering some amazing Christian volunteers, particularly my English teacher, who shared Jesus with me and convinced me that God had a purpose and a plan for me. When I made a decision to follow Christ, I was overwhelmed with a sense of love, and the heavy burden of years began to lift off me. Don't get me wrong – I wasn't totally transformed at that point, but it was the start of a journey of healing and faith for me. Likewise for yourselves, don't expect instant transformation with all your failure and weakness dropping off, but do know that the deepest, darkest parts of yourself will be opened up to the light, and you can't not be changed by that.'

I still didn't really understand who Jesus was, but Visal's emotional response as she shared her experience and thoughts with us was enough to let me know that here was something that was unmistakeably liberating, serious and life affirming. A few girls around the room were weeping quietly to themselves.

It had been a long first day for me and it was almost 9pm. The devotional session had gone on much longer than the billed one hour. Not wanting to engage in conversation with anyone and suddenly feeling the full weight of my exhaustion, I avoided all eyes and made my way from the main courtyard in the direction of my room.

Chapter 18
Cambodia, May 2008

I moved the mouse so that the cursor was flashing next to the word 'Thai', clicked and held until the whole word was selected. 'Next click control and C, which is a short-cut for copy.' Uncle Bob was giving us very careful instructions in Khmer, which had to be repeated and rephrased several times as some of the girls just couldn't keep up with what he was saying. This was only my third or fourth time on a computer as I had used Helen's laptop a couple of times when I was learning English with Amy, but this was already so intuitive to me that I was becoming impatient with the pace of the lesson.

'Excellent work there, Song, you're doing great,' Bob murmured to me as he circulated the classroom, checking our progress, 'especially as you missed the first couple of lessons in this sequence.'

Although the pace was slow for me, it was so good to have the opportunity to learn again, and I really looked forward to the morning lessons. Aunty Visal was my Khmer teacher and a middle-aged African American lady named Betty was my English teacher. I knew how to speak Khmer but I'd never learnt to read and write, so Khmer was almost as new to me in many ways as English was. In both, within a matter of months I had progressed rapidly enough to be able to move up to the next level.

The skills were a different matter. The computing classes were easy for me, but I found it so dry that the thought of specialising in this made me kick myself mentally with boredom. I had loved all manner of paper-related crafts such as origami when I was staying with you, Lydia, and I enjoyed card-making skills, but couldn't see myself doing that in the future as an economic venture. The other craft skills eluded me. My fingers couldn't keep up with the instructions that were being given, and I ended up with tightly knotted pieces of embroidery or crocheting which had holes in places where there shouldn't be holes. Photography, though, was unique. I lost track of myself while doing photography. I'd get so engrossed in the composition of a piece that I'd almost forget where I was. However, until a few months after I arrived, no one perceived photography as a way of making money. It was just being taught to us as a way of unleashing our creativity. That was all to change in good time.

The outer shell of my numbness had been penetrated, but there was still a good way to go in terms of getting through to my emotional core. Helga's next job as my counsellor involved finding out more about my experiences of sex slavery. You now already know my story, but there's a good deal of difference between telling someone 30 years after the event and telling someone a few days after your escape from bondage.

I'd spent the previous day talking about the emotional highs and hinting at some of the dark realities, but I hadn't got close yet to the molten centre of my experience. I made things hard for Helga that second day, skirting around the questions she asked and deliberately avoiding too much detail. It's difficult to articulate why I behaved in that way, other than a sense of distorted pride and a desire to hold it all together on my own. You got thus far through my shell. Don't think you can get any further without my permission.

After 45 rather painful minutes, Helga pushed back her loose strands of hair and said with resignation, 'You're clearly not ready to share today. Do you want to finish there? I don't want to hold you against your will.'

As soon as she said that, I felt liberated to let slip a detail in my own way, tantalising her with a taste but refusing to give her any more. 'Radha sold me to a pimp, you know. Isn't that horrible?'

Helga looked at me, visibly shaking with frustration. 'Of course it's horrible, Song. I could have guessed that already. Have you any more to give me?'

I looked at her darkly and silently, willing her to keep pressing me. In retrospect I'm ashamed of how I behaved on that day. The revelations of the day before together with Visal's story had caused a subtle hardening in me, in reaction against the vulnerability I had felt then. As I left the room something gripped my voice box and I breathed an obscenity to Helga, almost against my will. Shaking her head and looking at me with downcast eyes she said, 'IF you're able to treat me with a little more respect, I'll see you at the same time tomorrow.'

The inflated sense of power I imagined I had to control her soon began to deflate as I wandered the corridors, kicking my heels. The thought began to run through my mind: What's so great about kicking someone else when I'm down? I'm not the only one who has suffered. I couldn't understand the nature of my reactions, having never treated anyone in such a deliberately cruel way before.

At 4.15 I went back almost nonchalantly to see Dr Anchaly for the results of my test. I don't remember being overly concerned about what the results would be. I was surprised to see Aunty Visal sitting cross-legged beside her. Aunty looked up at me and beckoned me to sit down next to her, smiling sadly. I sat down and looked at her, wondering what she was doing there. Dr Anchaly raised her eyes from the papers in front of her and said, 'Ah, Song. It's good to see you again. I've just received the results of your HIV test. Visal is here with me to help me tell you the news.'

Visal looked me directly in the eyes, held my hand and said, her mouth a big Oh of compassion, 'There's no easy way to say this, Song. The results have come back that you're HIV positive. Nobody wants to hear this news, but we can help you as much as possible to deal with the reality of it. In fact, we've got a whole team of support including the doctors, your counsellor and myself. We're in this together with you.'

Still not understanding what this really meant, I looked from one woman to the other with my eyes glazed. As if reading my mind, Visal said, 'You don't know what this means, do you?'

'Um, yeah, of course I do,' I said, still in proud mode, 'but you can tell me more,' in acknowledgment of my ignorance.

Probably used to this type of response, Dr Anchaly took over at this point and explained things as simply as she could to a novice like me. 'HIV stands for Human Immunodeficiency Virus. Basically, the human body has something called the immune system, which attacks any viruses or infections that you get. Eating well, sleeping well and generally being in good health can all help to keep your immune system high. HIV is a virus that attacks the immune system itself, and this means that your body won't be able to fight against other sicknesses properly. Aids is what happens when your immune system becomes so weak that it can no longer fight off other viruses, and your body succumbs to other diseases such as TB or pneumonia and leads eventually to death. If all is well and we can treat you effectively, you can stem off Aids for a good many years and even your whole lifetime, but there is no guarantee.'

'But I've not been unwell...' I responded, the word death hitting me with a g-force.

'It's not uncommon for people with HIV not to show any symptoms for a long time, and this is our lifeline really. You're really lucky to live in a generation when antiretroviral drugs are available, and even luckier to be able to have access to these drugs as the World Health Organization has contributed funding to Safe Hands to be able to pay for HIV treatment for our clients. If you're happy to, we'll start you off on a dose of antiretroviral drugs straight away. Please be aware, though, that once you start the drugs you need to continue to take them every day to maintain their effectiveness, so if you prefer you can take away a leaflet and read about the side effects and talk to your counsellor about them. Every medicine has possible side effects, but normally the positive effects outweigh the negative. If you were to find that the negative side effects were making your life a misery, then we could look into trying an alternative drug for you. What do you want to do?'

As she talked, I felt chilly tentacles wrapping themselves around my heart. Dr Anchaly was so matter-of-fact about all this, whereas I was learning of a dire consequence to my life as a prostitute that I had never contemplated seriously before. I didn't know how to respond to her question. What I really wanted to do was to climb to the top of a really high mountain away from anyone else and scream at the top of my lungs, but I knew that wasn't what she was asking me. I swallowed hard and responded with a choked voice, 'I'd like to take the leaflets, please.'

Dr Anchaly was all sympathy when she said, 'I know this will be hard for you to take in, and you may well have all types of emotions to deal with in the coming days.' Reiterating Visal's words of support, she continued, 'One thing you can be extremely grateful about is that you're in the best place here to be taken care of. No one pushes you to share anything you don't want to, but you've got the best counsellors and the best workers who can all get alongside you to support you and encourage you.'

'Are there others here who have HIV, too?' I asked.

'Yes, one or two, but, for reasons of confidentiality I can't disclose who they are, in the same way that I'm not going to tell anyone else your result. You can choose who you want to tell, if you want to tell anyone, as you're old enough to make that decision yourself. But obviously that means that *you're* responsible for making sure you take your drugs in the right way and at the right time.'

Aunty Visal's eyes were ringed with compassion when she added, 'Whatever you do, don't do this on your own, Song. Make sure you share all your fears, anxieties and frustrations with someone, whether it be Helga or someone else you trust. My door is always open if you want to talk to me in particular.'

I closed my eyes. This was not something I wanted to have to deal with right now. Who had dealt me this hand of cards? Out of the prison camp of sexual slavery into the hot coals of HIV, I felt as though my nose was being rubbed against the wall, forcing me to feel, when all I wanted to do was hibernate like a squirrel in the winter. Humbled, I was reminded that even though I'd just pushed Helga away, I couldn't do this on my own, that I would need her and others to get alongside me and help me not just to survive, but to thrive.

Walking back to my room in a daze, I saw Thida coming down the stairs to meet me. 'Aren't you coming to dinner?' she said.

'Not today,' I responded, trying to sound cheerful, but failing miserably. 'I'm not hungry.' This was a lie: in fact, I was ravenous, but I couldn't face seeing other people right now. I just wanted to spend time on my own, unravelling my thoughts and avoiding others seeing my face.

I spent a long time thinking and pondering. My reading skills weren't strong enough yet to be able to properly read the leaflets the doctor had given me, so my thoughts took me down a maze of wonderings. Sometimes I came up against a dark wall, seemingly with no way out, and at other times I found myself coming into an open space filled with light, but as I looked around I still couldn't figure out my next move. I listened to the music coming up from the devotions below and stuffed my fingers in my ears, trying to ignore the persistent voice kneading my brain, reminding me of Visal's words, 'When I made a decision to follow Christ, I was overwhelmed with a sense of love, and the heavy burden of years began to lift off me.' Who on earth was this Christ, and why should I follow Him?!

At around 8pm, Thida came up to our room on cat feet and, seeing my face hidden under the pillow, I imagine she thought better of engaging in conversation with me and slipped out again after a few moments. Martyr-like, I felt slightly disappointed that she hadn't attempted to converse with me in my suffering, although I totally understood why she hadn't. I ignored the grumbling in my stomach that reminded me of my hunger, and gradually drifted into a fitful sleep that was broken frequently through the night by disparate sounds: a random sound of laughter from one of the girls, a racking cough outside my bedroom door or a gecko slithering its way under my bed. As each sound broke into my consciousness, my thoughts began flickering and leaping again, drawn like a magnet to the molten core of pain in my centre.

I woke at 5am and flung aside the clammy sheets with a new sense of urgency, having made the decision a couple of hours earlier that I wasn't going to hide any more. After a rapid shower, I padded downstairs and wandered into the kitchen, knowing that most people would still be sleeping. The cook, a sprightly Khmer lady called Botum, was sitting cross-legged on the floor with a bowl of potatoes in front of her that she was already peeling. 'Good morning, little one,' she chirped cheerfully. 'Can I help you with anything?'

'No help, Aunty, just company,' I smiled. 'Everyone else is sleeping.'

'And that's where you should be, still.'

'No thanks. It's been a long enough night.'

Raising her eyebrows she said, 'It's been a rough one, has it?'

'Yeah, something like that...' I said, being truthful, but giving nothing away.

I sat there quietly for a few moments, just enjoying having a human presence near me, and listening to the scht, scht, scht of the knife. A slender black and white cat came up and rubbed its body against Botum's, purring contentedly. Smiling, I looked questioningly at the cook. Botum nodded her head in acknowledgment, and said, 'That's Stripy; he belongs to Teacher Bob. He often comes and keeps me company while I'm preparing food, so I'm getting quite fond of him.'

'What time do you have to get up?'

'When I'm working, which is most days, apart from Mondays when Lina takes my role, I'm up at 4.30. I've never needed more than six hours' sleep so it suits me perfectly.'

'When I was in prostitution, I often had no more than that too, so I got used to it, but I've been making up for it the past couple of nights. The tiredness has caught up with me.'

Botum kept her head down and gave me a terse 'hmm', making me feel as though I was bothering her. I got up from my seated position, stretched and made some pathetic excuse about needing to go and do something else, and wandered aimlessly back up to the bedroom, where Thida was just beginning to stir. She yawned and rolled over in the bed, looking up at me with sleep-filled eyes. 'You're up early, spring chicken,' she murmured.

'Yeah, I just got up early for a morning wander. Already had my shower and raring to go.' She didn't mention anything about my mood last night, and for that I was grateful. I was ready for exposure again, but I wasn't ready to let my defences down to Thida just yet. Instead, Helga would get everything I'd stored up inside.

'Are you feeling hungry now?'

Actually, my feelings of hunger had been put to rest temporarily, but as she asked me the question it reminded me of the physical reality, and so I could honestly answer, 'Oh yes, can't wait. I'll be first for breakfast this morning.'

'Missed you being around yesterday evening.'

'You know how it is when you need extra sleep,' I said vaguely.

'Yeah, I remember when I first came here. I was the same. Sleeping about 10 to 12 hours a night. It's perfectly normal. At least we can do that here, rather than being expected to cater for men's so-called *needs*.'

I lowered my eyes, not ready to even mention sex to her at this point, although we all knew that was the reality we'd come from, so ultimately there was no point in denying it.

Holding on to the tight little ball of determination to reveal my all, I lived that day going through the motions, smiling as was expected and doing what was asked of me. By the time it came to my counselling session, that tight ball was coiled so tightly that it was ready to spring open to release the tension. Helga welcomed me into the room, all ease and gentleness, as if I hadn't sworn at her so rudely the day before.

I sat down, and the first thing I did was to open my mouth to apologise. 'I'm sorry I was so rude to you yesterday. I don't know what got into me.'

Looking at me with a new sense of both compassion and astuteness, Helga said slowly, 'That's very brave of you to admit your failing. I appreciate it and I forgive you. But don't forget, this isn't really about me; it's about you learning to share and learning to let go and let others in.'

With a lump in my throat, the second thing I did was to show her the crumpled leaflets that I'd carried in my pocket all day.

'What's this? Oh no, I'm so sorry. You found out your results yesterday, didn't you?'

I closed my eyes, feeling the lump dissipate and hot tears drip onto my cheeks as I gave all the contained emotion permission to be exposed. Helga brought her chair close to mine and held my hand wordlessly, while I sobbed and choked. After some time, I sighed heavily and began to speak, 'Until the doctor explained it to me yesterday, I didn't know how serious HIV was. I don't know what to do, I really don't. Can you read these for me, please. I can only read parts of them myself and I don't understand many of the words.'

Helga perused the leaflets and said to me, 'Are you suffering any symptoms now?'

'I don't think so. I haven't been ill for a while, apart from a short bout of flu just recently.'

'Well, you have a choice to make, because once you start taking antiretroviral drugs you need to keep taking them every day for the rest of your life. The aim is to keep the amount of HIV in your body at a low level to prevent the weakening of your immune system. The problem is that they can cause side effects, like nausea and diarrhoea, or sometimes worse. So you could put off taking them until you do experience more illness, or you could start taking them as soon as possible and risk any side effects.'

'I feel like I can't make this decision. Can you make it for me, please?' I said in a small voice.

Helga raised her eyebrows sympathetically and said, 'No, I can't make the decision for you, but I can advise you.'

'And what would you advise?'

'I'd advise you to start taking some tablets soon. There are potential side effects with all drugs, but usually the good outweighs the bad, and it sounds like if one drug causes too many side effects they can switch you to another. If you don't take anything, the HIV will start the process of gradually weakening your immune system, and eventually you'll get sick, whereas if you take the drugs you could put off getting sick for a long, long time, perhaps your whole life. My understanding is that we only have two options here in Cambodia, even with the WHO funding, so there's not much choice of antiretrovirals. They'll be minimising costs that way while still providing you with the chance to manage your HIV.'

'I didn't do this to myself – it was done to me. How is that fair?'

'It's not fair. Many things in life are unfair, I agree with you there, but the question is what are you going to do with what you have been given? What choices are you going to make to deal with the hand you've got?'

'You know, the person I feel most angry with is not the man who gave me HIV, whoever he is, but with Uncle Radha. He's the one who got me into this situation in the first place. I'm angry with him for hurting Aunty Lydia, and I'm angry with him for taking me away from her and the life I had with her, and I'm angry with him for selling me into prostitution and exposing me to all this shit.'

'So are you going to tell me more about him now, then?' Helga gently probed.

Feeling as ready as I ever would be, I began a slow drip-feed of revelation about Radha and the details that had led to my sexual slavery. My anger was not pure anger as it was confused with the other feelings I'd had for him, including affection, and that made it all the more painful to acknowledge what he had done to me.

'Can I also conclude that you're angry because you loved him?' Helga said when I was halfway through telling my story.

Pausing mid-flow, I didn't even have to search for an answer, but I felt the bitterness marking itself on my face. 'Of course!' I spat out, as though I'd chewed on a red-hot chilli.

'Betrayal can be one of the most painful human experiences,' she said after some time, before asking me something unexpected. 'Who do you think is suffering most from his betrayal of you? You or him?'

Stupid question, I thought. 'Me,' I said edgily, wondering where this was going.

Helga shifted in her chair and leaned forward to look at me intently. I turned my eyes away, uncomfortable. 'How does it make you feel to hold on to the anger you feel about what he did?'

'Angry?'

'What does that do to your mind and your body?'

'Well, to be honest, most of the time I'm not thinking about it, but when I do the anger grips me so tightly I almost feel like I'm going to explode, if that makes any sense?'

'Yes, it makes total sense. My point is that if you forgive him and let go of the pain of what he did to you, you'll feel much better.' I opened my mouth to protest, but she held up her hand and continued, 'Just wait till I've explained something. Forgiveness doesn't mean that you accept the wrong he's done. What he did was clearly heartless and selfish. It means that you give him over to God to deal with the consequences of his sins, and you release yourself from bondage. You'll be the one suffering most from unforgiveness, while Radha won't feel the effects of that. He may feel his own pain if he has any conscience, but you may think deep inside that if you hold on to your anger he'll be punished in some way, but this is actually not true; you only punish yourself.'

I pressed my fingers tightly against my eyes and watched the black and gold flickering kaleidoscope behind my eyes, and breathed deep and hard. 'I don't know if I can do that – at least, not yet. It's too painful.'

'That's totally fine, and you can take as long as you want, or never forgive him if you choose, but remember that forgiveness will actually make the pain less in the long run.'

174

'But who can I blame if I don't have Radha to blame?!' I blurted out.

Helga turned her head away thoughtfully. 'That's a very good question, and there's no straightforward answer. Let me start by telling you a story.

'There was a wealthy businessman who had two sons. The oldest son, Bourey, was hard-working and always did well at his studies, and was obedient and devoted. The youngest son, Kosal, was good-looking, a little arrogant and always pushed the boundaries. When he was 18 he figured he'd had enough of the restrictions of being at home, and decided to leave. But he didn't just leave; he came to his dad and asked him if he could have all of his inheritance – in other words, all the money he would get when his dad died. Can you imagine how his father must have felt?

'His dad didn't argue with him or try to stop him. He gave him the money and said to him, "I hope all goes well with you," and Kosal left without a backwards glance, flicking his credit card in his pocket and calculating how he was going to spend his money. Because he had loads of money he found it easy to gather lots of companions around him, and he spent all his money on meals out, fancy cars, wild parties in hotels with prostitutes, and he basked in the sunshine of his popularity.

'After one particularly long night gambling in a casino, he lost the remains of what money he had left and he found himself spiralling further and further into debt. In the end he no longer had any money left to pay for even a decent hotel, and he was exhausted, unshaven and beginning to feel the rumblings of hunger. His companions all drifted away, having lost interest in him once he was no longer spending money on them, but he knew he couldn't blame them as he'd never invested any real concern or friendship into them. He wandered the streets near the river and watched the people begging and selling things on the pavements, and he asked himself, "Is that going to be my lot in life?"

'Kosal had vivid memories of his father coming down the stairs and laughing warmly, his whole body shaking with the laughter, and of his mother holding his hand tightly and calling him her little pumpkin when he was small, and a lump came into his throat as he was struck by how ungrateful he had been for all the good things in his home life.

175

"I've been away for three years now and haven't called once to see how they're getting on. Do you think they'll accept me if I come back now? I know I've done wrong. Maybe I can ask Father if he'll take me on as one of his employees for a while until I've paid back the debt I owe him."

'So Kosal went into some back alleyway bathroom and shaved himself as neatly as he could without a mirror, washed his clothes in a bucket and begged a neighbour for use of an iron. He rehearsed over and over what he was going to say when he got home, expecting a cold response from his father. But when Kosal knocked on the door, his father flung the door open and his arms wide and called out, "Kosal's back!!" He pulled him into the house with a bear hug, bouncing up and down with childlike glee. Kosal kept trying to open his mouth to grovel and beg, but his father so overwhelmed him with his love and acceptance that he couldn't find the words. He prepared an enormous welcome back party for him with party hats and the best champagne – the full works.

'Meanwhile, Bourey was on a short business trip away for a couple of days and arrived back while the three-day celebration was in full flow. "What's all this? Has Dad managed to clinch himself another good deal?" One of his younger cousins rolled into the entrance hall on a toy bicycle, blowing a trumpet. Seeing Bourey's look of surprise he yelled out excitedly, "Kosal's back! Kosal's back!"

'Bourey was not exactly impressed. In fact, he felt quite resentful and went up to his private gym to have a good workout to get rid of the anger he felt. The cousin went and told Bourey's dad that Bourey was home. When he didn't come down to join them, his father slipped away from the party to have a quiet word with his eldest son. "Hey, my son, why haven't you come downstairs to greet Kosal?"

'Bourey growled and changed his pace on the treadmill so he could talk. "Dad, Kosal has been away for three years and hasn't given a thought to any of us, and you throw him a slap-up party as soon as he waltzes back in!"

'"Bourey, Bourey. You have been with me the whole time, enjoying the good life and spending time with your family. Kosal has been lost to goodness knows where, doing his own thing, and now he's come back again: he's been found. Shouldn't you be happy for him?!"'

Helga raised her eyes to me searchingly and said, 'And that's where the story ends. Why do you think I told you that story?'

'I don't know,' I said. 'Something to do with not blaming?'

'You're on the right track. This story is actually based on a story that Jesus told in the Bible, and the father represents God. The father accepts the youngest son back in spite of his wild ways, because he loves him and in the end he came back to him. As a Christian, I believe that God accepts us all, whether we're like the rebellious younger son who later turns from his selfish ways, or like the resentful older brother, feeling like we've always done the right thing and haven't been noticed. Jesus turns on its head the whole tendency of humans to blame by saying that we're all to "blame" in some way, and all in need of the father's love. How did you feel about the brothers in that story? Which one could you relate to the most?'

'I hated the youngest brother to start with, especially the way he was so selfish and uncaring, and I know I would have felt most sympathy for the older brother, but I could also relate to the younger brother feeling so dirty and unworthy to come back home.'

'Yeah, it's an incredible story that gets right to the heart of what it means to be human. I think it speaks to us all in some way or another.' Helga glanced at her watch and said, 'You know what, we've been talking for two hours now. Time has flown. I'm sure you still have lots of questions and doubts, and you probably don't have many of your fears related to HIV resolved yet, but I hope you're feeling a bit better anyway. We'll meet again at the same time tomorrow if you're up for it?'

'Definitely,' I said, sensing that a doorway had been prised open, and fresh air was blowing through.

Part 3
Full circle

Chapter 19
England, November 2036

'So you did, didn't you?' Lydia sat forward in her seat, half willing Song to resist, but knowing that it wasn't going to happen.

'Did what?' said Song, sensing the defensive tone in Lydia's voice.

'Succumb to the God squad?'

Song bubbled with laughter, a peal of laughter that chimed out like bells. 'I don't know that I would put it that way. I certainly gave in to the pull of God's love eventually, and I did give my life to Jesus, yes.'

'How long did it take?' Lydia leaned back in her seat and looked at Song quizzically. She was not being deliberately antagonistic. She'd experienced real compassion for Song's suffering throughout the telling of the tale, but was struggling to square this scale of suffering with her bona fide faith in God.

'It was probably only a matter of months. With Helga and Aunty Visal having a strong influence in my life, and even thinking back to how Dara had been so different to other men, I didn't have much chance of resisting. Well, I did in one sense. There's always the option to say no, and many did and of course do, but with me it was a slow drawing in to a foregone conclusion.'

With many interruptions, questions and tearful interludes, Song's story had taken some hours to tell. It was 1am, but both women were on an adrenaline high and had no desire to sleep yet.

Tired of sitting, Song began pacing the room and picking up trinkets and photos, mostly of Lydia's friends and birth family. 'Did you keep any photos of Radha?' she asked.

'No, of course not,' Lydia responded flatly, and after a prolonged pause she asked Song her own question. 'Did you forgive Radha in the end?'

'Yes. That took as long as it took me to accept Jesus.' Song fingered a photo frame of Lydia's mum when she was young, and then turned cautious eyes to Lydia. 'In fact, when I was about 21, I actually met him again.'

'You did?! How did that happen?'

'Well, it's another longish story, but if you don't mind...?'

181

'Please.' That was all Lydia needed to say to release a further torrent of words.

'I'll have to backtrack a little bit if you want me to explain fully.'

'You can get to the parts in between later if you like. I want to know about this, not that I… Anyway, you understand.'

Song exhaled, knowing that this was not going to be easy for Lydia. 'Do you remember Jars of Clay?'

'Yes, I do. A lovely café.' Jars of Clay was a café run by a Christian organisation in order to give girls from difficult backgrounds the chance to earn an honest living. It was used predominately by expats and other foreigners.

'Well, at 21, I was developing my photographic skills and contacts, but in the meantime, before that became my main thing, I was working as a waitress in Jars of Clay. One day I was making a cappuccino for a customer and had my back to the door, when I heard a customer behind me place an order with my colleague, Lena, in Khmer. "A black coffee, please." That was all he said, but I recognised his voice at once. I turned around as slowly as I could to the customer I was serving, but I began shaking so hard that the cup clattered on the saucer and the coffee spilt over the edge.

'"What's wrong with you, Song?" Lena said under her breath, as I was normally very efficient at my job. I didn't say anything in response, knowing that she wasn't really looking for an answer, but began apologising profusely to my red-haired customer. "No problem, no problem," he said, waving his hands. I could see Uncle Radha out of the corner of my eye. He had noticed my name being used, I was sure of that, but I couldn't read his expression. It was only ten years later, and he must have recognised me as, although now a woman, I was still recognisably me. As you can imagine, my heart was pounding and everything in me was on high alert. I had forgiven Radha, but it's very different to do something like that when someone's not around, and I wasn't expecting to ever see him again. There he was, in the flesh, only a few feet away from me. He didn't try any of his charm, but just sat there quietly, drinking his coffee and reading *The Cambodia Daily*.'

'Did he talk to you? Did you find anything out?' Lydia's questions tumbled over themselves in an urgency to get out.

'Yes, but not then and there. I didn't want to miss what would probably be my only opportunity to find out the truth, but Radha didn't give any signs of wanting to communicate. In the end I summoned up all my courage and whispered to him as I was clearing a nearby table, "Can I talk to you sometime?" He glanced over at me, took a pen out of his pocket and showed it to me, then wrote something on the edge of his newspaper. As I sidled past his table I saw a few scrawled words in English. *Café Yejj at 4pm? What day?*

'I mentally checked my rota and figured I would be free at 4pm the next day as I only worked a half-day on Wednesdays. "Tomorrow, Wednesday," I mouthed to him and he nodded imperceptibly. He clearly didn't want to communicate with me in a place where I was known, which made sense really from his point of view, even if it was cowardly.'

'Interesting, as Café Yejj is only just round the corner from Jars of Clay!'

'Yes, it was until about 2016, and then it moved to bigger premises along Sisowath Quay.'

'Where were you living at this point?'

'I was living in an apartment with two of my friends from Safe Hands – Lena and Thida – in the area near Psar Orussey. I mentioned to Thida that I was planning to meet Uncle Radha, and I also mentioned it to the leader of my church, a trustworthy man called Pastor Phirum. Thida thought I was mad. Pastor Phirum kindly suggested that he could hang around nearby so that he would be within reach if anything untoward were to happen.'

'So was the meeting revelatory?'

'What do you mean "revelatory"?' This was one of the few words in English that Song did not seem to know.

'Did you find out things that you didn't know before?'

'Ah, yes, like revelation!' Song chuckled. 'It was, actually. I had the sense that he was really torn up about what had happened. He kept lifting his eyes and giving me searching looks, then scrunching them up as though he couldn't bear to imagine what had happened to me. Conversation was stilted. It was really hard. He kept saying, "I'm so sorry. I'm so sorry," and told me about his endless sleepless nights. He even tried to put a considerable amount of cash into my hands in an attempt to compensate for all that I'd gone through, which I obviously refused to take. I think he was relieved that I hadn't suffered too much at the hands of my pimps or clients as I was there and well in front of him. The main thing you want to know is why, isn't it?'

'Of course,' Lydia said with expectancy, picking up an empty mug from the floor and rotating it in her hands.

'Do you remember the letter he received that he wouldn't show you? It was from his mum. She had cancer and the treatment was going to cost the family more than they could afford, and you know he'd have done anything to help his family. She was asking him to help financially but he knew he wouldn't be able to afford the treatment himself without going into debt, and as you know, he hated the thought of that. I guess selling me for a good US $1000 was an easy way to make some cash.'

Lydia scrunched her hands together around the mug, and her knuckles whitened. 'What a complete idiot. He could have asked me to help. We could have found a way somehow. I don't understand how he could have sacrificed all that we had together by going to such extremes! My God, it makes me angry to know the truth; it could have been so different. But at least I know now, and I don't have to feel so in the dark as to why. Not knowing is worse, even though after all these years I've tried to make a show of moving on. Did you seek any form of legal redress?'

'Do you know what? I couldn't bear to do anything about it after all those years. As far as I knew, I was the only one he'd ever done that to, and Radha somehow seemed so lost and tormented that I genuinely saw him as an object of pity rather than anger. I didn't want to take any money from him as my heart cried out to me that the spiral of moneymaking and debt needed to be broken. I can't fully explain it though, as a part of me knows that he needs to experience justice for what he did, but I feel as though he's already experienced enough emotional punishment in the years since. And somehow I don't feel bitter about it. You probably think I should, but the anger I did experience has genuinely gone now as I can see the hand of God in it all, turning around the awful situation and bringing good out of it.'

Song paused and said quietly, 'I hope I did the right thing in coming to see you and telling you everything that happened.'

'Yes, yes! I wish you'd come earlier.' Lydia's cheeks reddened with the emotion she was feeling.

'I understood from what Uncle Radha said that it was his pride that stood in the way of asking you for financial help. I'm so sorry.'

'Don't be sorry for me. You're the one that suffered the most,' said Lydia, tears seeping down the lines of her face. Song came and sat next to the older woman on the couch and they held each other tightly, both weeping at the memories and the lost years, the younger bringing comfort to the older.

'So why didn't you come to see me earlier?' Lydia asked after some time, throwing another sodden tissue into the wastebasket.

'There are several reasons. One is that I wasn't sure if you would want to see me again – silly, I know. Secondly, it took me a long time to track down where you'd gone and what you were doing. You only joined Facebook recently, although for the life of me I can't understand why. I had searched previously for Lydia Philips but not found you, though of course I wasn't sure if you'd got married and changed your name. Also, I didn't have enough money to travel to England until I'd built up a name for myself in the photography world, and it took some time to save up the money needed, as well as obviously having a family in between.'

'I feel like we've got so much catching up to do. You're a real daughter to me, even though the time we had together was so short...' Lydia's breath caught in her voice, as though she had stumbled back from tripping over the edge of a cliff. 'My goodness, I've forgotten to ask you something really important. How is your health? You look well, so I'm assuming...?'

'I'm absolutely fine. I'm healed,' Song smiled.

'You mean that the antiretrovirals are keeping the HIV under control?'

'No, I mean that I'm no longer HIV positive.'

'Wait... have you been healed by medicines?'

'No. That of course would be possible now, but I can honestly say that in my case that's not what happened.'

'Well, what then?' said Lydia, impatient with this slow drip-feed of information.

'God healed me. All the test results have been verified scientifically. This is real.'

Lydia exhaled slowly. She couldn't hold off the gentle pressing-in any longer. 'I need some fresh air. Do you want to come outside with me into the back garden? You came with a coat, right?' Song nodded, bemused at Lydia's sudden need for a late-night walk in the cold November air. 'I can lend you a hat and scarf if you need it?'

'Thank you,' Song said politely.

'You can tell me more of your story outside.' Song fumbled into unfamiliar layers of winter woollies while Lydia slipped into her coat and hat and fumbled into thick boots. Lydia led Song out through the French windows at the back of the room where they'd been talking. A biting wind blew inside as the windows opened. It must have been about five or six degrees Celsius but the wind made it feel quite a bit colder, and the women were glad of the layers once they stepped outside into Lydia's pleasantly patioed garden. The patio stretched out for a few metres before disappearing into dark shades of lawn and bush.

'I've been hiding a long time,' Lydia revealed, opening up before Song had the chance to tell the rest of her story. It was as though the fresh air was opening up a new vista of possibility for Lydia.

'Hiding from what?'

Lydia paced the patio, not looking directly at Song. 'From myself and from God. All those years ago, when I was in Cambodia, I kept God away by taking the typical liberal approach of doubting Christians' intentions and viewing with a cynical eye everything the Bakers and others that I knew said or did. Then after Radha took you away I couldn't reconcile the idea of a loving God with what had happened. Even now I don't get it, but having listened to you and your story I'm starting to believe that perhaps God is so much bigger than your or my tragic little stories. I've been viewing everything spiritual through a narrow lens, thinking I was being open-minded, when actually I've been the complete opposite. I hate to admit that but it's true. I thought that being nice was enough, but I've realised it's not. Being nice only papers over the shaky walls of self.' Lydia turned to face Song, who was listening quietly. 'Ha, ha. I bet you weren't expecting that!'

186

Song smiled wryly. 'You're right, I wasn't. But I'm glad to hear you say it.'

Lydia was in the mood to talk so Song let her continue. 'I never married, did I? That was my way of protecting myself from being hurt again. But keeping men at bay was also my way of keeping myself from God, invulnerable and impenetrable. When you said that God had healed you of HIV, I felt that invulnerable wall being pierced; I don't know any other way of explaining it. Is that all it takes? One word?' Lydia was laughing and crying all at once.

'That's the power of the Holy Spirit,' Song responded gently. 'Using powerful and convincing words won't change anyone unless the Holy Spirit is working in that person's life.'

'But now, I really do want to know more about your healing.' Lydia clapped her gloved hands together with glee, like a young child.

A gust of wind sallied past, bringing a sharp tingle of tears to Song's eyes. Lydia turned to her and said with apologetic recognition, 'It's really cold out here, isn't it? We can go back inside if you want. My head is clearer now.'

'Yes please. I would prefer that, to be honest.'

'Another drink?' Lydia asked Song as they thawed their hands under the cushions and allowed their tense muscles to relax in the warmth of the room.

'Drinking, drinking, drinking…' Song laughed. 'I'll say yes, not because I'm thirsty but to have something warm to hold.'

'What did you decide about the antiretroviral tablets in the end?' Lydia asked, as she placed a steaming mug into Song's hands.

'Well, naturally, because of the advice Helga and the others gave me, I decided to take them. My body responded with a certain amount of nausea in the first three months of taking them, but it wasn't too bad and didn't actually lead to vomiting, so the doctor decided to keep me on that drug. After the first three months the nausea settled down and I barely noticed any negative effects after that. So you might ask, how did it come about that I even thought about being healed?'

'You read my mind!'

'It was,' Song counted on her fingers, thinking to herself, '2014. I was almost 18 and I'd been at Safe Hands for a number of years,

187

building up my photography skills and language abilities and coming to terms with what had happened through a process of continual counselling and emotional healing.'

'Was Helga your counsellor the whole time?'

'Yes, she was, which was brilliant. Some of the others had three or four different counsellors, and with each one they felt they had to start all over again in terms of building a relationship and trust.

'Anyway, about two years after moving into the centre I joined a church that met outside, the one led by Pastor Phirum, who I've already mentioned.'

'How did it come about?'

'Pastor Phirum was a distant relative of Aunty Visal's and he used to come into the centre now and again to lead devotionals. One time he gave an invitation to us girls to come and visit his church (with the permission of Visal and under security). I and one other girl, whose name I don't remember now, were the only ones who took up his offer. For me it was out of curiosity and a strong liking for this man who displayed many qualities of character similar to Visal's own. When I visited I encountered God in a real way and came into contact with people who showed me what genuine family could be like.'

'What do you mean by that?'

'Good question. I mean they showed selfless interest in my life, genuine kindness, patience and a desire to see me change and grow, but without putting undue pressure on me to do so. As time outside the centre was restricted I didn't have many opportunities to get to know them really well until I was 16 and had freedom to come and go as I pleased, but nevertheless, what I did see was real and not superficial.'

'Is it a Khmer or a Western church?'

'It's Khmer but the leaders had built very good relationships with Westerners so there were and still are frequent Western visitors of different backgrounds. Anyway, getting back to the point, in January 2014 Pastor Phirum arranged a healing meeting in the church, to which we were free to bring guests who were in need of physical or emotional healing. There was no outside speaker, as you might expect at a healing meeting.'

'I had no expectations one way or the other,' Lydia smiled. 'I'm merely learning to step out of Miss Cynical Pants' shoes.'

Song chuckled at this description and continued, 'Pastor Phirum doesn't believe in building up unnecessary hype in order to release God's miracle-working powers. He wanted people to come not because of some well-known name but because they genuinely wanted an encounter with God. You know, when I came to the meeting that day, I wasn't even thinking about needing healing from HIV. HIV had affected my life so little that it wasn't on the radar of my major concerns. That might sound strange because obviously it was a big deal when I first found out that I was positive, but other than the first three months of taking my drugs I wasn't physically affected by them. I almost feel as though there are others suffering with HIV or Aids who deserved – or should I say needed – healing much more than I did. Don't take that to mean I'm not grateful. I am so, so grateful, but totally overwhelmed at the same time by God's small kindnesses to me.

'This is how it happened. We were in the middle of singing and praising God. No invitation to come forward for prayer or word about healing had been brought at that time. I was simply standing near the back of the room about two feet away from the closest fan. I remember exactly where I was standing. I can see the spot of yellowed paint on the ceiling above my head even now and remember the red T-shirt of the girl standing next to me. Suddenly what felt like an electric shock pulsated through my body from head to toe. I began to shudder all over and fell backwards as I was unable to hold myself upright. I felt pinned to the ground for what must have been ten minutes, and for all that time waves of joy and peace were washing over me. When I stood up again, I had no idea what had just taken place other than that I'd been bowled over literally by the power of God. A few minutes later, Pastor Phirum began calling out words of knowledge for people who needed healing.'

'What do you mean "words of knowledge"?' Lydia asked, frowning.

'Words of knowledge are basically when God gives someone an insight into someone else's life. Usually these are things that the receiver couldn't possibly know on their own so they're clearly received supernaturally. It'll become clearer when I give you the examples from Pastor Phirum. He called out from the front, "There's someone here with a right toe that is causing them problems, possibly from an ingrowing toenail. I can see a person bowed down with a spiritual oppression that is caused by a trauma that took place two years ago." He gave a couple more words, which I can't remember now, and then he spoke the words that were relevant to me. "Someone here has just been healed of HIV. Go and get yourself tested as soon as possible to check that this is true."

'Can you imagine how I felt? My heart thrilled with the certainty that this was me. I'd never have known I'd been healed, though, unless he'd given that word of knowledge. I just thought I was experiencing God's power and love in a general sort of way, so I wouldn't have dreamt of getting myself checked out medically. I didn't go and share what had happened with the whole church that day as I didn't have evidence yet, and that's what the word had asked me to do, but at the end of the meeting I went and spoke to the pastor about my experience and he was delighted – he'd not known I was HIV positive – and reminded me to go and get evidence for my healing.'

Song looked at Lydia, watching for her reaction. Lydia sat forward in her chair with her eyes wide open, opening and closing her fists gently, not saying a thing.

'I went to visit Dr Anchaly a few days later. To get an appointment I told a white lie that I'd been having some disturbing side effects related to my illness as I didn't want the receptionist to know the reason.

'"You want to retest for HIV?" the doctor said wearily when I explained my real reason for being there. "But you already have a positive result. That's not going to have changed."

'"Pleeaase!" I begged. "I really want you to do this for me. I believe it has changed." I said this with a dry mouth and palpitating pulse because, despite having had a certainty in my spirit, natural doubts and fears about being wrong had wormed their way into the forefront of my thinking.

'Dr Anchaly sighed, bit her lip and looked at me in frustration. I murmured a silent prayer to God that she would relent. She said, "You know it's a waste of time and resources to do this, but other than that I can't see any reason why we can't."

'"Thank you!" I said. Not wanting to overdo the excitement and risk her changing her mind, I kept it to one thank you. Her face was pinched and hard as she took the blood from me, and she simply told me that the result would be available in three days' time.'

'And it came back clear?' said Lydia, impatiently.

Song looked at Lydia with a discreet pleasure showing around her eyes and her mouth. 'Yes, as I said before, it did.'

'Wow! I don't know what else to say. Wow!' All Lydia's previous measured, conscientious thinking about what was possible and impossible began to tumble, each delicately placed book shifting one by one in her mind. Even though Song had already told her that she'd been healed of HIV, the knowledge of actually *how* that had happened produced a seismic shift.

'You don't have to say anything if you don't want to,' Song said delightedly.

'What did the doctor say?'

'Dr Anchaly was quite amusing in her response. She said, "Well, it certainly is a miracle – an unusual and disconcerting result." She didn't express any sense of delight or joy for me not being HIV any more! I, of course, told everyone I knew who had known I was HIV positive, and even those that hadn't known, as I wanted as many as possible to know how God had healed me.'

'Of course you did,' Lydia assented, then looking at her watch, she turned to Song and said, 'It's 2.30am. Really, let's go to bed now. You must be shattered. I know I'm getting that way. I still have a few questions left to ask but they can wait, I assure you!'

Song yawned widely, as though only now allowing herself the luxury of doing so. 'Yes, please. That would be wonderful.'

Late morning came, and a half-glazed sense of unreality tinged Lydia's mind as she awoke. She had a disorientating feeling that it was her friend Sally in her house, and began mentally preparing for further banter about school dramas and politics, when she recalled that it wasn't Sally; it was Song. Her world had undergone a cataclysmic change in 24 hours, and that earlier world and her place in it seemed so artificial now.

She shuffled downstairs to prepare brunch, planning on leaving her guest to sleep as long as she needed, but just after putting her slippered feet on the stairs, Song's door inched open and a bleary-eyed Song poked her head out. Lydia smiled at her and said, 'The shower's next door to you on the left-hand side if you want to freshen up. I gave you a towel, didn't I?' Song nodded. 'Do join me downstairs when you're ready.'

'I didn't imagine everything you told me last night, did I?' Lydia asked in a bemused way, placing a pile of hot, buttered French toast between them on the kitchen table. 'Please, help yourself to honey or jam, and have as much as you want.'

'Of course you didn't; it's all real. I'm real. Look, touch my hands!' Song replied, joining in with good humour.

Lydia laughed. 'How did you sleep?'

'Beautifully. The bed was the most comfortable I've ever slept in.'

'Really?' Lydia asked rhetorically, pleased. 'I slept better than I have for a few nights now, though the details of your story kept me on a high level of adrenaline for the first hour, in spite of being totally ready to sleep by then.

'I'm so happy to have you back with me.' Lydia addressed Song's steady gaze. 'It's ok, I know you're not going to come and live with me in England as you have a family and an international career, but at least we can have regular contact now.'

Song paused before speaking with measured words. 'Actually, I was going to ask you: would you like to come and live with me back in Cambodia? You don't have to respond straight away. I know it would be hard for you in many ways.'

'You mean because of memories of Radha?'

'Well, yes.'

Lydia psshawed and said with a new lightness, 'Come on, it was all a long time ago now, and if there's one thing I've learnt over the course of the night, it's the need for forgiveness. There's not much chance of me bumping into him now, really, is there? And if I did, I'd deal with it, somehow.'

'So, you're thinking…?'

Lydia spoke over Song in her determination and said, 'Song, it sounds wonderful. We could catch up on many lost years, and there aren't many ties holding me to England, to be honest. Plus, I was always more comfortable living in a foreign climate in some ways. I know I'm getting on a bit, but...'

'Don't be silly. You've got a good 20 years left in you, I'm sure!' Song said affectionately.

'I'm certainly stirred by the idea of coming to live with you, but I'll need to think through the practicalities more before I make any final decision. As I said last night, I've still got a couple of big unanswered questions, but there's no hurry. When do you need to leave, by the way?'

Song flicked her eyes to one side, as though glancing at an internal calendar and said, 'Sara is performing in the school band in four days' time, a performance I've promised I'll be back for, and my return flight is booked for 8th November, so we've got a couple of days for now, and then after that...'

Lydia scraped some honey onto the toast in front of her and began munching thoughtfully. A companionable silence descended while the two of them sat together like mother and daughter.

'One thing I'd like to know is whether you ever overcame your fear of alcohol? I'll never forget that time you reacted so strongly when you were at Helen's. It really scared me.'

Song looked down at her toes and wriggled them. 'To an extent, yes, but I think that's one of the areas that hasn't been fully healed in my life. I still don't like to see people getting drunk. It fills me with a sense of overwhelming panic to the extent that I just have to get away and breathe deeply to stop me hyperventilating. But it's not like it was before. I won't react now when I simply see a bottle of alcohol. I can handle it when people are drinking, as long as they're drinking in moderation.'

'How did your experiences of sexual slavery impact on your growth into womanhood and eventually handling a loving sexual relationship? I feel like I'm interviewing you, sorry!'

'No need to apologise; it's fine!' Song said, though her voice did shake a little. 'Do you want the honest and full answer or the half-baked answer? I don't know how much you can handle, after all.'

'What a question! Of course I want the full answer. I'm past pretending.'

Song exhaled through pursed lips and closed her eyes, 'That's what I thought you'd say. It wasn't an easy process, to be honest. This might sound very odd to you, as clearly sex was something that had been forced upon me and was painful in the early days, and in many ways it did repulse me. But early sex, even unwanted sex, had opened up natural sexual feelings in me that I shouldn't have known at such an early age. I craved sexual fulfilment for many years after coming out of prostitution, but it was so tinged with perverse imaginings and disturbing memories that I knew it wasn't good. Once I felt comfortable to, I shared these thoughts and feelings with Helga and we prayed through them. I had to be set free from demonic oppression, and only then the disturbing imaginings lifted, though the sexual feelings were still there.'

'What do you mean by "set free from demonic oppression"?'

'That's something else that would need several hours to explain properly.' Song scratched her head and wrinkled her nose.

'Try me.'

'I'll try to explain as simply as I can. As Christians, we believe in the reality of the spiritual world and that any form of sin can open up the door to demonic forces, especially if it's repetitive sin. That's not to say that all sin is demon inspired. It certainly isn't; most of it is just from our own human desires that have strayed away from God's will. However, when there's ongoing or perpetual sin that's hard to break or addictive, or when abuse has taken place, chances are that the demonic has taken hold. It doesn't mean you're completely possessed and are unable to function as yourself, as you might have seen in films. It just means that certain areas of your life come under demonic influence. Jesus is stronger than all those forces and they can't stand against His power, but I had to allow Jesus to take control of my imaginings and sexual desires and to cast out those ungodly elements.

'This may sound all very fantastical but I can assure you it's real. I was so much lighter and felt less dirty once Helga and others had prayed for me to be set free from demonic oppression. When I eventually married and began having sex again, it was very different. It felt much purer and more joy filled than prostitution. I won't pretend I didn't struggle at all with fears and wrong imaginings. It was a process. However, without the deliverance I'd already received I think it would have been much harder and perhaps impossible to have established a truly healthy sexual union.'

'It's unfamiliar territory to me and I won't say it makes complete sense,' said Lydia thoughtfully, 'but it certainly has a ring of truth about it. I told you, my Miss Cynical Pants hat has been removed! Some more toast?'

'No thanks, I'm stuffed. I haven't had French toast since I lived with you and it takes me back to that special time.'

'So you still see it as special, in spite of the bad that came out of it?'

'Oh, definitely. And, in fact, I wouldn't change any of it now as it was all part of the learning curve and growth that God took me on, into and out of slavery and ultimately to Christ.' Song glanced at Lydia with her turned-up lips and furrowed brows and said, 'I can see you're confused by that.'

'Yes, because it implies that God wanted you to go through all that hell, and how could He want that if He's a loving God?'

'That's the same sort of question I wrestled with in the early days. You know, I don't think there's an easy answer! I do know that if a loving God could send His only son to suffer on the cross because of the love that He bore the whole world, then that tells us something about the nature of God's care for us. There's a bigger picture in mind when God allows us to go through suffering. He wants us to know Him better, to develop and strengthen our character and perseverance. He doesn't want robotic followers – people who pretend to love Him but don't do it wholeheartedly. God doesn't bring about suffering, but He allows it in order to achieve His good purposes. In my case, when I think about what I went through, it was through it that I ultimately came to know Him. I can also use my experiences to share with others going through challenging circumstances and encourage them.'

Lydia closed her eyes and rested her forehead on the heel of her hand. 'It all sounds too pat. I've heard arguments like that before and just interpreted it as brainwashing, but when I hear it from your mouth, knowing you and the way your mind works, I know you've not been brainwashed.'

195

'Not in the sense of having no control over my thoughts, you're right, but in some ways I have been "brainwashed", in the sense of allowing God permission to gradually transform my thinking and make my mind more like His.' Song laughed as she saw Lydia's mouth open loose and shapeless like a dumbfounded teenager.

'I should have given up being surprised by you, Song, but somehow you're still managing to do it. Brainwashed but not brainwashed – where's the logic in that?!'

Song shrugged and said, 'Exactly as I explained.'

'One thing I can't shake from my mind is your friends in the brothel – Sodarath and the others. Do you have any idea what happened to them, and did you ever attempt to make contact with them again?'

'Soda.' As she repeated her name, Song's voice cracked and a single drop of sorrow appeared around the rim of her eyeliner and rolled down her cheek. 'Somehow I managed to blank that out of my memory when I was telling you my story yesterday. I did find out what happened to her and I can only say that she was one of those that tragically no one was on hand to rescue until it was too late.' Lydia waited breathlessly for Song to continue. 'When I met her again it was quite by accident. It wasn't a planned meeting. I had left Safe Hands by then and had recently got engaged so my life was spinning in happy new directions. One day, I'd finished printing some of my photos at one of the local stores and was crossing the road at the north end of Monivong Boulevard, near where that small supermarket Thai Huot is based. I don't know how much you remember about beggars and the way some of them would use small children to draw custom in?'

'I remember very well,' Lydia said grimly.

'As I was crossing the central barrier between the roads, I felt a tugging on my ankles and looked down to see a small child pulling at my feet and the plaintive cry of "N'yam bai"[6] being uttered again and again. My heart turned over as I could see sores around her mouth and the beginnings of a pot belly, indicating severe malnutrition. I looked around to see if there was any adult nearby, prepared to leave if I could see one. I remembered my own childhood situation and bent

---

[6] N'yam bai literally means 'Eat rice'. Here it is being used by a small child to indicate a need for food, or hunger.

down and handed the girl a couple of thousand riel.[7] You can't help all the children and, as you know, helping them on the streets is not always the best way of genuinely providing support, but something in me tugged at me and compelled me to give. The child pocketed the money and I continued to cross the road over to the other side. I looked back, unable to let this go yet, and saw a scrawny female adult appear. It was obvious that she'd seen me as I could see her staring at me across the melee of traffic. Presumably the fact that she had seen me and recognised me had drawn her out from wherever she'd been hiding.'

'Soda?' Lydia gasped.

'I'm afraid so.' Song drummed her fingers archly on the kitchen table as though typing rapidly on a keyboard, and breathed out. 'The young woman picked up the child and crossed the road to join me on the other side, signalling to me with one hand to wait, and ignoring the beeping of the four-wheel drivers indignant at her defiantly breaking the unspoken rules of the road. I waited with bated breath, not having a clue who she was. As she drew closer, she stared into my eyes, which showed me that this was someone who knew me well as a peer, and clutched my hand in a not-too-friendly grip. "You did forget about us!" her voice hissed in my ear. "You said you never would!" When she spoke, a shock wave went through me as I both recognised Soda by the unmistakable sound of her voice and could see how changed she was in physical demeanour and mind. She was shrunken and shrivelled. Her face had lost all of its softness and sweetness and she seemed to have aged about 20 years.' Song gulped and moved her tongue around the edge of her teeth.

'Did she tell you what had happened to her?'

'Not exactly. It's not one of those neatly rounded-up stories, I'm afraid, but I could see that she was a woman who had been brutalised by life, and she seemed to be demonstrably mentally ill. She hissed at me, which somehow shocked me more than anything I had experienced while in prostitution, and stared at me accusingly. I tried to open my mouth to speak, but I have to confess that the words just wouldn't come. Just as I mustered up some words that I could say to

---

[7] Four thousand riel are approximately equivalent to US $1, depending on the fluctuating exchange rates.

her, she picked up the child, who may well have been her own, and slipped off like an eel into the traffic again. She didn't give me one backward glance, which hurt me so much.'

'How do you square that incredibly meaningless example of pain with your theology of suffering?' Lydia's cynical persona edged sideways.

Song arched her back against her chair and tilted her head back, thinking about how to answer. 'You know what? Sometimes we don't have all the answers. Suffering can seem to be intensely meaningless, and I certainly don't have any specific answers to Soda's situation. The only thing that gives me peace about it all is knowing that God is a God of love, and that even without having all the answers I can trust Him. Love doesn't mean that everything is going to go smoothly in the world, though, because ultimately people have free will to mess things up for others and for themselves, to let go of pain or hold on to it, to choose God or not to choose God.'

Lydia flicked the edge of the table, which she had been gripping tightly, and raised her eyebrows. Then she stood up and shifted to the other side of the kitchen where she picked up the kettle and refilled it with water. 'I should never have said I had one or two questions. One question leads to another question and to another and so on. This will be a long process, I'm sure.'

The sound of the ticking from the old-fashioned teak clock on the kitchen wall gathered momentum as the two women paused in companionable silence, one standing and the other sitting. Lydia listened to the clock, each pulse beating a rhythm of time passing inescapably, and sighed. Song closed her eyes, her lips moving almost imperceptibly, and hoped. Outside the house the street light rattled in the early November wind, and the sun streamed a silvery square of light through the closed window.

Epilogue

The camera pans in and pans out, highlighting a sequence of images being repeated in various guises around the world. Layla sits by her phone waiting for it to ring: the birth father whom she's never met is in town. Will he ring? Does he care?

The locked door rattles. Joe curls up under the bed, shaking, and wills his father to stay away. A pile of screwed-up pieces of paper under the bed testify to his fear.

Mary keeps her face as emotionless as possible, aware that every expression is an excuse for her mistress to fire false accusations at her. She concentrates hard on polishing the trophy in front of her, hoping against hope that the perfection of her work will mitigate any threat.

The muscles in Jed's back stiffen even more as he fights the cold by wrapping his arms tightly around his knees and breathes warm air onto his gloved yet freezing hands. Yet another faceless pedestrian walks past without a sideways glance in his direction.

Jasminder closes her eyes for a moment, takes a deep breath, picks up her pen and begins writing her exam. The voice of her dad rings in her ears, demanding that she achieve an A: nothing else will be good enough for him, even if she has done her absolute best.

Behind the closed door is another victim of sexual slavery, cleaning herself perfunctorily at the sink after her second customer. Robin clears his throat and steps away, pushing down the bobbing head of guilt that threatens to engulf him.

The purple-robed man of sorrows, His eyes wells of compassion, draws near to each bruised reed, touching them gently on the shoulders and beckoning them into His enormous embrace with the scent of sunshine, a promise of purifying spring air and a hint of something more.

Bibliography

Arensen, Lisa, Mary Bunn and Karen Knight. 'Caring for Children from Commercially Sexually Exploitative Situations: Current Practices in Cambodia and Recommendations for a Model of Care'. Written for Hagar with funding from World Hope International via the US State Department.

Brown, Louise. *Sex Slaves: the trafficking of women in Asia*. Virago Press, 2000.

Cambodian National Council for Children. 'Five-Year Plan Against Trafficking and Sexual Exploitation of Children 2000–2004'. Cambodia, 2000.

Haugen, Gary A. with Gregg Hunter. *Terrify No More*. W. Publishing Group, 2005.

Himm, Sokreaksa S. *After the Heavy Rain*. Monarch Books, 2007.

Hudd, Sandy. 'Sold Like Chickens: Trafficked Cambodian Girls Speak Out'. NGO Coalition to Address Sexual Exploitation of Children in Cambodia (COSECAM), 2003.

Mam, Somaly. *The Road of Lost Innocence: The True Story of a Cambodian Childhood*. Virago Press, 2008.